W9-AOT-743

WICKED WOMEN

WICKED WOMEN

Stories by
FAY WELDON

THE ATLANTIC MONTHLY PRESS

NEW YORK

Published simultaneously in Canada
Printed in the United States of America

FIRST EDITION

Library of Congress Cataloging-in-Publication Data
Weldon, Fay.
    Wicked women : stories / by Fay Weldon. — 1st ed.
        p.   cm.
    ISBN 0-87113-681-3
    1. Women—Social life and customs—Fiction.   I. Title.
PR6073.E374W53   1997
823'.914—dc21   96-37499

DESIGN BY LAURA HAMMOND HOUGH

The Atlantic Monthly Press
841 Broadway
New York, NY 10003

10 9 8 7 6 5 4 3 2 1

CONTENTS

TALES OF
WICKED
WOMEN

END OF THE LINE

"There's a girl called Weena Dodds on the end of the line," said Elaine Desmond.

"Tell her I'm busy," said Defoe Desmond, her husband. They were fifty-fiveish. Both were personable and attractive. They lived in a secluded Grade I listed property.

"She's from the *New Age Times*," said Elaine. "And she wants to talk to you about Red Mercury."

"Red Mercury's a hoax," he said, "and the *New Age Times* is a streak of shit. Tell her to go away."

Elaine couched his response in gentler terms, but Weena Dodds would not go away.

"What's he fucking afraid of?" Weena demanded. "What's he so guilty about? Ask him!"

Elaine did.

"I am afraid of nothing and guilty about nothing," said Defoe Desmond to his wife. "Tell Weena Dodds she can have her interview."

Elaine explained to Weena that Drewlove Village was at the end of the line. Weena would need to change at Westbury Junction, and start out from London at 9 a.m. to arrive at midday. Then she should take a taxi. The interview would last an hour. Elaine was sorry she could not offer lunch, but there would at least be coffee.

"All that way and no lunch," said Weena to her editor, Dervish Wilton. "What a bitch she sounds. Just like my mother."

"Find out why the Defoe Desmond show was really axed," said the editor of the *New Age Times,* who was thirtyish and had dark eyes as cold as Stalin's. "You're not going for the food."

"I'm going First Class," warned Weena Dodds. "I'm not roughing it in Standard."

"You're lucky I don't make you cycle down," said the editor. "There's a dozen Vegan girls out there already lining up for your job."

"Let 'em line," said Weena. She was safe enough. She blowjobbed the editor on Friday afternoons, and not many Vegan girls would do that these days, not even for the sake of employment. The old world and the new criss-crossed each other. You could turn them both to your advantage if you had the instinct. She was a pretty girl with a prim mouth and wide eyes, a smooth high forehead and a great deal of frizzy hair, and a bosom plumper than she wanted it to be. Sometimes she shaved the hair back from her forehead: then she had a bland, medieval look. But it was a problem when the hair was growing back. She had to stay at home.

"What do you reckon the girl from the *New Age Times* looks like?" asked Defoe.

"Lank-haired," said Elaine, "from the sound of her voice. It had a nasal whine."

"Ah," said Defoe. He was sketching a nuclear warhead on his architectural drawing board, prior to Weena's arrival. Six slugs of Red Mercury backed six slugs of plutonium, all focusing in

4

on a central point, where he helpfully wrote, "POW! CRITICAL!"
Underneath he wrote, "A neutron bomb in a golf ball!"

"Isn't that rather too jokey?" enquired Elaine. "You don't want
even the *New Age Times* to do a hatchet job."
"I have been so hacked to pieces already," said Defoe, "a hatchet
would have nothing with which to engage."

Defoe's TV science show had recently been pulled. Ratings had
fallen with the end of the Cold War. No one feared nuclear
extinction any more. Death by passive smoking seemed a more
prescient danger. The world was bored by Defoe's pacings, up
and down, up and down across the studio floor, as he explained
the mechanics of the nuclear apocalypse at length for the home
market, in snippets for CNN, and many a broadsheet and yellow
sheet had remarked upon it, and he chafed.

"Tell me more about how you see Weena Dodds," said Defoe.
"Unblinking," said Elaine. "Therapists, New Agers and Born
Again Christians seldom blink. A blink marks the mind's regis-
tration of a new idea. Converts have no intention of receiving new
ideas. They know already all they want to know."
"I see," said Defoe, "that you already have a prejudice against
the girl. Well, I will have to be nice to her to make up for it."
"She has a strange name," said Elaine. "Weena Dodds! What kind
of parents name their child Weena? How did they expect her to
turn out?"
"I expect they were fans of H. G. Wells," said Defoe. "I expect
they had read *The Time Machine*. Weena was the name of the little
creature who befriended the Time Traveller. She was an Eloi. In
the distant future, Elois skipped about and danced and sang on
the surface of the earth; Morlocks toiled below the ground, deal-

ing with the intricate workings of the universe. They lived in the fetid dark, dwarfish mechanics, and surfaced only to herd the Eloi for food." Defoe liked to give instruction.

"And the Time Traveller brought her home with him?" asked Elaine.

"I seem to remember," said Defoe, "that the Morlocks ate her before he could."

"You are the chief Morlock," said Elaine. "I am glad I didn't ask her to lunch, for her sake."

"I can't stand wives," said Weena Dodds to her mother Francine that night. They were doomed to live together, it seemed, mother and daughter, for reasons of commerce and comfort.

"I was your father's wife," said Francine. She was an elegant, unemotional woman, doing a further degree in Clinical Psychology.

"Exactly," said Weena. "You always acted as if you owned him."

"I did," said Francine. They decided, mutely, not to take the argument further. Both were tired.

"What a bitch!" said Weena, playing for sympathy instead. "All the way to the end of the line and not even any lunch."

"You could do without lunch," said Francine, who had been born thin and attributed her daughter's tendency to put on weight as lack of self-control. Weena burst into tears and ran from the room.

Weena called her friend Hattie.

"My mother is such a bitch," Weena said. "She killed my father, you know. People only get cancer if they're unhappy."

"My father killed my mother," said Hattie gloomily, "in that case."

"It was stomach cancer," said Weena. "Even after it was diagnosed, she wouldn't go over to health foods. She kept on feeding my father meat, not to mention animal fats."

"My mother was the worst cook in the world," said Hattie. It wasn't so much that they conversed, these two, as set each other off. "My father says it contributed to her early death. It was stomach cancer, too."

"It isn't healthy to live with one's mother," observed Weena. "I'd move out, only I know my father always intended me to have the apartment. It was just the inheritance laws stopped him so now we have to share."

"Couldn't one or the other of you buy the other out?"

"Yes, but which one? We both want it. Guess where I'm going tomorrow?"

"Where?" asked Hattie.

"To interview Defoe Desmond."

"That man who used to be on the TV?"

"That's right," said Weena.

"What on earth for?"

"There's this new stuff called Red Mercury they say could blow up the world."

"Never heard of it," said Hattie.

"That's the point," said Weena. "It's used in neutron bombs. Neutron bombs kill people but preserve property. So they're keeping it a secret."

"They are awful," said Hattie bleakly. "What news on the Bob front?"

"Still pattering along behind," said Weena, "breathing halitosis over my hopes." Bob was Senior Editor at a Publishing House, and forty-fiveish.

"Men are awful," agreed Hattie. She was trying to paint her toenails and speak on the phone at the same time.

"I blame his wife," said Weena. "First she said she loved him, and wouldn't leave him alone; then she threatened to burn us alive in our bed, so we had to go into hiding; then she changed her mind and left him, and now it's over between us and he needs her she won't even go back to him. God, women can be bitches."

"It sometimes seems to me, Weena," said Hattie, "that once they've left their wives for you, that's when you lose interest."
"I suppose you could see it like that," said Weena, "or you could see it as men trying to reduce you to wife status the moment they get you, and me fighting back. I would have thought a friend would see it the second way."
"Sorry," said Hattie. "I thought friends were the ones who were meant to tell you the truth. Well if Bob's going free, perhaps I should take him up? He has money and influence. I think you're mad to let him go."

Weena shivered and drew the conversation to an end. Once a man was rejected, he ought to stay rejected, and by everyone she knew. She went and said she was sorry to her mother, for no rhyme or reason, and took herself off to bed. She still had teddy bears on her counterpane and liked to cuddle them.

Elaine showed a couple called the Swains, David and Lila, around Drewlove House. The property was for sale.

"I like the way the house is at the end of a line," said Lila, "and then you take this journey into the woods, and suddenly there it is, a little piece of old England." Lila was from Bangladesh and had an American accent. David nudged her and she said, "Oh, sorry."
"It should perhaps be better described as remote, not secluded," said David. He was tall, thin, whiter than white, blond and had a receding chin.
"Just you and me," said Lila, twitching her sari to stop the gold and red fabric trailing in the cat's saucer of milk. They were in the kitchen, Aga-warmed. There were spring flowers on the table especially for the occasion. "You and me. Safe from the world's stare. Nature is so much kinder than people."

"We were looking for somewhere more accessible to London," said David Swain. "That wait at Westbury Junction certainly lowers the value of the place," and as Lila opened her mouth to speak, he nudged her and she shut it again.

"I'm surprised you want to sell," David Swain said as they walked through the garden, and Lila fell on her knees in front of a frilly double tulip of particular attractiveness. "If, as you say, it's been in your family for some generations."

"There has been a rather sudden change in our circumstances," said Elaine.

"The names on the deeds of Drewlove House are a matter of public record—one likes to get these details straight before contemplating purchase. Do get up, Lila. You are making your sari dirty."

"I am a Drewlove," said Elaine, pleasantly. "My mother lost the house, gambling, in 1941, when I was little, which as you can imagine caused quite a family upset. My mother lost to a local builder, a Mr. Malcolm Trott. Had she won, she would have owned the Trott farm. Mr. Trott, being no gentleman, held her to her gambling debt. She would have done the same to him, no doubt. The house was presently requisitioned by, and later bought by, the Ministry of Defence, who then sold it to my husband, on our marriage. My husband was at the time a young scientist working for the Ministry. So the names on the Land Registry should read, since 1785, Drewlove after Drewlove, with various mortgaging, surrendering, conveyancing, further charging, of various lands and buildings to the Family Trott; the whole lot going to Malcolm Trott in 1941, who won in the end; to the MOD in 1947, and from MOD to Desmond in 1963. Okay?"

"That was a very full explanation," said David Swain, appearing satisfied. They were back inside the house by now. Elaine had talked all the way. David Swain drummed his sweaty fingers on an Aga especially cleaned and polished for his visit. "Thank you

for it. I know you understand that in the circumstances some explanation was certainly called for."

"Would you like to see the Granny flat?" asked Elaine.

"I don't have a family," said Lila. "They have disowned me."

"One moment," said David Swain. "There is something fishy
going on here. How come your mother's name was Drewlove?
There should be another name there somewhere if that cock-and-
bull story is true."

"My mother," said Elaine, "never married. She was a very fishy
woman. I am illegitimate. And I do not want you living in my
family home; it will take you twenty minutes to walk to the station, the end of the line. My phone is out of order, or I would call
you a taxi."

"I heard it ringing just now," said Lila.

"It does that sometimes," said Elaine. "The lines round here can
be very bad. You had better go now, and hurry, or you will have
to wait hours for your next connection."

"The Swains went away quickly," said Defoe.

"Not soon enough," said Elaine.

"We don't have to sell this house," said Defoe.

"You haven't seen this morning's letter from the bank," said
Elaine. "We do. They say it's the end of the line."

"Perhaps this house is unlucky," said Defoe.

"It was okay until they extended the railway line, in 1919. That
was the year my mother was born," said Elaine. "And things go
wrong anyway. One can hardly attribute all cosmic events to a
verbal pun. One can hardly say we lost our income because you
lost your job because the world lost interest in the nuclear threat
because our house is at the end of the line."

"Some could," said Defoe. "Someone like the girl from the *New
Age Times* could very well. New Agers drive winsome thoughts
between ordinary notions of cause and effect."

And his eyes drifted towards the window, to see if Weena Dodds was coming up the path. She was.

Elaine opened the door to Weena. Weena saw a woman who was a dead-ringer for her mother Francine, but without scarves and earrings. Her nails were broken and she was without eye make-up, which for someone of her age was foolish. This woman had clearly lived in the country too long.

"There wasn't a taxi at the station," said Weena. "I had to walk." "Walking would do you no harm," said Elaine, "from the look of you." Weena seemed to be a heterosexual version of her own daughter Daphne. Just one of those things.

"The bitch, the bitch!" said Weena to Hattie that night on the phone. "I expect she was jealous," said Hattie. "Probably flat as a board herself." Hattie had a nice little bosom herself, just about right. Weena giggled.
"Not flat," said Weena. "There are advantages to flat. Just shape- less. You know how wives and mothers get."
"I expect you had your revenge," said Hattie.
"Oh, I did," said Weena. "I did."

"Well," said Defoe, waiting until his wife had left the room, "this is a surprise. I didn't think you'd have the nerve. I want my £20 back."
"What £20?"
"The £20 you stole from my wallet while I was asleep."
"That was the point," she said. "I always take money from a man's wallet if he falls asleep after sex. It's policy. It repairs my self-esteem."
"I was tired," Defoe said. "It was after the show. You had no mercy. I am a tired old married man."

"You could have fooled me," she said. "And the wallet was so stuffed I'm surprised you noticed."

"That was before Nemesis fell," he said. "I could do with every penny now."

"Not Nemesis," she said, "but Karma. We all get what we deserve. But I know the feeling."

"We get what we deserve!" he marvelled. "Do you honestly believe that?"

"I got you that night," she said, smiling her pretty smile, "so I must have done something right."

"When I called the number you gave," he said, "the woman who answered said she didn't know who you were."

"The bitch! The bitch!" Weena moaned to Hattie later. "That's my mother's idea of a joke. 'I don't know who she is.' She's always driving my men away."

"Better than stealing them," said Hattie, but Weena wasn't listening. "Everyone I know has mothers on hormone replacement therapy," continued Hattie, "who're a real problem, but me, I'm motherless."

"I can't stand women who make jokes," said Weena. "Men don't like them either. The way to a man's heart is through total solemnity."

"If you want to get there in the first place," said Hattie. "It seems an odd ambition to me."

"Well I fucking, do," said Weena. "I have simply got to get out of my home situation."

"So you gave up," she complained.

"Guilt undermined my intent," Defoe said. "And then my world crumbled about me."

"Of course it did," she said, briskly. "Guilt is a destructive emotion. I never feel guilty about anything, especially sex!"

* * *

Elaine came into the room with a tray on which there were two mugs of instant coffee and some sugar in a little white-lidded bowl.

"I don't take sugar," said Weena, looking under the lid. "It's poison."

"Well, dear," said Elaine, "don't take any, then." And she went out of the room, raising her eyebrows at Defoe. Weena caught the look. Very little escaped her.

"She doesn't like me," said Weena. "But then I'm not a woman's woman. My mother doesn't like me either. But you're not interested in me."

"I am interested in you," he said. She was sitting silhouetted between the desk and the window. The fabric of her white blouse was fine. She wore no bra and the outline of her full breasts was visible: when she moved to adjust the tape recorder the nipple of her left breast flattened against the wood.

"Well," said Weena briskly to Defoe Desmond, at Drewlove House, "I didn't come all this way to talk about fucks past. I came to talk about Red Mercury and its implications for the future of the world. My editor says, though the nuclear threat is far from the top of the world survival agenda, it still has implications for concerned people everywhere."

"It does," said Defoe.

"I don't actually drink coffee," said Weena. "Most people nowadays don't."

"My wife is old-fashioned," apologised Defoe.

"I can tell that," said Weena. "Now, where were we? Oh yes, my editor said it didn't matter I was science-illiterate, you were such a brilliant populariser even a Gaian could understand you."

"Did he really say that?" Defoe was pleased.

"He did," said Weena.

"Your editor seems to loom large in your life," said Defoe.
"What's a Gaian?"
"There!" she said, pleased. "At last something I know, and you
don't. Gaia is mother earth as gestalt, a self-healing entity."
"Self-healing? How consoling a notion," Defoe observed.
"You get so gloomy, you scientists," she said. "There's a whole
world of hope and happiness out there you know nothing about.
Do you think your wife would allow me a glass of water?"

Defoe went to the door and called Elaine, and asked her to bring
Weena a glass of water. Elaine did.

When Elaine was gone, Weena said, "She doesn't like me much,
does she?"
"Why do you say that?" asked Defoe.
"She didn't even bring the glass on a tray. It's all thumb-printy.
Shall we get on with the interview?"
"I'm at your command," said Defoe. Now Weena's skirt was
rucked up to show her long bare legs to advantage. She bent to
adjust the tape recorder and again flattened her left nipple against
the wood of the desk. It looked an expensive desk.
"It's a nice desk," she said.
"Eighteenth century, burr oak. It's been in my wife's family for
a long time. It will have to go to auction."
"That's a pity," Weena said. "There's usually some way round
these things."
"Not this time," said Defoe. "Or so my wife tells me."
"Some people are just doomy," said Weena. "Life falls into their
expectations."
"You may be right," said Defoe.
"I love nice things," she said.
"You deserve to have them," said Defoe. "Someone like you."

* * *

Elaine showed Harry and Rosemary Wilcox around the house. "A little less than a manor house," said Elaine, "a little more than a farm house. It grew, like a living thing. It began as a single stone structure, without windows, this room here, we believe, back in the ninth century. There's a dwelling here in the Domesday Book: 1070-ish. See how thick the walls are? The farmer, his family, his hangers-on, the animals, all sheltered in here together. A few good harvests, no wars and some clever barter, and the humans can afford to separate out from the animals: they get to live above them. That way you get the warmth but not the stench. You build a staircase up the side of the structure: even get windows with glass. Later you build out and the farmhands and servants live apart from the farmer. You enclose the staircase. You build a big hall and panel it; you begin to get grand. A major upheaval moves the animals out to stables and byres: the servants move up to the attics; the family moves down. You send the farmhands to war and ask the monarch to stay: you get given land, or buy it. Now you've got more land, you've got more trees and can afford to heat the place. You get more confidence: separate bedrooms for the kids. An elegant frontage gets built in the early eighteenth century, and bathrooms in the twentieth. Farming's no longer the family business. Second half of the twentieth you sell some of the land off. So, yes, it's historic: it's also a mess. Some of the improvers had taste, some didn't. The bathrooms being a case in point. Wretched little things tucked under the eaves."

The Wilcoxes looked at her blankly.

"None of the doors are flush," said Rosemary.

"We could soon replace them with something more modern," said Harry. "You could really do things with this house."

"Look at the state of my heels!" she said. "There are actually cracks in the kitchen floor."

"Those are flagstones," said Harry. "We could tile them over easily enough."

"I expect what moved your editor to send you over to me," said Defoe, "was the documentary on TV last week. I was the nuclear expert he saw, sitting in a Moscow hotel with my face in shifting squares, electronically blurred, to no real purpose; experts are never in real danger. Everyone needs them. The chambermaid always survives the palace revolution. Someone has to make the beds. In my hand I held an anti-rad flask, and in it was a helping of Red Mercury, looking just like goulash. I tilted the flask, and it sloshed around as would any oily stew in a cooking pot, only with a paprika tinge, which is why I compare it to goulash, and why it is called Red Mercury. Hoax or not? A fictitious substance devised by the Russian Mafia—and in fact goulash? Or a real and dangerous addition to the nuclear arsenal, a substance so secret governments deny its very existence. A new element which will give the terrorists' A-bomb in a suitcase the fillip required to turn it into an N-bomb in a golf ball, capable of destroying life for miles around—with one quick fizzle, one flash of radiation so profound it kills all living things, while leaving buildings, highways, transport, microwave towers, post-office towers to you—and water supplies untouched."

"You're very good at this," she said, admiringly.

"I earned my living at it for twenty years," said Defoe. "I should be."

"One thing," said Weena, "wouldn't the water supply be contaminated?"

Defoe brushed the comment away, and accidentally brushed her breast.

"I'm sorry," he said.

"That's okay," she said. "I don't have a thing about body space. I'm the touchy-feely type, as it happens. Aquarius. You're Taurus, aren't you?"

"I'm a man," he said. "That is all the definition I need. Where was I? Red Mercury, fiction or fact? Oddly, until the stuff was in my hand, I had assumed it was a fraud, a con. But there was a kind of reluctance of movement in the stuff, something about the sluggish way it shifted in the flask, as I said earlier, like chunks of meat in oil, which made me think it was authentic. The natural world hesitates when it's on the verge of self-destruct. Surface tension prevents the lava spilling out: simple air pressure keeps shifting tectonic plates in place—to bring two pieces of plutonium together to reach critical mass requires a gigantic effort: as improbable as slamming together two pieces of magnetised metal with similar polarity. Everything in nature cries out no, no!"

Defoe paused for breath.

"You're very romantic," said Weena, "for a scientist."

"Scientists have hearts, too," Defoe said. "Who better than scientists to understand the romance of the universe, the mystery of matter?"

"Tell me," said Weena, "if it's true, if this stuff exists, why do governments deny that it does?"

"The function of governments," said Defoe, "is to hold truth in reserve, as a last resort. If it doesn't exist, so what; if it does exist, then the technology required to fit it into warheads is available only to governments, and major armies."

And Defoe produced his diagram.

"I think it's wonderful!" she said. "Did you draw that circle freehand?"

"I did," he said.

"I thought Leonardo da Vinci was the only man ever known to draw a perfect circle freehand."

"Leonardo da Vinci and me," said Defoe.

Elaine put her head round the door.

"Do you want to explain the boiler to some people called the Wilcoxes?"

"No," said Defoe. "I'm in the middle of an interview."

Elaine went away.

"Does she always do that?" asked Weena. "Interrupt you in the middle of things?"

"If in her judgement her needs are more urgent than mine, yes."

"Well," said Weena, "I think it's rather rude to me. As if I was unimportant. You mustn't worry about being temporarily out of work. The world can't do without you. You talk so really well. Very few people can do that. That night in the hotel after the show I should never have let you go."

"I was tired," said Defoe. "I don't suppose I did much talking. Have you read any of my books?"

"No. I know I should have. But I don't get to read much. But I love reading, all that."

"I'll give you a copy of my latest," said Defoe. "*Science the Terminator.*"

And Weena actually clapped her hands with pleasure, and dropped her pen in so doing.

Perhaps Defoe would have helped Weena find the pen under the desk, but Elaine entered with Harry and Rosemary Wilcox.

"It can't be," said Rosemary, "but it really is! Are you *the* Defoe Desmond?"

"I know of no other," said Defoe wearily.

"We're Harry and Rosemary Wilcox," said Harry.

"*The* Harry and Rosemary Wilcox?" asked Defoe, but Elaine frowned at him so he added, "Just a joke! We're all *the* whoever it is to ourselves, aren't we! The centre of our universe," and Rosemary and Harry's hurt puzzlement turned to smiles.

"Sorry your programme was axed," said Harry. "But we must all take the rough with the smooth. So now you're selling?"

"We always planned to sell when the children left home," said Elaine firmly. "This is the library—note the original panelling."

"I just love the atmosphere," said Rosemary Wilcox, who had turned, as Weena put it to Hattie later, from a moaning cow into a buzzy bee. A glimpse of a celebrity can do that to some people, albeit one teetering on the brink of has-been-ness.

"Let me show you the Conservatory," said Elaine. "We haven't had the staff to keep it up properly, but there's a very good fig tree, nearly a hundred years old. It was planted the day my grandmother was born."

And she moved the Wilcoxes on, looking at her watch and raising her eyebrows at her husband, as if to suggest he hurried things along with Weena if he could. Weena caught the look.

"The bitch!" said Weena to Hattie later. "Treating me like dirt and thinking she'll get away with it. I don't know how Def stands her."

"Def, now, is it?" said Hattie. "As in blind and deaf?"

"Calling him Def makes me feel owned and owning. Like a child."

"And another wife bites the dust!" said Hattie.

"Oh, Elaine—" said Defoe, as his wife left the room.

"What is it, Defoe?" asked Elaine.

"If you're going upstairs, could you bring down a copy of *Science the Terminator?* I want Miss Dodds here to have one."

"We only have the shelf copy left," said Elaine.

"Then we'll lend it to her and she'll have to bring it back."

"I am very good with other people's books," said Weena. "I always return them."

"Oh, so you live locally?" enquired Elaine. "I thought you told me you'd come up from London."

"I visit the area quite often," said Weena. "And I do so love this house."

"You are welcome to buy it," quipped Elaine. "Unless outbid by Mr. and Mrs. Wilcox here."

"There's a lot of modernising to do," said Harry Wilcox to his wife as the party moved on. "To bring the place into even the twentieth century, forget the twenty-first." Defoe overheard. His ears were finely tuned and trained, after years of studio work, to catch remarks on the fringes of discussion.

"What did you have in mind," demanded Defoe, now on his feet and pursuing Harry Wilcox. "Flush doors and an avocado bathroom suite?"

"Defoe dear," said his wife, "calm down! And please remember we already have an avocado bathroom suite." And she smiled cordially and led her guests to view further features of the house. It was clear, from the look exchanged between Mr. and Mrs. Wilcox, that she was now wasting her time. This was a property they were unlikely to buy.

Defoe, his object obtained, calmed down quickly. He and Weena discussed his motives in leaving the field of theoretical nuclear physics, where he had started his career, his move to the Ministry of Defence on his marriage to Elaine, and thence into weapons development, and finally, when his children were born, into the media. "So, because you had a family to keep," said Weena, "you couldn't follow your chosen path. Just think of it—you could have been the one to harness the power of the sun. Nuclear fusion, and all that."

"I was not a world-class scientist," Defoe said. "With or without my marriage."

"I don't believe that," she said. "You get a kind of aura off some people. I get it from you. Charisma."

"In the eight weeks since the programme ended," said Defoe, "I fear mine has somewhat faded. But it's good of you to mention it."

"Your wife shouldn't have humiliated you like that," said Weena.

"Like what?"

"Showing you up like that in front of those people," said Weena, "about the bathroom suite. As if you didn't know your own house. But some men just like bitches. Or else they get so they don't notice."

Elaine came into the room with a copy of *Science the Terminator,* and found Defoe scowling at her.

"Is something the matter?" she asked, surprised.

"Consult your conscience," he said.

Elaine did, finger on chin, a mockery of anxiety on her face.

"If it's about the bathroom suite," she said, "we'll talk about it later, when this interview is finished."

She handed her husband the book he had asked for.

"What shall I write in it?" Defoe asked. "My mind goes blank."

"It's the shelf copy," said Elaine. "The one that's not supposed to leave the house. You're lending it, not giving it."

"So I am," said Defoe. "You will be sure to bring it back, won't you, Miss Dodds? Next time you're in these parts?"

"Or you could post it," said Elaine. "If you registered it first."

"And when you come next time," said Defoe, "you must be sure to stop for lunch. Now the children are grown, now I'm out of TV, now I'm confined to quarters, as it were—"

"Oh I will," said Weena, reluctantly moving herself from her place in the sun, so the light no longer made a halo of her hair, so the curve of her bosom could no longer be seen. "I will."

"Let me see you to the door," said Elaine.

"Thank you, Mrs. Desmond," said Weena, "you've been ever so kind. Can I call you, Mr. Desmond, if my notes don't make sense? Or the recorder hasn't picked everything up?"

"Of course you can," said Defoe. "These days I have time to spare." But he did not catch her eye as she left the room, and she thought that was a bad sign.

"You went too far, too fast," said Hattie on the phone that evening, "from the sound of it. You shouldn't have slagged off his wife. Men like to do that themselves; they don't like others doing it."

Weena called Bob Ratchett in his bedsitting room. Lawyers had got him out of the matrimonial home and his wife and children back in it. He was in debt. None of his family would speak to him. This is what love can do for a man.

"Oh God, darling," he said, "it's you."

"We're just good friends," said Weena. "Remember?"

"Come round and we'll talk about it," said Bob.

"What I want to talk about," said Weena, "is the possibility of my writing a biography of Defoe Desmond, for a ginormous advance."

"Well," he said, cautiously, "I think the time for Defoe Desmond is past. He peaked five years ago. And since the Berlin Wall came down, forget it. On the other hand—"

"On the other hand what?"

"Come round and talk about it," said Bob Ratchett.

"Okay," she said.

* * *

The next morning Defoe and Elaine got up before breakfast to go mushrooming in the fields behind the house. Their golden Labrador gambolled ahead. Little circles of white amongst the short horse-cropped grass drew them first here, then there. They held hands.

"Everything has to change," observed Elaine. "I may be the fifth in the line of generations who have walked about this field and gathered mushrooms, but I no longer own the house. You do. I live here by your courtesy. I never wanted you to put it in our joint names. When you offered, I resisted."

"Yes, why did you do that?" he asked. "I used to think it was your desire to be dependent."

"I married you for your money," she said, "or rather for your ability to buy back the house I loved. Then I came to love you more than I loved the house. I thought I should be punished."

"I'll have to think about that one," he said. They picked more mushrooms. He no longer held her hand.

"Now when we sell the house I love," she observed, "the money will be yours."

He thought a little. The basket filled to overflowing. Still they wandered.

"But you and I will live on it," he said. "I could put half in your bank account, if you prefer. But I have been supporting you for many years, and you have never worked."

"When the mortgage and the overdraft are paid," she said, "there won't be much left. How uncomfortable change is, that it should oblige us to have such difficult conversations."

The dog set off a rabbit. The rabbit raced down one side of the hedge, the dog down another. The rabbit won. The dog sat down and panted, looking daft, which he was.

* * *

"Of course," Defoe said, "the English landed gentry always lived by selling their sons and daughters in return for land and money."

"I sold myself," she said, "being an orphan and having no one to sell me."

"We're too near the hedge," he said. "We might mistake a death cap for a mushroom."

"Or vice versa," she said. They moved back towards the centre of the field, in the bright light where the death caps never grow.

Later in the day the phone rang. It was Weena.

"Hello, Miss Dodds," said Elaine.

"How did you know it was me?"

"I recognised your voice," said Elaine. "You were here only the day before yesterday. Do you want to speak to my husband?"

"Yes," said Weena. "I would like to speak to Def, Mrs. Desmond, if that's okay by you."

"I should warn you," said Elaine, "he doesn't like being called Def unless he has given express permission."

"That's strange," said Weena. "He didn't seem to mind the day before yesterday."

"So you have some kind of problem today?" enquired Elaine.

"My editor's looked at my piece and isn't too happy. He wants some changes made."

"It seems some women have editors the way some women have husbands," observed Elaine.

There was a pause while Weena considered this.

"You're really quite funny, aren't you?" she said.

"Thank you for the compliment," said Elaine.

"I really admire that in you," said Weena. "People say I don't have a sense of humour, and then I feel bad. But humour goes with being smart, doesn't it, and I guess I'm not all that smart. I think it's more important for people to feel, and respond."

"Then that's just as well," said Elaine, "isn't it?"

"What I'm trying to say," said Weena, "is that I'd like to come back and ask Def a few more questions."

"I'm sure you would, Miss Dodds. I'll get my husband to call back if he's interested."

"Do you have some sort of problem with me, Mrs. Desmond? I get the feeling you're hostile to me. What have I done?"

"Miss Dodds," said Elaine, "most journalists manage to get what they want in the time allocated. That said, I am not in the least hostile to you."

"I'm not really a journalist," said Weena. "I'm more sensitive than that. I'm a writer. I was trying not to be personal, not to ask him what it feels like to be a has-been, that kind of thing, and these are all the thanks I get."

"Defoe is taking the dog for a walk," said Elaine. "I'll get him to call you back. Can I have your number?"

"Def's got that."

"He'll have lost it," said Elaine. "You know how it is; people write numbers on bits of paper and then the cleaner tidies it up."

"In my world," said Weena, "we do our own cleaning. Tell him I look forward to hearing from him."

"Oh I will," said Elaine, "I will."

Francine stopped Weena as she was going out of the apartment. "Weena," she said, "I am tired of doing your laundry. Is it too much to ask for you to put your own washing through the machine?"

"It's in the laundry basket waiting for me to get round to it," said Weena. "Do you have a problem with that?"

"Just that the laundry basket is overflowing, and smelling," said Francine. "And has been for weeks."

"You resent me being my own person," said Weena. "You want me to keep to some kind of mythical timetable, in which you are always the mother and I am always the child."

"I am always the mother," said Francine, "and you are always the daughter; there is no denying that. And now I am a widow, not even a wife, and you are still jealous. Just get that laundry basket cleared."

"I will not be spoken to like that," said Weena. "And I do my own washing in my own time."

But she could feel her mother getting nearer and nearer some essential part of her being, and she could tell that, if she wasn't careful, she'd be the one to move out.

When she'd slammed out of the house she paused and pressed the bell of her own apartment.

"Hello?" enquired Francine.

"It's my dirty knickers you can't stand," said Weena. "It's the smell of sex. You need treatment, Mother."

"My dearest," said Francine, "I don't. You do. I had an excellent sex life with your father, and you had better face it."

There were no more doors to slam, so Weena strode down the street towards the bus stop, head held high, glowing with anger and frustration, and attracting many a glance, both male and female.

Defoe returned from his walk with the dog.

"Anything happen?" he asked.

He professed to love the country, but lack of event bothered him. Anything happening is better than nothing happening. Who wants the last days of peace, when they could have the first days of war? Most things are good at the beginning.

"Very little," said Elaine.

"What am I meant to do with my day?" he asked.

"Sell the house and move to town," she said. "Invest the money, and live near to our children: pick up what work you can. We have reached the end of the line. The end of the Cold War put thriller writers out of business: the end of the arms race is the end of those whose business it was to comment on it."

"It hasn't ended," he said. "It has just gone underground. I need to say that to people."

"They're not listening," she said. "There are other threnodies being sung."

"You're very hard," he said.

"We should never have hoped for permanence. Even this house won't stand. If they do away with the local line, the road will come instead, bear everything away. What are five centuries in the history of a house, the story of a family? Let's leave with dignity, while we can, before the others realise."

"But I love this house."

"You love the theory of this house, and the history of this house, and the way you came into possession of this house. And the way it reflects status upon you. But the house itself? Harry Wilcox was right. It needs modernising. It could burn down tonight, and us with it, the wiring's so bad. Let Lila Swain fight the closing of the branch line. She won't win, and if she does, worse will happen. In fifty years this house will not be here; or you and me either. We will be underground, or burned and scattered. The cities eat up the countryside: it is time they did. People must eat, must have space to move in and air to breathe: they'll kill to get it."

"So nothing happened in my absence," he said, "except you started brooding. What you say is nonsense. The cities are more dangerous than the countryside: everyone knows that."

"To live in isolation anywhere is a luxury," said Elaine, "without a perimeter wall, steel gates, and an entry system."

He yawned. He was bored. He was accustomed to sound bites, not stretches of speech. What would he do now the dog was walked?

Peter was Defoe and Elaine's son. Now the phone rang in his penthouse. Peter was thirty-one, and an investment broker for a direct insurance company. He had a cold in the nose, or so he said, and was not going in to work today. His new partner Rick, aged twenty-three, had stayed home from his antique shop to keep him company. Rick picked up the phone and handed it to Peter.

"It's your sister Daphne," said Rick in his soft, sweet voice.

"I called the office," said Daphne accusingly, "and they said you were ill. Are you shirking again?"

"I've made enough money for them lately," said Peter. "I'm taking a day off."

"Was that your new young man?" asked Daphne. "If so, it sounded suspiciously like a girl. Can I meet him/her soon?"

"It's a him," said Peter, "and I'd rather leave it for a while. I am not sufficiently convinced of your gender orientation to risk losing him to you."

"Honestly," said Daphne, "these days I am only interested in hers."

Daphne and Peter had looked so similar when young, one had often been mistaken for the other. They had enjoyed that. There was a mere ten months between them. She was the younger. Peter would have his hair cut short: Daphne would take the scissors and do the same to hers. Peter would grow his: so would Daphne.

"Did you know they're going to sell the house?" asked Daphne. "Mum's already showing people around."

"Dad won't like that," said Peter. "What, sell the old homestead? Out of the family? That's terrible. Why?"

"There isn't a family left," said Daphne. "Only you and me, and we're not going to propagate. We're the end of the Drewlove line: the Desmonds are nobodies—they go on and on, but mostly in America, believing they're somebodies."

"But selling the house!" lamented Peter. "Without reference to you and me!"

"They're like that," said Daphne. "Entirely selfish. Just an announcement. Five hundred years in the family and just like that— our family home, our childhood refuge—to be sold!"

"But do you want to live in the middle of a wood?" asked Peter.

"Certainly not," said Daphne. "It's okay for weekends, I suppose."

"I don't want to live in it either," said Peter, "and Rick gets dreadful hay fever."

"Then that's that," said Daphne. "They'll get a good price and leave us the proceeds."

"If they don't spend it first," said Peter. "They may have been living beyond their income. I hope they haven't run up too many debts."

"I hope they're not upset. Dad won't have liked losing his job."

"He'll have liked the fuss that went with it," said Peter. "Ought we to go down?"

"Oh God!" said Daphne.

"Oh Jesus," said Peter. "Heaven preserve us from these turbulent parents."

He sneezed so much they had to abandon their conversation. Rick brought Peter herbal tea: Alison, Daphne's partner, brought her coconut cookies she'd made herself that morning, and served them with grubby hands. Peter and Daphne always attracted simple, loving, dedicated others. It was their talent.

Back at Drewlove House, Defoe came downstairs again. "You're sure no one called?" he asked. "While I was out walking the dog? The phone was completely silent?"

"Actually the boring girl from the *New Age Times* called," said Elaine. "I forgot about that. She wants to come back and do the interview again. For all you and I know, she is in league with robbers and is simply casing the joint. I should be careful if I were you. I did what I could to put her off, but obviously not enough."

"Pity. Witness to my humiliation. Vis-à-vis your jibe about the avocado bathroom suite," he said.

"It isn't like you to be so sensitive."

"You think I am without sensitivity?" he asked, prickly.

"I did not say that." She was patient.

"So is she coming back?" he asked. He looked in the crazed glass of the mercury mirror and thought he looked good. Early nights and a domestic bed and less stress opened the eyes and firmed the skin. He would leave the decision to his wife: whether Weena came, or stayed away.

"I said you'd call her."

"Then I hope she left her number? She gave it to me but I think I lost it."

"I took it again," she said, and found it for him, and left the room. Mrs. Mary Hadfield was at the front door, to beg Elaine to join the committee which was to defend the branch line.

"Your wife wasn't very nice to me, Def," said Weena on the phone. "She seems to have some problem where I'm concerned."

"I can't think what that can be," said Defoe.

"It's not as if she knew," said Weena. "At least, I presume she doesn't."

"Know what?" For a moment he was baffled.

"That we fucked," she said.

"Hush!"

She laughed. "You're so guilty!"

"Of course she doesn't know," said Defoe. "Tell me, in your world, would Elaine have a right to object if she did know?"

"She might come at me tooth and claw," said Weena. "That would be real. That would be okay. But objecting in a clinical way, no. People have no right to be sexually possessive."

"No? Give me the wisdom of your generation. I love it!"

"Because that limits lives, Def. It's the opposite of liberation. We've got to learn to love one another."

"What, all in one great flower-strewn bed together? I am back in my youth."

"Don't mix me up, Def. It isn't fair. I'm not very smart. Anyone can take advantage of me. Please don't you, Def."

"Sorry," said Defoe. "What are you wearing?"

"Nothing," said Weena, which was a lie. She was wearing a designer white satin blouse of her mother's. It had gold embroidery down the front and Weena wore it over her jeans and a black T-shirt, the better to save the latter from the slops of cornflakes and milk she had consumed before making the phone call, lying on her front on the floor; the black fabric too easily picked up cat hairs from her carpet. Her mother had worn the white satin blouse to her father's funeral underneath a tailored black suit. Weena had thought the outfit unspeakably vulgar. The crematorium chapel had been hot. Francine, her taste for once impugned, had taken off her jacket, and thereafter glittered like a beacon in the funereal gloom, attracting eyes away from the coffin as it slid on its rollers into its suggested immortality behind pink silk curtains. "She never loved him," Weena thought, finally seeing the proof she sought. "Never, never." Now she thought that the sooner the blouse was accidentally ruined, the better: certainly before the anniversary of her father's death, fast approaching.

"Don't do this to me," said Defoe. "You are provoking me on purpose."

"No clothes at all," said Weena, "and I am lying on my back on a white carpet. When I do this my breasts turn into kind of fairy cakes, but at least not pancakes, as, for example, my mother's do."

"I know that," said Defoe. "I remember your breasts well. And is your hair all spread around? Over your shoulders, framing your face?"

"I guess so," said Weena.

"Just tell me when you're coming to visit me," said Defoe, "before someone interrupts us. For God's sake!"

31

"We have a right to talk," said Weena. "Even people in prison are allowed to talk. Wives don't own a man's soul. All no-no's exist to be broken. The brave break them. I'll come down on Tuesday."

"Monday," said Defoe. "Come in the morning: stay to lunch. Elaine goes to her pottery class on Monday afternoons."

"Pottery! Wet clay draws the spirit out of people. After that they develop a kind of hard crust. Sometimes they get crazed. Lots and lots of little lines."

Elaine had never shaded her face from the sun. It was indeed lined, and could be thus described. But she remained attractive: intelligence animated her and gave her grace.

"That way there'll be time between Elaine going to her pottery class and the 5:15 train."

"Time for what?" asked Weena. She wiped her nose on the back of her hand and wiped that down the front of the satin blouse.

"I don't know what for," said Defoe. "I don't care. Just for us to be together, in whatever way you like."

"I haven't much time to think about any of this," said Weena. "I'm trying to get an article on fluoride pollution to Dervish by Friday afternoon."

"Is that your deadline?"

"No. The editor's usually in a good mood then, that's all."

"I never knew anyone in a good mood on Friday afternoon," said Defoe. "Peak time for good moods is Tuesday afternoon."

And so they chattered on, as lovers, or almost lovers, will.

"What can you see in a man like me?" Defoe asked.

"Charisma," said Weena. "Brains, good looks, charm and practicality."

"You don't mean that, Weena."

"I do," said Weena. "I've always moved amongst pygmies. But

you're a giant amongst men. My editor would say careful, persons of restricted growth or look for another way of saying what I mean, but that's the way it came out. He gives me a really hard time, sometimes."

"Fuck your editor," said Defoe, and there was a short, surprised silence from Weena.

"I'm sorry," said Defoe. "Bad language on the phone is never a good idea."

"That's okay," said Weena. "A giant with a wife who wants to cut him down to size. Avocado bathroom suites! Perhaps your mother was the same? What was she like?"

"A nightmare," said Defoe, "but someone's coming. I must go. Monday morning? I'll meet the train at Abbots Halt at 12:15."

Weena put the phone down, took off the blouse and went along to the bathroom where the laundry basket overflowed with her dirty clothes—blacks, reds, navies and greys. She carefully shoved the blouse into the sleeve of a sweatshirt, so no glimmer of white could be seen, and dumped both back in the basket. She knew that presently her mother's nerve would give and she would shove the lot, unchecked, into a too-hot wash. And serve her mother right, and Weena could play the innocent when the blouse was discovered, grey and ruined, its sheen and its memories gone for ever.

Francine answered the telephone to Dervish, Weena's boss. She held her ruined, once-white blouse in her hand.

"Can I speak to Weena?" he asked.

"I don't know who she is," said Francine, and put the phone down. It rang again.

"Wrong number," she said this time, but before she could hang up Dervish spoke.

"You're Weena's mother," said Dervish, "and I don't know who she is either, so we're on the same side. Is it a child, is it an employee, is it Superbitch? Since her father died, she's been a nightmare! I'm her employer. Hello."

"She's been a nightmare since the day she was born," said Francine. "Daddy's little jail-bait. So why don't you fire her? Does she have some hold over you?"

"She's a good little writer," said Dervish, "with a certain flair, and has a future in journalism if she can get over this bad patch."

"She has a hold on you," said Francine, flatly.

"But if she doesn't deliver her piece on fluoride pollution by Friday afternoon, she loses her job. Will you tell her that?"

"No," said Francine. "Supposing I were to deliver a piece on fluoride pollution by Friday afternoon in her place, would I get her job? Literary style is inherited too, you know; part of the genetic gestalt."

There was a pause at the other end.

"Well, you'd better come up and see me sometime."

"I'll be there Friday afternoon," said Francine.

"That was Weena," said Defoe. "I think you upset her."

"And why should I not upset her?" asked Elaine. "She irritates me."

"I'd rather you didn't let it show. It's always unwise to upset the press."

"When you had a TV show to run, perhaps. Now it can hardly matter."

"Thank you very much, Elaine," said Defoe, with irony.

"I didn't mean it like that. I meant you were doing her the favour. When is she coming?"

"On Monday," said Defoe. "I asked her to stay for lunch. I thought she should be pacified."

"But I go to pottery class on Monday," said Elaine.

"Oh goddamnit, I forgot," said Defoe. "Call her up and put her off."

"It doesn't matter," said Elaine. "I'll serve something simple and go, and you two can linger. She won't think I'm too rude, I hope. It's not as if her generation sets much store on manners."

"No, but she's an Eloi," said Defoe. "A throw-forward. They are easy to hurt; prone to bruising. Unlike the Morlocks. Those of us who have dwelt too long in TV studios can't help being Morlocks."

"She would make an insubstantial lunch, I fear," said Elaine.

"You know your problem, Elaine?" asked Defoe, and answered the question himself. "You suffer from high self-esteem."

"I didn't know I had a problem," she said.

The telephone rang. Defoe took it. It was their daughter, Daphne. "Well?" barked Defoe. His daughter, who had delighted his younger years with her wide-eyed charm, her curly-headed, little-girl ways, had little by little turned square-jawed and mirthful: she had ceased to adore him in a way he understood. She was too like her mother—the irony had entered her soul. It had descended when she was seven, as a soul descends into a five-month foetus. He remembered the occasion. Daphne had fallen down a well in the garden. She crouched twelve feet down, unharmed, her little face grimy and tear-streaked, the bones of dead cats about her. Fire appliances, ambulances, police cars were assembled: their crews milled about: media men arrived: DEFOE DESMOND'S DAUGHTER TAKES PLUNGE. Peter wailed his distress about the garden, rightly, he being the one who had removed the well's protective planking. Up above, the noisy business of her extrication began: down below, Daphne stared up at her distraught father. "Are you all right?" he enquired.

"I'm bored," she called up, and they laughed together. But he knew it was the beginning of the end. She double-took the world, experiencing it in its shifting experience of her: this was not a gift a woman should have. To be all jokes and intelligence—the world got worse and worse: the dawn of self-awareness came earlier and earlier: these days even infants sprung into the world fully post-modernised, gave you a glance before latching onto the nipple as if to say, "Look at me! I'm a baby, but I won't be for long." For both his children, heterosexual relationships had seemed too head-on, too upfront to be properly real; they preferred the inbuilt jokes of same sex love: the brushing of breast to breast, penis to penis, like to like; the very lack of outcome of such intimate encounters appealed. For some reason Defoe found Peter easier to accept than Daphne.

"Well?" barked Defoe again.

"If you want phone calls from me," said Daphne mildly, "you will have to be more polite."

"Why are you calling? What do you want?"

"I don't want anything," said Daphne. "People do sometimes call home. You are my family."

"You know your mother and I disowned you years ago," said Defoe.

"Can't be done," said Daphne blithely. "Your blood is my blood. All you have to do, Dad, is reconcile yourself to your genetic responsibility. Can I come home for a few days?"

"You and Alison?" Defoe was wary.

"Is something wrong with that?" asked Daphne. She allowed the frown in her voice to be heard. These days she worked for Her Majesty's Customs as a senior European negotiator: the youngest ever in the service. She was both ruthless and light-hearted: talks which had dragged on for years found themselves completed in weeks. Bureaucratic stumbling blocks dissolved beneath the astonishment of her gaze.

"Nothing at all," said Defoe hastily, "except your mother doesn't like the dog."

"I need some space to sort out a personal problem," said Daphne.

"What's the problem?" asked Defoe, as a father should.

"You know Alison used to be Alistair before the operation—" said Daphne.

"The entire yellow press of this country obliged me to notice," said Defoe.

"Well, we've now just about decided I want to change to being a man."

"What?" asked Defoe. "Sew on to you the bit they took off him? Wouldn't it have been simpler to both stay the way you started out?"

"Simplicity is not the object of the exercise," said Daphne. "And I think you misunderstand the nature of the surgical intervention, which in any case is symbolic rather than sexual: more to do with gender integrity than anything else. But it's a big step, and I'd like to come home and brood about it for a few days. Now don't get all old and stuffy, Dad."

"When do you want to come?" asked Defoe, defeated.

"The beginning of next week?" suggested Daphne. "The Brussels talks broke down and I have a window."

"From Tuesday on is okay with me," said Defoe. "I'll put you through to your mother," and he called for Elaine to take the phone, and went upstairs to use the mobile in his office.

"Dad says it's okay if Alison and me come to stay," said Daphne.

"Is it essential?" asked Elaine, not unkindly but wanting to know.

"Yes it is," said Daphne. "Our apartment's being de-flea'd by the Department of Health. We have an infestation. We had to have something done. The hall rug seemed to quiver whenever you looked at it: it turned out to be fleas leaping about. But the stuff they use is poisonous, so we thought we'd come and stay for a couple of days."

"With Alison's dog?" asked Elaine. "I love it but your father hates it."

"We can hardly put her in kennels. Jumper hates change. She'll be traumatised. And they're not her fleas. It's a local epidemic."

"Perhaps Jumper started it," observed Elaine. "If Jumper comes too, your father will only kick her."

"Then Alison will kick him. Only three days, Mum. We'll come on Saturday, leave Monday on the 5:15 train. Dad wanted us to come midweek but that was just his power-trip. Don't mention the fleas. I told him I was contemplating a sex-change operation. That quite moved him."

"Oh?" Elaine was interested. "What to, male or female?"

"Cheap jibes!" said Daphne amiably.

"You shouldn't tease your father," said Elaine. "I don't know how you came to be so good at lying, Daphne."

"It's in the blood," said Daphne. "You and Dad have to decide which one of you it's from, and reconcile yourself to it. It comes in handy for the job: a past spent playing one parent off against the other. See you on Saturday."

"Please don't bring Alison or the dog," said Elaine. "I'm trying to sell the house."

"That's another thing we need to talk about," said Daphne. "Peter and I feel we should have been consulted. So that's settled. We'll come Saturday, leave on Monday evening, then. If Alison and Jumper come, we'll go by car, otherwise by train."

"Bring Alison and then you can drive the Red Mercury girl back to the station," said Elaine. "Save your father doing it."

"Who's the Red Mercury girl?"

"Weena Dodds. Some young fan of your father's drifting into our lives and out again."

"I thought all that kind of thing would be over now," said Daphne. "What kind of thing?"

"Never mind," said Daphne. "You never could see what was under your nose. It made coming out a real problem, for both of us."

"Coming out of where?" asked Elaine.

"Never mind," said Daphne. "And what's Red Mercury?"

"Some kind of sinister nuclear substance," said Elaine, "half-way between a catalyst and an explosive, man made, which if used properly destroys life but not property. Your father knows all about it, and Weena Dodds wants to pick his brains."

"She sounds quite bright," said Daphne.

"Not exactly the stuff of genius," said Elaine.

"Pretty?" asked Daphne.

"I haven't really looked," said Elaine.

"Are you offering her as some kind of alternative to Alison? Does she not smell perhaps? Does she not have dogs?"

"I shouldn't think so," said Elaine, "she's too self-centred. You could even drive her back to town, if you left Alison and still brought the car."

"Lesbians are not like heterosexuals," said Daphne. "They do not jump people."

"I just thought in my quaint old-fashioned way," said Elaine, "you might like some company on the way home. And you could both leave before the 5:15. It's such a bad service. They don't even man the station, except on Friday and Sunday nights."

"I don't believe this! You were trying to throw us together," croaked Daphne, whose voice lately had been getting deeper and deeper.

"For a trained negotiator, you can be very tetchy," said Elaine. "And I'm sure I never complained of Alison smelling, but it does rather get into the upholstery, along with the dog hairs."

"I wash too much," said Daphne. "Alison doesn't wash enough. I'll come by train, and that's that, but I won't bring Alison, or the dog. Okay?"

"Okay!" said Elaine.

"Jesus!" said Daphne, as she put the phone down.

* * *

Francine Dodds sat in Dervish's office. Dervish was a good-looking young man run so much to plump that his thighs spread of their own accord. Unmade-up nice girls with straight hair, soft voices and unblinking stares ran in and out of their editor's office, with faxes, copy and cups of herbal tea. Some were tall and gangly, others very short: many had buck teeth. A proportion wore saris or ethnic dress of one kind or another.

"This is an equal opportunities concern," said Dervish, "as you may notice. We run things on a point scale here. We make an exception for Weena, who is white and privileged and would not normally be eligible for employment, but she comes from a broken home and was a child-abuse victim. But we see the perpetrators as victims as well; and one of my staff pointed out we must not become ageist—no one on the *New Age Times* is above thirty and we need to address that—so I felt able to call you in, Ms. Dodds. You are a widow, too."

"Call me Francine," said Weena's mother, perched on the desk, legs dangling, high heels half-on, half-off her elegant little feet. "And let me point out that Weena is the victim of no more than her whiteness, her privilege, as loving a family as she would allow, her education and her looks, all of which have hopelessly spoiled her until now she is as poisonous as a pampered rattlesnake. That is not chatter you hear, that is the noise made as the serum is working through. Weena's home was broken only by death, and no abuse occurred, although her father and I occasionally wished to beat her to death. Sometimes, if the truth be told, and though it is unfashionable to say so, a monster springs from the loins of the nicest people. Weena may have picked up on the vibes, I don't deny it. For that I take responsibility. In my time, as I think you know, I have run a chain of magazines from *Management Consultancy* to *Industrial Strategy*, all of which did very well under my management. I am now training further in the field of Clinical Psychology with a view to research work, but could be tempted back into the commercial field. I abandoned my career when my husband fell ill: the better to nurse him, to devote myself to his last days. This Weena may have told you."

"No. She implied you were sacked for forging your time-sheets and shuffling your expenses. But the expenses we offer here are minimal—"

"So it seemed a risk worth taking? Of course it is! Fire Weena, employ me as a contributing editor. I need the money. You need me. Circulation is falling. Fifty per cent of your staff need to go; I expect you know that. You just lack the courage to do it. Make me assistant editor—I'll do it. Years with Weena have toughened me up."

"But they're such nice, good girls," said Dervish helplessly. "What would I fire them *for*?"

"For being too young, inexperienced, half-starved and in need of animal protein to liven them up, but which they are too principled to eat. The media is no place for principle. Even the *New Age Times* must be a hot-bed of expediency and cynicism if it is to succeed. Look at it clearly—their T-shirts are grey and stiff from ecologically sound washing powder, but they are too full of integrity and regard for the environment to throw them away. Even Weena has this unhealthy obsession with old clothes. But at least she eats meat."

"Weena eats meat?" Dervish was startled.

"Weena eats meat at home, and she can sleep herself into a job anywhere."

"So could you, if you wanted it enough."

She stared at him; he stared at her.

Weena was on the phone to Hattie. She lay in Bob's bed. It smelt agreeably of toothpaste, old socks, lust and despair. He had snivelled and wept into the pillow. Now he had gone to work.

* * *

"Hattie," said Weena, "I think I can see my way through my life."

"I'm really glad for you, Weena," said Hattie. "I can't. I have my niece to stay. She's three."

"Why are you so masochistic? Why do you do it?" asked Weena.

"To help my sister out, I suppose," said Hattie.

"I think you're being the opposite of helpful," said Weena. "Parents should be left to get on with it. Then they'd have fewer children."

"Whose phone are you using?" asked Hattie.

"Bob's," said Weena. "I'm in his bed."

There was a short silence.

"I thought you'd finished with Bob," said Hattie.

"I have," said Weena. "This was just a one-off."

"Do you think that's fair?" asked Hattie. "You ruined his life: now just to go scrabbling about in the ruins!"

"The problem with Bob is he never had much of a life to ruin," said Weena. "His wife is well rid of him. I don't suppose his children want to see him anyway. I don't mean ever to fuck an employed person again. Employment saps a man's soul. They're forever having to get to work or find sick-notes. A man must be self-employed if he's not to end by sweating like my editor or grovelling like Bob. Status games make lovers sweaty and grovelling. In future, I'll stick to the self-employed."

"Then what are you doing there, Weena? In his bed?"

"I need a commission. Bob can get it for me. I need to write Defoe Desmond's biography. I'm tired of my job. I'm tired of living with my mother. I want to live quietly in the country in a grand house and be a chatelaine. I want to be acknowledged, Hattie. I want to take my proper place in life. This bed is just a starting point. The sooner I'm out of it the better. This bed is damp, sweaty and full of crumbs."

"Then you will be out of it soon?"

"Of course. I just need to make another phone call. Why?"

"Those are my crumbs, Weena. Bob and I had toast and marmalade in that bed yesterday morning."

Again a short silence. Then Weena spoke.

"Your problem, Hattie, is you try to be good to men. Men prefer it if you're terrible."

Weena made another phone call.

"I really ought to be at the *New Age Times,*" said Weena to Defoe. "But it's such a boring place. No one there likes me, except the editor. And he just lusts after me. Sometimes he writes my pieces for me. But since I met you, he's rather gone off me."

"Why's that, Weena?"

"I guess it sort of shows I'm into someone else, Def. So if I lose my job, it's your fault."

"I'd rather you didn't work for a boss who lusts after you," said Defoe.

"A good job's hard to find," said Weena. "And a hard boss is good to find."

"What did you say just then, Weena?"

"Forget it. Just a saying. I feel really soft and happy and lazy today. It's the thought of seeing you on Monday. I've been so upset about my mother."

"What's the matter with your mother?" asked Defoe.

"She used to abuse me when I was a child, but we won't go into that. I got away for a couple of years, but somehow I drifted back. People say she has an unhealthy hold over me. I had a pure white satin blouse and she put it through the hot wash on purpose, with all her dark things, and of course it's ruined."

"That certainly seems a symbolic thing to do," said Defoe. "I know if anyone shrinks a shirt of mine, I get very wound up indeed. Shouldn't you leave home?"

"I can't," said Weena. "I can't afford anywhere on my salary. I need someone to take me in."

"Drewlove House has lots of rooms," said Defoe, "and I'd love to, but you have your work to do and I don't think Elaine would like it."

"But why not? Is she very jealous?"

"She can be," said Defoe.

"But not of us, surely," said Weena. "You shouldn't give in to her. It's so low and ungenerous to be sexually possessive. And it smacks of a bad sex life. I'm never jealous because I know I make men happy." She yawned, languorously, the smell of the male bed-sitting room and its desperate sex flowing into her nostrils.

"Where are you?" asked Defoe.

"At my friend Hattie's," said Weena. "Shall I go to work? Tell me what to do."

"Stay where you are, sweet as you are, and talk to me," said Defoe. "Forget the *New Age Times*."

"But if I lose my job?"

"I'll look after you," said Defoe.

"I've always wanted to do a biography," said Weena. "I have such an inquisitive nature, I think I could really make it work. I suppose I could always do one of you. I feel I know you so well yet there's so much more to know. You're so deep."

"Who would want it?" asked Defoe. "An old has-been like me!"

"All kinds of people," she said. "I'd have to come down and stay, wouldn't I, if I was working on your biography? I'd have to know everything, go through old photographs—"

"You would," he said, his voice lightening. "Indeed you would. We'll talk about it on Monday."

"If you like," said Weena. "But I wasn't thinking of doing much talking. Well, only over lunch, when your wife's there. Before pottery."

Defoe came downstairs to find Elaine brushing out the ashes in the grate.

"Cinderella!" he said.

"Daphne's coming down by train for the weekend," said Elaine, "without Alison or the dog. She'll be leaving Monday on the 5:15."

"I thought she was coming down on Tuesday," said Defoe. "She can't be here on Monday."

"Why not?" asked Elaine. Her face was smudged with soot.

"I have an interview," said Defoe. "The journalist's staying to lunch, you're going off to pottery. Call Daphne now and rearrange it."

"No," said Elaine. "You do it."

"I don't like having my time taken for granted," said Defoe.

"Daphne doesn't need entertaining," said Elaine. "She's family."

"I suppose she is," said Defoe. "Perhaps she's Saunders' child."

"I beg your pardon?"

"Saunders had a queer brother. I always thought he was a bit of a poofter himself. Saunders, your Australian lover?"

"He was not my lover, Defoe."

"Then I don't know where Daphne gets it from. I certainly don't want Daphne round the same luncheon table as a journalist. HAS-BEEN CELEB'S OLD AGE SHAME CRAWLS OUT OF CLOSET."

"I'll call Weena Dodds and put her off, shall I?"

"I don't have her number."

"I do," said Elaine.

"Then please don't use it. Weena Dodds is thinking of writing my biography."

"Your biography!" exclaimed Elaine.

"Why not?" asked Defoe. "Do you think no one's interested?"

"But all you've done is interview people," protested Elaine.

"You want to pull me down," said Defoe. "You think finally you've got me to yourself and defeated me and I can't get away. Well, you're wrong."

"Defoe, I think nothing of the kind." Elaine stood up to face him. She struck the ash-filled dustpan against the fire irons, by mistake, and fine pale grey powder swirled up and around her in a mist before settling on hair, face, limbs, dress. It was wood ash, almost white. "I have waited many years for us to be together, that's true enough. What is the matter with you?"

"You are the matter with me," said Defoe. "You make me doubt myself. You always have. You stand there like a ghost. You are my old age. You make me decrepit before my time. You drew me away from the power source of the universe: you doomed me to mediocrity. You are right, all I ever did was interview people. Oh, you have a low opinion of me!"

"The power source of the universe! When I met you, you were developing nuclear weapons," stated Elaine. "Your ambition was to destroy the universe, so far as I could see."

She shook her dress. Wood ash puffed around. He stood further away from her so as not to be infected.

"At least on TV," she said, "you have done no harm, though I can't see you have done much good."

"You are polluting me!" he cried. "I don't want to be a ghost."

"Though it's rare for one person on their own to do much good, so don't reproach yourself," she said, ignoring what she clearly saw as his childishness.

"Did you say Weena Dodds of all people wanted to write your biography?" she asked. "And you're encouraging her in this madness?"

"Yes," he said.

"Isn't she rather young?"

"The nation is full of young people," he said.

"But not young ones who read biographies," said Elaine, "or can afford to. I think we're quite safe. I don't think any publisher will see their way to doing it."

"Safe! I want it done. My life needs to be written. Those people, those experts, whom I merely interviewed, hold all existence in their hands. The human race is at the end of the line, the doomsday clock ticks on. It's stopped for a decade at four minutes to midnight, but there the hands still stand. Any minute now they'll begin to move again. Red Mercury gave the clock a nasty judder, quite a jar: perhaps all that was needed!"

"My dear," said Elaine, "I am not a camera, and not a sound boom. Pray do not address me as if I were a TV audience."

"Bitch!" he cried. "Bitch! You're so circumscribed here in your life, in your rightful place. So serene in your self-righteousness. So unemotional, so reserved, so without self-doubt. We hear a quaint tale or so about your mother the aristo alley cat, the gambler, the child-deserter. But they're stories told to make people laugh, not cry. To keep the yobbos out, not let them in. Here we are, so quaintly eccentric. Why, even our children are gay! Have I ever made you cry? Never!"

"You're my husband," she said. "Why should you want to make me cry?"

If he put his foot forward and stamped, just a little, the floorboards carried the movement through. He tried it again. Yes, when the floorboards vibrated, yet more ash puffed out of his wife. For some reason this phenomenon reminded him of Hiroshima. You never get rid of radioactive elements. Never. Plant a dahlia in Hiroshima, even today, turn over the earth, apply a geiger counter and hear its ruthless rise. You could vacuum Elaine's dress one day and still next day the stuff would ooze out. He longed for Weena, who at least had spent fewer years in the world than anyone else around. So little strontium in her bones!

"Well," said Elaine, "I do what I can for you. I am selling this house so you don't have to live here. I won't go to pottery on Monday, if you prefer."

"But I do want to live here," he said. "I just don't want to live here with you."

He awed himself with his capacity to say it. It came out as a howl.

He'd been reared in the back streets of Deptford. The howl contained the notion of estuary flooding the mouth of the Thames, and the snarling and yapping of dogs at swirling and unusual water. In extremis his origins showed. So did Elaine's.

"I'm such a mess," she said vaguely. "All over ash! I think I'll take a bath."

"And if you don't go to pottery," he said after her, "I'll kill you."

"In that case I'll go," she said, startled. "But why?"

"You have to keep your own life going," he said. "You don't want yours to get swallowed up in mine. We agreed."

"Did we? I expect you're right. Anyway, I like it. I'll try to go."

As she went she pressed her lips lightly on his cheek, leaving a lurid cupid's bow of powdery ash upon it.

"Poor old darling," she said. "It's no fun growing old."

He went upstairs and did press-ups, and felt the sofa cushions to see if they were soft. They were.

"Justice, constancy, endurance, honesty," said Elaine to her daughter Daphne, as she put salad from the garden on to the table, "those are the virtues. Those and a few others, abstract terms of a kind unknown to contemporary youth, but which those of us who learned the classics threw around with ease, are what we are on earth to pursue. They now cluster, undetected, only vaguely understood, under the heading 'good.' Just as under the heading 'bad' come minor vices such as procrastination, dishonesty, capriciousness, falsity—as in 'we must teach our children the difference between good and bad. Thus we will put an end to all juvenile crime.' But without the ability, the inclination, or indeed the intellectual wherewithal to break down good or bad into their component parts. The language of distinction ceases to be available; is no longer available. We must search CD Rom for meanings which once were clear, but now are obscure. The words are too big for the narrow column of the contemporary newspaper. We are all one-syllable people now, two at most. So we mumble and stumble into our futures. But it is still our task and our reward to scavenge through the universe, picking up the detritus of lost concepts, dusting them down, making them shine. Latin was the best polishing cloth of all, but we threw it away."

"Shouldn't Dad be back by now?" asked Daphne, who had learnt to ignore a speech perfected when Daphne refused to learn Latin and Elaine thought she should. "Perhaps the train was late?"

"Perhaps," said Elaine. The vinaigrette was made: the egg mayonnaise prepared. Dishes were displayed, rather bleakly, on the round, polished mahogany table.

"It doesn't look very lavish," said Daphne. "But then it never did."

"I have the habit of my class and generation," said Elaine. "We were never a particularly sensuous lot. So your father complains."

"It's been a really sticky weekend," complained Daphne. "I haven't enjoyed it much."

"You only have to stick it out till the 5:15 train," said Elaine. "It was your idea to come here, to hide out from the fleas. Don't complain. Your father and I bicker. It isn't serious."

"I made up the fleas," said Daphne. "Actually I came for a little breathing space. Alison's putting pressure on me. She thinks I ought to turn into a man. I need to be sure. Though my operation would be reversible, just about, as it isn't for Alison."

"But you wouldn't be a fertile man?"

"No. Of course not. I am fertile now. That's one of my main problems. As it is, I could have a hysterectomy, but I'd still be just a woman, only without even a womb. I'd rather have a bit put on to balance it all up. And then we could adopt. If Alison has legal female status, I can argue that I want male status."

"I can go so far in understanding," said Elaine, "no further. Frankly, I don't want to. Work it out yourself. Which bit of you and Alison go into one another is neither here nor there, but then I am not an interested party."

"I knew I shouldn't have brought the subject up," said Daphne. "I might have known you wouldn't be interested."

Elaine groaned. "Are you like this at your meetings?" she asked.

"Of course not," said Daphne.

Defoe and Weena came in. Both were flushed. Defoe's longer piece of hair fell not across his scalp but down behind his ear. He did not care. Weena put her hand on Elaine's arm. She wore a black T-shirt and no bra beneath it, and a pair of skimpy blue faded denim shorts with frayed hems around the thighs. A big green leather bag was slung over her shoulder. Her hair had been shaved well back from her brow.

"Behold your husband's biographer," said Weena to Elaine.

"How nice," said Elaine, removing Weena's hand. "I must go and drain the potatoes. But do meet my daughter Daphne."

Daphne regarded Weena with more interest than Weena regarded Daphne. Elaine went through to the kitchen.

"Not only is Weena to do my biography," said Defoe, following her to the door, "but a Sunday newspaper is to buy it in instalments, for a sum well into five figures, which Weena and I will share, fifty-fifty. So your doubts were unfounded, Elaine. I am not a nobody; I am still a somebody."

"I'm so glad," said Elaine, bringing in the boiled potatoes. "And the train was late, I take it?"

"Very late," said Defoe, sitting at the head of the table, in a high-back upholstered chair which had been given to Elaine's great-grandfather by a nephew of the King of Denmark.

"Actually," said Weena, "it was on time. Defoe and I had a celebratory fuck on the way to the house, down in the reeds by the river. Why hide it, Defoe? What's to be ashamed of? I hate lies."

"Don't make jokes like that, Weena," said Defoe. "Don't try and shock people."

"There's only one shocking thing round here, Def," said Weena, sitting down at the table on a chair bought by Elaine quite recently, at an auction. Very few things in the house actually matched any more, but had been chosen with care and sensitivity to fit in. "And that's your hypocrisy. Well, people are easily cured of that. Just don't tell me what to do: and don't patronise me. Can I dig in? Sex always gives me an appetite. Def says I can stay here, Mrs. Desmond, while we work on the book. I hope that's hunky-dory with you."

Defoe went upstairs to fetch his glasses. Elaine looked at Daphne for support and advice. These two women were still on their feet. Daphne seemed flummoxed, but presently said to Weena, who had helped herself to egg mayonnaise, potatoes and salad, and was now eating well—"I think you should withdraw your remark about fucking down in the reeds by the river. I think it was the Great God Pan did that—'What was he doing, the Great God Pan, down in the reeds by the river?' The answer, to the horrid children, being obvious!"

"The way this whole family speaks alike!" said Weena. "It's too much. I might make recordings. We might market the books of Def Desmond with tapes attached. He's such a listening-to kind of person, isn't he? Brilliant! It's what first attracted me to him. And a good fuck, too, to coin a phrase, if a little slow at the beginning. But that might just be his age."

"Withdraw the remark," said Daphne.

"No," said Weena. "It's true. Def and I have been having an affair for almost a year now."

"You're lying," said Elaine. "My husband wouldn't do a thing like that."

"Well, he would," said Daphne.

"Not with someone like her," said Elaine.

"He said yours and his sex life was over anyway," said Weena to Elaine. "You don't want to do it any more."

"The liar!" cried Elaine, but Weena did not want to hear that. "I suppose that's natural as you get older," said Weena, "though I don't see it happening to me. It's been hard on Def. So I don't see I'm poaching on anyone's territory: if anything, I'm a help. Don't you put mint in your potatoes?"

"It's vulgar," said Elaine. "Too obvious."

"Def says you never notice anything," said Weena, "or you might have noticed he's on the vulgar side himself, not to mention the obvious. You do to Def what my mother did to my dad: you shame him and expose him and laugh at his achievements. You suck his life out of him to keep yourself going."

"You've got it wrong," said Daphne. "It's the other way round."

"I'm the one who loves Def properly," said Weena. "I'm the one who can make him happy."

"I want you to leave my house," said Elaine. "I want you to leave it now." And she looked round desperately and automatically for help from Def, who wasn't there.

"The thing is," said Weena, "it isn't your house, is it? It's Def's. He told me so. So it's not up to you whether I go or stay, it's up to Def. And he needs me to stay because he won't get his money other-wise, and the money is enough for him to pay off his debts and stay here in the house he loves. With me to love him and look after him."

"She's insane," said Daphne, "or seriously disturbed. But ever so fanciable. Perhaps I should borrow your car, Mum, and drive her back to London for treatment."

"No thanks," said Weena. "Not if you're as dykey as Def says. I'm not sitting in a car with you!"

* * *

Defoe returned with his glasses.

"I want to make it clear," he said, "that Weena was merely using a tactic common to biographers today. Her train was late—check with the station if you like—we came straight here. Our relationship is, of course, perfectly proper. The rest is shock tactics, designed to sweep away our conventional habits of restraint and repression when it comes to our own lives. After this, we will all be as frank and open as she requires."

"And you're old enough to be her father," said Daphne.

"It's the last station at the end of the line," said Elaine. "It's unmanned, as you well know. I couldn't check if I wanted to. Either way, Daphne will drive me back to London now. I will stay with her and Alison."

"Peter has a bigger apartment," said Daphne. "Rick is smaller than Alison. There is no dog. You'll be happier with Peter."

"I will stay with one of my children," amended Elaine, "until you've come to your senses, Defoe."

"One dyke and one queer," said Weena. "Even my mother didn't do as badly as that!"

"Shut up, Weena," Defoe had the grace to say, but Weena made a dive for his crotch and he giggled. "That is so profoundly politically incorrect. God, I love you!"

"What have you been taking, Dad?" demanded Daphne. "What has she been giving you? Shall we go upstairs, Mum, and put a few things in a suitcase?"

But Defoe was smiling too hard to hear. Elaine seemed to be in shock: ashen. Daphne helped her from the table. For the first time, Daphne envisaged her mother as old: and what was more, quite possibly old without a husband. Defoe would quickly find a woman to nurse him, even one of the likes of Weena. But who would Elaine have? Daphne? Peter? The needs of an older generation would not spark sympathy in Rick's mind, let alone

Alison's. Jumper would not mind. Daphne must get home to nurture Alison. She had been away too long.

"No need to make such a scene, Elaine," Defoe reproached his wife. "Weena's just an Eloi. She's easily upset. You're turning this into a real embarrassment. It's unforgivable."

"Is she really going?" asked Weena, watching Elaine and Daphne leave the room, leaning into one another for strength and comfort. "Just like that? She's not exactly Boadicea. Do you know about Boadicea? I was reading up on her the other day."
"My wife has her dignity," said Defoe. "Let her live by it. And constancy, endurance, honesty and all the rest. Me, I have you."
"And the house to ourselves," rejoiced Weena. "What an innocent Elaine is. It never pays to leave the matrimonial home: doesn't she know that? Possession is nine-tenths of the law. Once she's out, it'll take her a year and ten thousand pounds at a minimum to get back in. If she ever does. Not so much an innocent, more of a fool."

Defoe's hand travelled up Weena's thigh and under the edge of one of the frayed denim hems, but she pushed his hand away. "Not while Daphne's in the house," said Weena. "A daughter's a daughter and they suffer. My mother and father never closed the door. They never cared what noise they made. That counts as abuse, doesn't it?"
"Poor little Weena," said Defoe. "I'll make it up to you."
And he took his hand away and gazed in admiration at the angel who had now taken Weena's form, though she floated a little before his eyes. Down in the reeds by the river she'd given him a tablet or two to take, and he'd swallowed them because she'd said so, and took a step backwards away from him for every second he dithered, her naked body translucent, greeny-white and firm like some plump

serpent, miraculous in its existence, threatening to disappear. Once he'd swallowed, she came nearer: her turn to swallow him up.

Hattie tried to lull her niece Amy to sleep. She sang every lullaby she knew: that is to say "Rock-a-bye Baby" and "Hush, My Darling."

"Boring, boring," said the child, and used the remote control to get to Sky and the Pop Channel. Then she put the volume up really loud and fell asleep contentedly. The telephone rang. It was Bob.

"You'll have to forgive me, Hattie," he said. "Let me get this over. It's Bob. I'm not worthy of you. Last week I asked Weena round. She stayed the night. It won't happen again. It's taken me three days to get up the courage to tell you. I don't want it to spoil things between you and me. Please God it won't."

"Are you at home?" asked Hattie.

"I got fired," said Bob. "There was a letter on my desk Friday morning. Now I'm so far down I guess there's no way left but up, and I'm almost glad."

"But why?"

"I guess it was Wednesday's management meeting. First of all I was late—that was Weena's fault, the little bitch. I know she did it on purpose—"

"Don't tell me; just don't tell me," begged Hattie.

"Then I said how about Defoe Desmond's biography, and there was a kind of silence. Well, it was a crazy idea, I know, but Weena wanted me to put it to them, so I did. In the letter it said my editorial suggestions weren't in tune with managerial and financial goals, so I guess that was it. Suggest a has-been to the powers that be, get to be a has-been too."

"I see," said Hattie. "So now you're fired you'll go on the dole and there'll be no maintenance for your wife."

"I hadn't thought of that," said Bob.

"I bet Weena had," said Hattie.

"You used to be her friend," said Bob.

"Not any more," said Hattie. "And I'm glad she suffered from our crumbs. If you promise to change the sheets, I'll come round."

"When?" asked Bob.

"I'm looking after my sister's little girl Amy," said Hattie. "I'll wait till she wakes and then take her home and come on to you."

"Wake her up now," said Bob.

"Certainly not," said Hattie. "That would be immoral. She has to wake naturally."

Elaine moved stiffly round the bedroom, frowning and inefficient. Daphne stuffed the more obvious items of clothing and personal necessities into a suitcase.

"Dad's been taking something, Mum," she said. "He's not himself. Let's just get away, shall we?"

"Perhaps it would be better if I stayed," said Elaine. "It doesn't feel right just to go."

"I can't leave you here on your own," said Daphne. "And I can't stay, so you'll have to come."

"Why can't you stay?"

"Because Alison is taking Jumper to the vet at 7:45, and the vet's a woman and just her type. I've been away for three days and I want to get to the appointment too."

"Do you mean the vet is Jumper's type, or Alison's type?"

"Alison's type," said Daphne patiently.

"Oh," said Elaine. "And then you could have an operation to get to be an animal and then you could be Jumper's type. Just a thought."

"Not a very good joke, Mum," said Daphne.

"Probably not," said Elaine gloomily, and waved at the furniture. "What are you doing, Mum?"

"Waving goodbye to the matrimonial fourposter," said Elaine. "I was born in that bed. I had you in hospital. Peter too. Perhaps that's what went wrong. Lack of faith."

"You're talking strangely even for you, Mum," said Daphne. "Let's just get out of here."

"No, wait a moment," said Elaine, clinging to one of the four posts of the bed. "I could compose a curse. I could curse your father and all his line."

"He doesn't have a line. Just Peter and me."

"My mother cursed my father and all his line before she went," said Elaine. "Before she jumped in the river. They found her down near the reeds. Why shouldn't I do it too? It obviously works." Daphne tried to prise her mother's arms from the post, but failed. "Jesus, what a nightmare!" she said. "Compared to home, International Relations is a piece of cake."

The phone rang. Elaine let loose the bedpost and answered it. "Hello," she said. "Yes, as it happens, someone called Weena is in the house. An Eloi. We're just Morlocks."

"Is that Mrs. Desmond?" asked Hattie.

"Lady Drewlove to you," said Elaine. "Who ever wanted to be married to a mere commoner?"

"Lady Drewlove! Wow!" said Hattie. "I thought you were just a Mrs. It was you I wanted anyway, not Weena. I need to warn you. Weena's no well-wisher. I know: I'm her friend. She's after your husband. She'll drive you out, suck him dry, spit him out as a husk. I can't go on, because you're out of town and this is my friend Bob's phone. One of the husks I'm talking about. There are hulks and there are husks."

"She's writing my husband's biography," said Elaine. "She seems to be plumping him up well enough, making him rich and famous again: I see no sign of any husk—"

* * *

Downstairs, Weena said to Defoe, as she helped herself to rasp-
berry mousse with a meringue topping, done to a turn overnight
in the Aga's plate-warming oven, "As soon as she's gone, call
the locksmith, change the locks. Then she can't get in without
breaking in, and you can call the police if she tries. Communi-
cate only through lawyers. Accuse her of violent behaviour. She'll
soon give up and go away and leave you in peace, to be yourself
at last. I'll be here to help you; it's all going to be just fine!"

Defoe's head was clearing. The fronds of Weena's shorts were
beginning to separate out, lie still; had ceased writhing and weav-
ing round her leg.
"Wasn't that the phone?" he asked.
"Not any more," said Weena.
Defoe picked up the silent instrument to hear Hattie's voice.

"Weena's got no commission to do Defoe Desmond's biography.
She tried but she failed. There's no Sunday newspaper serialis-
ation. All that's for your husband's benefit. A commission just
acts as a pregnancy used to, when a girl wants a man and a home.
When she's got what she wants, the baby, the commission just
somehow fades away. She has a miscarriage: the editor changes
his mind. She's installed, though. She's okay. Too late for the
guy to go back. It happens to the good guys, not the bad. Don't
give up on your husband just because Weena's around."

Defoe put the receiver down. The words might have been real,
or they might have come from heaven. He did not recognise the
voice, but the statements made were the more convincing for that.
His hand tightened round Weena's thigh.
"You're hurting me," she protested. "I bruise so easily. I'm Weena
the Eloi. My mother named me after the girl in *The Time Machine*,

did I ever tell you that? She wanted to diminish me from the moment I was born."

"I'm the King of the Morlocks," he said, picking up the bread knife, "and I'm going to eat half of you for lunch, and the Queen shall have the other half for tea."

The knife was at her throat and she was on her feet in an instant.

"Get out of here now," Defoe said. "Just out."

"I'll tell everyone," Weena said. "I'll tell the press. I'll tell them you raped me. I'll tell them everything."

"Tell away," he said, "because who's interested? No one. It's the end of the line, Weena, for you and for me, and you're lost and I'm saved."

"Take me now," Weena pleaded, thrusting out her chest at him, but the T-shirt seemed unerotic, the breasts pointless. "This is so exciting! I've never wanted a man so much—"

"It won't work," Defoe said, brandishing his knife, pursuing her. "It worked once, it worked twice; three times and you'd have me. Serpent! Slimy, cold creature. I'll cut your head off!"

And Weena turned and ran out of the house. He followed her to the door and flung her green leather bag after her, and the bread knife after that, so it glinted in the air and almost got her: she stared up at it, mouth open and paralysed, as it arced towards her, over and over, and down, Elaine's best bread knife with the serrated edge. But the knife missed her, and buried itself haft-deep in the lawn. Weena grabbed her bag and ran. Defoe slammed the door after her and turned the locks just as his wife and daughter came down the stairs.

"I reckon I was just in time," said Hattie to Bob. "If I'd come straight round, if I hadn't waited for Amy to wake, I wouldn't have bothered to get through to Defoe Desmond's wife."

* * *

Bob had found no clean sheets, but had straightened those already on the bed and brushed away the crumbs, ready for next morning's breakfast. She could forgive him.

Weena went to her office and found her name off the door and her desk gone. She had no job: she was one of many similarly made redundant. Nor was Dervish there to cajole and persuade, blackmail and charm. He had left a message to say if she attempted to stay, she'd be thrown out. She could collect her wages the following week.

Weena went to her apartment and found the lock changed and her suitcases out, and the white satin blouse, now the same grey as Elaine's wood ash, hanging on the doorknob by way of explanation.

"She can't prove it," said Weena aloud, "she's got no proof!" but no one was listening. She thought she heard the sound of Dervish's voice, Dervish laughing in his particular pleasure, and knew that she had lost. She had gone too far.

Weena went to Hattie's apartment but there was no one there. So she went round to Bob's to cadge a bed for the night but Hattie was there and Bob wouldn't let her in. It was no good going to Bob's wife, who once had been Weena's best friend, because she wasn't speaking either.

Weena used the last of her money taking a taxi to the crematorium where her father was buried, but it was so vast, so many crosses, so many plaques, it seemed there were more people dead in the world than alive. She lay face down on the grass and tried to commune with her father, but failed. She reckoned he had gone and she was on her own. She had driven everyone away.

A man with a good profile in a good suit stood alone by a grave: the sky was rosy pink, the moon rising. She thought everything was beautiful. She would begin again. She felt reborn in goodness: her spirits rose: she was elated.

"I spent the last of my money on flowers for my mother's grave," she said softly to the man with the profile. He was perhaps in his mid-forties. "I didn't stop to think how I'd get home."
He turned his face to hers. He looked quite like her father, as she expected: intelligent, personable, interesting. It was the pattern fate made in front of you, laying out its crazy paving slabs. You got to anticipate what the next one would be. First you stepped on one, then on another: there was scarcely any choice. You tried not to fall between the cracks, and the attempt was the only free will there was. Lately they'd taken to shifting beneath her feet: she'd got things wrong. But you lost some and won some: you couldn't blame yourself.
"Otherwise it's the end of the line for me too," said Weena. "I might as well join those here gathered."
"They wouldn't have you," he said, having studied her for a little. "You're far too alive for that. Let me give you a lift in my Rolls. In the presence of the dead the truly living must stick together. And so few of us are truly alive."
They walked off together into the sunset, if not hand in hand, at least hip to hip; defiant, in anticipation of things to come.

RUN AND ASK DADDY
IF HE HAS ANY MORE MONEY
An Exercise in Italics

Well now! It was *Easter* and my friend *David* was helping his wife *Milly Frood* in the *shop* when he heard a *voice he recognised* crying loud and clear across the crowded room, "Run and ask *Daddy* if he has any more money," and his *blood ran cold.*

Easter is upon us now. It is a season when we should reflect upon our sins and consider the pain we cause others, especially those who have no choice but to put up with us; this trauma of self-knowledge, self-revelation, culminating on Easter Friday, leaving us Saturday to shop and recover, so that on Sunday we can wake exhilarated to our new selves—and then have Monday to calm down a bit and prepare to get back to work. Should, should! Mostly we just give each other cards and Easter eggs and are grateful for the holiday.

David is in his early forties. He has not very much reddish hair and an abundant, very red beard. He wears a tweed jacket. He is now a professor. He used to be a mere lecturer but his Polytechnic turned into a University and voilà! there he was, Professor Frood, a pillar of society: looked up to and trusted: a family man.

A really nice guy, too: the trustful kind, prone to loving not wisely but too well, as the best people are. But that is all in the past, of course. Professors can't muck about. There's too much at stake. All that a man can do is hope that the past, burrowing away like some mole through the pleasant green fields of his present, doesn't surface and spoil everything in an explosion of mud and dirt.

This particular Thursday before Easter, at two minutes past four in the afternoon, it seemed as if it very well might.

Milly Frood is sometimes spoken of by friends as Frilly Mood. They're being ironic. She's a really un-frilly, serious, nice, good woman. She has straight hair and a fringe and a plump, rather expressionless, round face and a body well draped in unnotice-able clothes. The Frood children, Sherry and Baf, now in their teenage years, have never wittingly eaten sugar or meat under their own roof: Frilly Mood has seen to that. The kids are healthy if a little thin, and very polite. Frilly Mood's done well by them. It is no crime to be serious.

The shop is between the Delicatessen and the Estate Agents, down the High Street. It's an upmarket gift shop, selling the kind of decorative things nobody needs but everyone likes to have, from papier-mâché bowls (French) in deep, rich colours, at £65; black elephant pill boxes (Malaysian) at £2.75; fluffy rabbits (Korean) at £12.35; little woolly lambs (New Zealand) at £8.50 and deco-rated Easter eggs (English) at £4.87, and so on. Pre-Easter is these days almost as busy a time as pre-Christmas. Everyone feels the need for a little unnecessary something extra, or what is life all about? Where are the rewards?

* * *

David was helping Milly out in the shop over the pre-Easter rush. And why should he not? The Poly (sorry, University) was closed for the holidays (sorry, vacation) and in Milly's words, David had "nothing better to do." His wage remained that of a lecturer no matter that he was called a professor. You can re-name everything you like, but harsh facts don't alter just because you've done so. In other words, money was tight and if Milly could do without extra staff so much the better. Nevertheless, David felt that helping out was a humiliation, and blamed Milly for it. In Milly's view a man was only working if you could see him working, and who can see a man thinking?

The voice he recognised was that of Bettina Shepherd; the voice had a most attractive actressy double *timbre* (that's in italics because it's French, not because it has significance for this story) and it was familiar because there'd been a time when it had spoken many words of true love, murmured many a sinful suggestion into his ear. But all that had been some seven years back, a long time ago: longer, surely, than was needed to make that man now feel responsible for the man then. Do we not all grow an entirely new skin every seven years? Should a man not be allowed to start anew; as with a driving licence, should the passage of time not wipe out past misdeeds?

Daddy was the man Bettina referred to: he was at the back of the shop where the inexpensive trinkets were. Bettina was looking peculiarly attractive in a cashmere dress, in seasonal yellow, belted by a linked chain which for all anyone could tell was made of pure gold; the whole setting off her bosomy figure, little waist and black hair to advantage. Daddy was grey-suited, good-looking, gentlemanly and wore a solid gold tie-pin. David thought he looked extremely boring and rather stupid, but David would, wouldn't he?

* * *

"David, this has to stop," Bettina had said to him in the History Tutorial Room one day, seven years ago. "You are a married man and I'm going to be married too. The ceremony is next week. I wanted to tell you earlier but didn't like to, because I didn't want to upset you. You are the only man I'll ever really love but I have to think of my future. We have to be realistic. You could never support two homes in any comfort and I'm just not cut out for employment. I'm not that kind of person." He'd thought his heart would break. He was surprised it went on beating. Later he'd told himself he was lucky to be out of a trivial, passing affair with such an unfeeling, whimsical person, but he'd never really believed himself. The truth was that he'd taken no real pleasure since in Milly's straight hair and earnest face. He could see Milly was good, but what a man wanted was something more than honest worth. Sometimes he felt guilty because others called his wife Frilly Mood, ironically, but then he'd tell himself she'd always been like that. Not his doing.

His blood ran cold—I say this advisedly. When David heard Bettina's voice—last heard on the floor behind the sofa in the History Tutorial Room—echoing through the shop at two minutes past four, he felt a chill strike down his head to his right shoulder, into his arm and down to his fingers, and he had the feeling that if that section of blood didn't warm up before it got back up to his heart, that organ would freeze and this time stop once and for all. So much a heart can stand, no more.

David turned his back on his customers, lest he be seen and recognised by Bettina, and busied himself looking for a *Peruvian crucifixion scene,* grateful that his heart had survived the shock. But not before he had seen *the little girl* obediently leave her mother's side and head through shopping bags and spring-clad elbows towards her father. Bettina, near the door, was clearly interested in purchasing the papier-mâché bowl at £65; Daddy flicked through *Easter cards* at the back of the shop.

The Peruvian crucifixion scene consisted of six pieces in brightly glittering tin—a crimson Judas, a gold Jesus, a navy Pontius Pilate, a scarlet Mary Magdalene, a pale blue Madonna, and a black cross.

The little girl had red hair like David's own. Bettina had black hair; Daddy's was fair and painfully sparse, as if responsibility had dragged a lot of it out. The little girl must be six years old. Her front teeth were missing, to prove it.

The Easter cards were the cheapest things sold in the shop. For 75p you could buy cards depicting bunnies and chickens; from there on up to £2 you could find anything an artist in a time of recession could invent. Milly and David Frood saw the innovation of the Easter card as one of the more sinister accomplishments of the Greetings Card Industry. Who ever in their youth had heard of an Easter card? All part of the commercialisation of religion, etc., etc. Obliged to live by commerce, the Froods despised commerce. Who doesn't?

Such things pass quickly through the mind when sights are seared into a man's heart, and he doesn't know what to think or feel, and he's gazing at a shelf.

David felt a *familiar hand* upon his arm. It was his wife's. "Perhaps we should have *another baby,*" she said, to his further astonishment.
"Why now?" he asked. "Why mention it now in the middle of such a rush?"

"Because we're always in a rush," said Milly Frood, answering back, quite out of character, "as anyone not on the dole these days is. And I just saw a little girl in the shop with hair the same lovely colour yours was when you were young: and I thought, last chance for a baby. I'm nearly forty now." Before David could reply, a voice behind him said, "Is there no one serving here?" and Milly Frood turned quickly back to her work and David was *let off the hook.*

The familiar hand had cooked his food, burped his babies, returned the VAT, encouraged him in love and in illness, and it was a whole seven years since he had even been grateful for it, he realised. Now suddenly he was. But the habit of disparagement remained. "Why mention it now?" he'd said, discouraging spontaneity, being disagreeable. He was ashamed of himself.

Another baby. David had not really wanted children in the first place: he had not wanted to get married. He would tell me about it when he lamented the everyday ordinariness of his life. The college, the kids, the shops, the bills, and never anything happening. But a man's seed bursts from him here and there, unwittingly, and a good man settles down to his responsibility, sometimes with a good heart, sometimes not. *Another baby?* David felt all of a sudden Milly could have anything she wanted. Suppose Bettina saw him; recognised him, greeted him? Then everything could simply fall apart. Supposing Daddy looked from his child's hair to the red beard, and remembered some clue, some time, some place? It's a wise man doubts his child's paternity, if his wife is Bettina. Supposing this, supposing that?

Let off the hook—but of course he wasn't let off the hook. The past may be another country, but there are frequent international flights from there to here, especially over the public holidays,

when everyone leaves their homes and mills about in search of
objects, not caring who remembers what. A papier-mâché bowl
here, an Easter card there.

 "Daddy," said the little piping voice: was it like Sherry's? Was
it like Baf's? It was. "Mummy says do you have any more
money?"
Silence fell upon the shop. All waited for the reply: mothers,
divorcées, widows, working women, and their escorts, should
they have them. It's mostly women who shop. Slips of girls. Red-
headed six-year-olds with gap teeth looking trustingly up at al-
leged fathers. An honest question, honestly asked, in time of
recession.

David turned: you cannot look at a single shelf forever. David
caught Bettina's eye. Bettina smiled, in recognition, acknowledgement. Bettina's mouth was not quite as plump and full as once it
had been. Everyone waited. A question publicly asked will be
publicly answered.
"Tell your mother," said Daddy loudly, "the answer is no. My
money's all gone and your mother has spent it."

Daddy tipped over the box of Easter cards onto the floor and,
parting customers with grey-suited elbows and gold-ringed hands,
made his way to the door and out of it. The little girl ran weeping
after him. David saw Daddy take his little girl's hand as they
passed the window: he saw her smile: evidently the little girl cried
easily and cheered up easily. Sherry had been like that.

If a woman has no money left, perhaps she'll turn back to love?
Bettina stood irresolute for a moment, all eyes upon her. She
looked at Milly, she looked at David. Then she said to Milly, "*I*

just love the shop," and followed her husband and daughter out. It was four minutes past four.

Bettina had found herself pregnant: perhaps by one, perhaps by another. Perhaps she had not been unfeeling, whimsical, in dismissing him, David, after all, behind the sofa in the History Tutorial Room. Perhaps the dismissal had been an act of love, to let the erring husband off the hook? Perhaps she had simply done what was right? In thinking better of Bettina, in forgiving her, David felt himself become quite free of her. And high time too. Seven whole years!

I just love the shop.
"What a nice woman," said Milly. "Saying that. Did she know you or something?"
"No, she didn't," said David. "And you're the nicest woman I know," and he found that, though the first was a lie, the second was true. *Happy Easter, everyone!* Which speaks for itself: no need for explanation, or excuse.

IN THE GREAT WAR (II)
The Gift of Life

Another story, friend, from the Great War, before the dawn of Equality and Peace, before Sisterhood, from the days when women were at odds with women.

My friend Ellen, a poet, lightly declared war on another man's wife, an artist.
"I can take any man from any woman," Ellen boasted.
"Oh no you can't," said the artist. "You can't take mine. We love each other too much. And we're married. Besides, your legs are short and your ankles are thick."
"We'll see about that!" said Ellen. "Too short and too thick I'm not talking about!"

What shall we call the artist? Y? Why not? Something universal! Ellen waited and worked and pounced, and stole a baby girl from Y's husband, or that was how Y saw it. Stole his sperm to bring into the world a new being, who had no business here. (We'll call the husband X: what else, the unconstant factor?)

Ellen called Y on the phone.
"I did it! I told you so. He loves me," she said, "not you. He told

me so. And here's the proof of it. I'm pregnant! And, what's more, I love him in return."

"I'd rather have her than you," said X, "now it's happened." So Y killed herself. X was sorry. But he didn't blame himself. In the Great War, men simply didn't. X turned cold and cruel to Ellen and her child. "Your fault!" he said. "I can never truly love you now, or anyone."

Now a ghost cries out for revenge. I hear it sometimes in the night, decades later. "Write me," she cries. "Write me, not them." I try to understand. The voice isn't Y's—Y rests easy, I think. No, it's Ellen calling. Ellen died too, by her own hand. Y reached out from the grave and stabbed Ellen in the back and dragged her down, and X made no attempt to stop Y, or save Ellen, which he could have, well enough, by smiling, forgiving, sopping up the harm Y did by her own dreadful act of self-destruction. He was the hook; he could have let Ellen off it. But no.

Well, it's true Ellen started it; it was a fierce war—no holds barred: Ellen deserved it: why should she lie quiet? Let her roam and reproach in the darkness. It's just that on the worst nights I hear two voices, sighing. I even see two ghosts. One is Ellen's: talkative and proud in death as she was in life, oddly robust: I don't mind seeing that: I'm rather pleased she's around, bearing witness to this and that. But there's another one, a little one, a shadow wraith, dancing and pattering at her mother Ellen's heels. I try to close my eyes but the pale image burns through the lids. Orchis was six when Ellen killed her. Six: a peculiar age, all spirit and not enough substance: of course Orchis won't lie down, why should she?

* * *

71

News of suicide travels fast, by telephone, contacts clicking, inter-locking! Oh God, oh God, grim news! News of murder comes faster still, runs by word of mouth from house to house. People knock at doors, stuttering, stammering. Add suicide to murder and the whole suburb reels and buzzes within the hour. Who saw them last? Whose fault can it be? If only this, if only that! We always knew, we never knew, we certainly never thought! Oh dreadful, dreadful! How could she, how dare she? Even as we grieve, anger breaks through. Don't we all suffer? What was so special about her that she found things intolerable? What was so special about her, that she had to do this to us?

More than you'd ever believe claim friendship, standing as near the frightful brink as possible, staring down into the black pit of blame, before drawing back into the sensible, recovering world. But it's never over. Decades later the sorrow still comes back, and the anger.

The Great War is now decades in the past, back in the sixties: those were the days when women fought over men, and died for love, or lack of it: but I suppose wars are never truly over, and shouldn't be, not while we remember their victims.

Well, consider it. Here's a fine picture for a War Artist. The little child, little Orchis, lying awake, the father far away, disowning, angry. The mother comes with whisky in the sleeptime cocoa: she brings with her a handful of pills. Take just another one, my dear, and just another one. Mother says so! For the cut on your finger, the bump on your head—see, soon all will be well: all troubles cured.

* * *

No wonder our children view pills with suspicion: they spit them out; they won't eat the green-and-red apple; they know the pink bit's poisoned. You don't need a stepmother for that. Mothers are dangerous things: they are all witches at heart: give me an apple the same colour all over.

How could Ellen do it? How could any woman do a thing like that? Kill her own child, and then herself? With more competence in death than she ever had in life? No hidden plea for help here: just surety, and certainty, that death is the proper answer to life.

But listen, I tell you, my friend, Ellen did the right thing. In retrospect I see it clearly. I didn't at the time. I know more now. If a mother kills herself, she must take her children with her: haul them kicking and screaming through the gates of finality. Let that be your deterrent, friend, if ever you're thinking of suicide. You look a little too sad, act a little too quiet, for your own good. Did it happen to you? The child who's left must live out the life sentence imposed by the mother. Few children truly survive the suicide of mothers: bodies go on living, but the mother has taken back the gift of life.

NOT EVEN A
BLOOD RELATION

"You are so selfish," said Edwina to her mother. Edwina was thirty-one. She hated her name. Her parents had expected a boy: "Edwin" had been ready and waiting. They'd just added on an "a" and ignored her thereafter. Edwina was Hughie and Beverley's first-born. Hughie, Duke of Cowarth, father: Beverley, a fortune-hunter from New Zealand, mother. Now, decades into family disapproval, Beverley was sixty-one; Hughie had died three months back. Edwina had affairs, rode to hounds and drank too much. The family had just about got over the shock of the death. Now it was all wills, or rather no wills, and inheritance, or no inheritance, and who got what title: that is to say whatever sad crumbs of comfort spilled out after death could be picked over and scrabbled for. Hughie had been much and genuinely loved. "But then," Edwina remarked, "you always were selfish, Mother." "What is so selfish," asked Beverley, startled, "about wanting to live in my own home?"

"Because it's far too big for you now," said Thomasina. "Sell the place and find somewhere small and sensible to live, and divide the money amongst us." Thomasina was the second daughter. She'd been meant to be a Thomas. She was thirty. Now she was

74

pregnant and had long blonde curls. That should show her mother a thing or two. "Little middle tom-boy," her mother had once referred to Thomasina: cropped her hair short and tossed her a gun so she could join in the shoot. How Thomasina had cried. So many poor dead birds, falling about her ears!

"We must hear what Mother is saying," said Davida, the third daughter. Honestly, it was beyond a joke, and Hughie had never even laughed in the first place. He'd wanted a male heir. Davida was twenty-nine. She was a therapist, married to a psychiatrist. Her once bouncy hair had flattened out and grown limp from the strain of wisdom: her bright eyes had turned soulful: her voice gone soft from understanding her own anger, and that of others. "In my experience it is counterproductive to cling to the past," said Davida, "though we must all find our answers within ourselves."

Beverley's answer was to stay at Cowarth Court, on her own, all thirty-one bedrooms of it, three dining halls, two ballrooms, three bathrooms—hopeless, hopeless, one to every ten bedrooms, but the water supply in these Elizabethan mansions is always tricky, and at least Hughie and Beverley's *en-suite* bathroom was properly serviced, plumbing-wise, and moreover warmed. In their childhood the girls had taken refuge with the horses whenever the weather got really cold. The heating never reached the nursery wing, but got to the stables okay.

Hughie had gambled and drugged the inheritance of generations away, spectacularly, with Beverley intermittently preaching prudence and common sense. The girls had taken the father's side: Hughie knew how to live in style; Beverley, the feeling went, had the mentality of a New Zealand sheep-farmer's wife—which was what she had been born to, after all—all practicalities and no *panache*. Now of course there was nothing left to inherit. The family seat, Cowarth Castle, and most of its lands, had been hived off in lieu of tax into the National Trust's care ten years back. Only dilapidated Cowarth Court and a rather ugly Titian, both made over to Beverley by Deed of Gift during one of Hughie's bankruptcy panics, remained. But the moral right to these was surely the girls'. They were Cowarths, after all. Their mother was not really even a blood relation, not if you were talking Cowarth. Which they so often were.

But Beverley was proving remarkably stubborn. She declared she would live in Cowarth Court staring at the Titian—which was profoundly under-insured—just as long as she liked. She was unreasonable; the painting would bring in at least four million: they could all have done with their share—who would not?

"Royalty alone is allowed a female succession," the family lawyer had once explained to Beverley, whose grasp of these matters was flimsy, no matter what her reputation as a fortune and title hunter. "It's no use looking to them for example. Royal daughters are treated as sons so long as they have no brothers. George VI dies leaving two daughters: Elizabeth gets the throne and all the goodies. The younger, Margaret, gets zilch. Elizabeth's first-born is Charles; when Anne comes along, she'll only inherit if Charles dies without heirs. Then Andrew and Edward come along anyway to keep her in her place: she can forget it. But Hughie's just an Earl, so normal rules of primogeniture apply. That is to say, girls don't exist. Forget any thought of equal opportunity: male winner takes all. That's how such a mass of wealth gets totted up to these families over the centuries. Napoleon got rid of the system in France, zonks ago: great egalitarians, the

French! Hughie being an Earl, you're technically a Countess, the girls are Ladies. If Hughie dies—heaven forfend, Lady Cowarth—without male issue, the title and property—such of it as survives his life—will go to the nearest male relative: in this case Hughie's younger brother, John. Your husband is Lord Cowarth only because his elder brother died in a hunting accident—all too frequent an occurrence in this backwater of English society. First-borns die; don't ask me to explain that."

The original Charter from Queen Mary by which the Cowarths—Catholic stalwarts all—held their land and wealth laid down that what the monarch gave only the monarch (i.e., alas, the Inland Revenue) could take away. It had, in the form of the National Trust, done so. But under the terms of the Charter not even the Inland Revenue could have kept the inheritance away from a direct male succession. Torn between the risk of Hughie's bankruptcy and the risk of an intermediate heir turning up, the Inland Revenue chose the latter. The husband, after all, was Catholic, the wife well over childbearing age.

"What option does an Earl without heirs have," Hughie would boom, "but eat, drink and be merry, and spend the lot! If you don't like it, Beverley, you should have given me a son!" (Three children in three years had finished off what little maternal instinct Beverley had in the first place.) In his apparently careless and scandalous contract with the National Trust, Hughie had ensured that if the girls got nothing, brother John would get nothing either, or only a title, and he had one of those already. Hughie made no will, although he'd had six months' warning of death, leaving the tricky business of satisfying the girls entirely to Beverley. That too was his habit.

* * *

And Beverley came up with the idea of not attempting to satisfy the girls at all: simply keeping what was hers by legal right. The girls settled down to the situation presently. When Beverley died, after all, Cowarth Court and the Titian could be sold, and the funds divided, and in the meantime their mother was quiet, and in mourning, and dwindling in a somehow satisfactory way: a thin, grieving figure in grand surroundings on a low income, wandering dusty halls but at least maintaining the fabric: keeping the roofs mended and the chimneys cleaned. And the Titian was improving in value year by year. The girls would visit from time to time to see it was safe, and their mother well.

John failed in his inevitable legal battle with the National Trust. He didn't even get costs. Beverley was unsympathetic. "You English nobs think you can live off your past," she said. "That's all finished, but you won't face it." Which was a bit rich, the girls agreed, considering how well Beverley had done out of exactly that past. And not even a blood relation!

Exactly a year after their father's death, Beverley asked her three daughters to tea. She told them she had an announcement to make. "She's going to sell the house!" they rejoiced. "She's going to sell the Titian! She's going to move into sheltered accommodation!"

The girls came together in Edwina's car, though fearfully. Edwina was a ferocious driver. They were surprised to see scaffolding up on Cowarth Court and workmen busy everywhere.
"Where's she got the money from?" They were wild! "Has she made some deal with the National Trust? If she has, we will have her declared incompetent by reason of insanity!"

* * *

But Beverley came down the steps towards them serene and cheerful. She was out of widow's black and into a pale yellow sweater and a very short skirt. She had on 15-dernier tights and the girls remembered how good her legs had always been. Accompanying her was a short but good-looking guy of, they guessed, around forty. Twenty years younger than she. An architect, perhaps? A lawyer? What was their mother up to?

"This is my *fiancé,* Brian," said Beverley. "We're getting married next week."
"Hi, Edwina, Thomasina and Davida," said Brian. "I've heard such a lot about you lot. I guess your mother wanted a boy!"

"You are completely disgusting!" said Edwina to her mother later, on the phone."What will people say? You have betrayed our father!"
"I know older people do have sex, but do you have to flaunt it?" asked Thomasina. "That short skirt! And you were holding that man's hand! It doesn't bear thinking about."

"Now Mother," said Davida, "you can't replace Father so why do you try? You can only make a fool of yourself. Pop stars and actresses can get away with toyboys but a woman like you simply can't. You just don't have the style. Can't you be content to just be yourself?"

"They none of them know what kind of woman I am," said Beverley to Brian later, in bed. "They've only ever thought of me as Mother, something you draw the strength out of till there's nothing left."
"Don't get upset," said Brian, "they were bound to take it hard."

"If I'd been the one to die," said Beverley, "they'd have expected Hughie to marry again. And someone younger too. What's the matter with them?"

The girls wouldn't come to the wedding. No. They wouldn't.

"We don't have to get married," said Brian, "if it upsets everyone so much. Perhaps that's the answer. We love each other. I'll just move in and we'll live as man and wife."

"Besides," said Beverley, "if I do marry you I become plain Mrs.; Countess is out the window."

So they didn't get married. The entire extended Cowarth family pretended Brian didn't exist. Beverley found herself marginalised. It made her angry. All those years of being on nothing but Cowarth sufferance! The male protection goes, and you're out, out, out.

"He's immensely rich," said Edwina to her sisters. "She's done it again!" Edwina had set a private detective on to their mother's lover. He was found to be an Australian without education—he had made a fortune in computers, and now, no doubt—so typical of the *nouveau riche*—felt he deserved to look at a Titian after a hard day's work. He had first met Beverley three years ago, one evening when he'd been installing—in his Aussie hand's-on way—the National Trust's great new state-of-the-art computer. Had their mother and this man been having a secret affair all this time? Was this why Hughie had got cancer and died? Suddenly, to believe anything about their mother, no matter how dreadful, became second nature to the girls.

"She used her title to trap him!" declared Thomasina. "Why else should one of the world's most eligible millionaire bachelors"— for that was what Brian had been before she nobbled him—"take up with a cowgirl from New Zealand?"

"She's a manipulative, greedy bitch," said Davida, for once losing her cool. "I hate her! She only didn't marry him so as not to lose her title."

Oh, the girls were angry with their mother. But as children will, they soon settled down to the new situation. Brian gave them a few thousand pounds between them and they looked at him with more favour. At least their mother was too old to disgrace them by having a baby. She'd had a shot in the arm, that was all, of life, love and energy. Grudgingly, they thought, Good for her! If Beverley left Cowarth Court away from them, or tried to give the Titian to her new lover or anything like that, they agreed they'd go to law.
"I don't know why they're all so difficult and moody," said Beverley to Brian, "it must come from Hughie's side of the family."

Two years to the day after Hughie died, Beverley summoned her children again.

"I'm going to have a baby," she said. "There's a clinic in Rome does it for women of my age. They take away one of your eggs, fertilise it with your lover's sperm, re-implant it and Bob's your uncle. Or at any rate your little brother. Sometimes one has to use a surrogate womb, but they think in my case it won't be necessary."

The girls would hardly speak to their mother. Sex at sixty was disgusting, but now to talk of a baby! Good God!

Edwina said she found something perverse about a baby emerging from withered loins: it was flying in the face of nature; the very idea made her feel sick.

* * *

Thomasina said poor little baby! It wasn't fair to it: its mother mistaken for its grandmother—even its great-grandmother—at the school gate: who would play football with the child at weekends? What happened when it found out its origins? The discovery could only cause unbearable trauma and suffering. She knew about babies! She'd had one. Society hadn't begun to think through the ethical implication of this kind of thing.

Davida said Beverley was being entirely selfish. She was trying to dance long after the music had stopped: it was pathetic; Beverley was sick in her head. For all her training, Davida said, she, Davida, just couldn't come to terms with this: it was too monstrous.

And the rest of the Cowarths said that to do such a thing was against God's will, or if God didn't exist—which as a family they increasingly believed—nature's plans for humankind. Hughie's widow, they complained, seemed indifferent to the fact that the Cowarths were, traditionally, a Catholic family. But what could you expect of a woman who used contraception and had thwarted Hughie of his heir and so driven him to his death? But Beverley was deaf to the lot of them.

She said to Brian:

(1) It was no more perverse and unnatural to accept medical help to have a baby than it was perverse and unnatural to use penicillin to stop pneumonia. If it could be done, what was the matter with it? Women commonly used HRT to postpone ageing: the menopause was not some sacred watershed, some divine punishment to women for their sexuality, just a gradual insufficiency of oestrogen. People just got hysterical about older women having babies. They became totally irrational and invented nonsensical arguments.

* * *

(2) She was sure that if you asked the child at any stage in its life it would state it would rather be alive than not born at all. If it decided otherwise it could soon enough take itself out of this world. But it should certainly at least be offered the choice. Who was her second daughter, anyway, to seek to deny her fourth child life? Had Thomasina's childhood been perfect? No! Then by what right did Thomasina insist on perfection for others on pain of their death—or non-existence, which was the same thing? Was it better to be met at the school gate by, say, an alcoholic, or an old mother? No one stopped drunken mothers having babies: or ill mothers, or poor mothers; or only surreptitiously. And at least she, Beverley, could meet the child in a Rolls-Royce. As for the football argument, that was pathetic. What percentage of the nation's children were taken to football matches by their fathers, anyway? Precious few! What made Thomasina think they'd enjoy it if they were? Beverley was glad, however, that her daughter recognised the next baby would be a boy.

(3) As for being sick in the head she was not: she, Beverley, was profoundly sane. She'd given birth to three ungrateful and ungracious girls who had been mean to her from the beginning, despised her for her origins and taken their father's part against her, whenever they could. She wanted a fourth child. She wanted another chance. Fourth time lucky. Dear God, she too wanted a boy, and now medical birth technology made it possible, she'd have one. It might not be pleasant, it might not be easy, but she was strong, happy, wealthy and wise. And the nursery wing, thanks to Brian's money, was finally properly heated. If she tired or weakened, a battery of nurses would be available to help, and though that too might offend some who felt only a mother's care would do, and a baby ought not to be born at all who couldn't experience it, her daughters had had her, Beverley's, total care

and were they grateful? No! They chose to remember the things that went wrong, not the things that went right. The worm has turned, said Beverley, and I'm off to Rome in the morning.

It was as well that the Rome clinic had taken its fees in advance—hundreds of thousands of dollars—because on the way to Rome news broke of a discovery in the field of artificial intelligence that would eventually put Brian out of profit, and probably altogether out of business within the year.

Three years to the day after Hughie's death, Beverley stood on the steps of Cowarth Court, Brian by her side, and showed her new baby to her daughters. "His name is Edwin," she said.
They sulked, especially Edwina.
"But that's a Cowarth name," they said, "and you're not even a Cowarth."
"This is a Cowarth," said Beverley. "This is Hughie's child and heir. Hughie had his young and healthy sperm deep-frozen years back, in case I died and he eventually re-married. It seemed the least I could do for your father, finally to bear his son—so this is the new Lord Cowarth."

John's claim to the title was outdated. The National Trust lost its gamble and its claim to the Cowarth estate. All now belonged to baby Edwin and, through him, in effect, to Beverley and Brian for the next twenty-one years.

"Just as well I didn't ever marry Brian," said Beverley to her daughters, "or the child would have been legally his, and not Hughie's at all, forget whose sperm was whose. Baby wouldn't even have had a title!" Put that in your pipe and smoke it, she could have added, but didn't.

Eventually Beverley married Brian and by nature of being mother to an Earl continued to call herself by the courtesy title of Countess. The College of Heralds are still arguing the rights and wrongs of the matter.

In time the girls came to accept their little brother and, I'm sorry to say, respected their mother the more, if only for being so thoroughly selfish and bad. They certainly became far more polite to her, and agreed that it was their father's doing that their names were what they were, rather than their mother's, though without much evidence either way. As to their being obliged to shelter from the cold in the stables, had they not liked horses anyway? They were good girls at heart.

TALES OF
WICKED
MEN

WASTED LIVES

They're turning the city into Disneyland. They're restoring the ancient facades and painting them apple green, firming up the medieval gables and picking out the gargoyles in yellow. They're gold-leafing the church spires. They've boarded up the more stinking alleys until they get round to them, and as State property becomes private the shops which were always there are suddenly gone, as if simply painted out. In the eaves above Benetton and The Body Shop cherubs wreathe pale cleaned-stone limbs, and even the great red McDonald's "M" has been especially muted to rosy pink for this its Central European edition. Don't think crass commerce rules the day as the former communist world opens its arms wide to the seduction of market forces: the good taste of the new capitalist world leaps yowling into the embrace as well, a fresh-faced baby monster, with its yearning to prettify and make the serious quaint, to turn the rat into Mickey Mouse and the wolf into Goofy.

Milena and I walked through knots of tourists towards the famous Processional Bridge, circa 1395. I had always admired its sooty stamina, its dismal persistence, through the turbulence of rising and falling empire. It was my habit to stay with Milena when I came to the city. I'd let Head Office book me into an hotel, to save official embarrassment, then spend my nights with her and some part of my days if courtesy so required. I was fond of her but did not love her, or only in the throes of the sexual excitement she was so good at summoning out of me. She made excellent coffee. If I sound disagreeable and calculating it is because I am attempting to speak the truth about the events on the Processional Bridge that day, and the truth of motive seldom warms the listener's heart. I am generally accepted as a pleasant and kindly enough person. My family loves me, even my wife Joanna, though she and I live apart and are no longer sexually connected. She doesn't have to love me.

Milena is an archivist at the City Film Institute. I work for a U.S. film company, from their London office. I suppose, if you add it up, I have spent some three months in the city, on and off, over the last five years, before and after the fall of the Berlin Wall and the Great Retreat of Communism, a tide sweeping back over shallow sand into an obscure distance. Some three months in all spent with Milena.

Her English was not as good as she thought. Conversation could be difficult. Today she was not dressed warmly enough. It was June but the wind was cold. Perhaps she thought her coat was too shabby to stand the inspection of the bright early summer sun. I was accustomed to seeing her either naked or dressed in black, as was her usual custom, a colour, or lack of it, which suited the gaunt drama of her face; but today, like her city, she wore pastel colours. I wished it were not so.

Beat your head not into the Berlin Wall, but into cotton wool, machine-pleated in interesting baby shades, plastic-wrapped. Suffocation takes many forms.

* * *

"You should have brought your coat," I said.

"It's so old," she said. "I am ashamed of it."

"I like it," I said.

"It's old," she repeated, dismissively. "I would rather freeze." For Milena the past was all dreary, the future all dread and expectation. A brave face must be put on everything. She smiled up at me. I am six foot three inches and bulky: she was all of five and a half foot, and skinny with it. The jumper was too tight: I could see her ribs through the stretched fabric, and the nipples too. In the old days she would never have allowed that to happen. She would have let her availability be known in other, more subtle ways. Her teeth were bad: one in the front broken, a couple grey. When she wore black their eccentricity seemed a matter of course; a delight even. Now she wore green they were yellowy, and seemed a perverse tribute to years of neglect, poverty and bad diet. Eastern teeth, not Western. I wished she would not smile, and trust me so.

The Castle still looks down over the city, and the extension to that turreted tourist delight, the long low stone building with its rows of identical windows, tier upon tier of them, blank and anonymous, to demonstrate the way brute force gives way to the subtler but yet more stifling energies of bureaucracy. You can't do this, you can't live like that, not because I have a sword to run you through, but because Our Masters frown on it. And your papers have not risen to the top of the pile.

Up there in the Castle that day a newly elected government was trying to piece together from the flesh of this nation, the bones of that, a new living, changing organism, a new constitution. New, new, new. I wished them every luck with it, but they could not make Milena's bad teeth good, or stop her smiling at me as if she wanted something. I wondered what it was. She'd used not to smile like this: it was a new trick: it sat badly on her doleful face.

* * *

We reached the Processional Bridge, which crosses the river between the Palace and the Cathedral. "The oldest bridge in Europe," said Milena. We had walked across it many times before. She had made this remark many times before. Look left down the river and you could see where it carved its way through the mountains which form the natural boundaries to this small nation: look right and you looked into mist. On either bank the ancient city crowded in, in its crumbly, pre-Disney form, all eaves, spires and casements, spared from the blasts of war for one reason or another, or perhaps just plain miracle. But Emperors and Popes must have somewhere decent to be crowned, and Dictators too need a background for pomp and circumstance, crave some acknowledgement from history: a name engraved in gold in a Cathedral, a majestic tomb in a gracious square still standing. It can't be all rubble or what's the point?

I offered Milena my coat. It seemed to me that she and I were at some crucial point in not just our story, but everyone's; that the decisions we made here today had some general relevance to the way the world was going. I could at least share some warmth with her. My monthly Western salary would keep her in comfort for a year, but what could I do about that? Not my doing. If she wanted a new coat from me it would have nothing to do with her desire to be warm, but as a token of my love. She didn't mind shivering. Her discomfort was both a demonstration of martyrdom and a symbol of pride.

"I am not cold," she said.

The city is a favourite location for film companies. The place is cheap; its money valueless in the real world and its appetite for hard currency voracious, which means good deals can be had. The quaint, colourful locations are inexpensively historicised—though the satellite dishes are these days becoming too numerous to dodge easily. And there are few parking problems, highly trained post-production technicians, efficient labs, excellent cameramen, sensitive sound-men, and so on—and cheap, so cheap. Those who lived in the city had escaped the fate of so much of the hitherto Russian-dominated lands—the sullen refusal of the oppressed and exploited to do anything right, to be anything other than inefficient, sloppy and lazy, in the hope that the colonising power would simply give up and go away, shaking the dust of the conquered land from its feet. And the power it had amassed lay not of course in the strength of the ideology it professed, as the West in its muddled way assumed, but in the strength of arms and organisation of that single, colonising, ambitious nation, Russia. Ask anyone between Budapest and Samarkand, Tbilisi and the Siberian flatlands, and they would tell you who they feared and hated: Russia, the motherland, announcing itself to a gullible world as the Soviet Union. Harsh mother, pretending kindness, using Marxist-Leninism as the religious tool of government and exploitation, as once in the South Americas Spain had used Christianity.

In the city they kept their wits about them: too sophisticated for the numbing rituals of mind-control ever to quite work; the concrete of the workers' blocks to quite take over from the tubercular gables and back alleys, to stifle the whispers of dissent, to quieten the gossip and mirth of café society. McDonald's has achieved that now with its bright, forbidding jollity, and who in the brave new world of freedom can afford a cup of coffee anyway, has anything interesting or persuasive to say now that everyone has what they wanted? Better, better by far to travel hopefully than to arrive, to have to face the fact that the journey is not out of blackness into light, but from one murky confusion into another. Happiness and fulfilment lie in our affections for one another, not in the forms that our societies take. If only I was in love with Milena, this walk across the bridge would be a delight. I would feel the air bright with the happiness of the hopeful young.

Be that as it may, the city was always better than anywhere else for filming, Castle and all. Go to Rumania and you'd find the castles still full of manacled prisoners clanking their chains; try Poland and you'd have to fly in special food for your stars; in Hungary the cameraman would have artistic tantrums; but here in the city there would be gaiety, fun, sometimes even sparkle, the clatter of high heels on cobblestones, sultry looks from sultry eyes, and of course nights with Milena in the fringy, shabby apartment, with the high, white-mantled brass bed, and good strong coffee in porcelain cups for breakfast. Milena, forever languidly busy, about my body or about her work, off to the Institute or back from it. Women worked hard in this country, as women were accustomed to all over the Soviet Union. Equality for women meant an equal obligation to work, the official direction of your labour, sleeping with your boss if he so required, the placement of your child in a crèche, as well as the cultural expectation that you got married, ran a home and emptied the brimming ashtrays while your husband put his feet up. Joanna would have none of that kind of thing; for the male visitor from the West the Eastern European woman is paradise, if you can hack it, if your conscience can stand it: if you can bear being able to buy affection and constancy.

I hadn't been with Milena for three months or so. Now, like her city, I found her changed. I wondered about her constancy. It occurred to me that it was foolish of me to expect it. As did the rest of the nation, she now paid at least lip service to market forces; perhaps these worked sexually as well. Rumour had it that there were now twenty-five thousand prostitutes in the city and an equal number of pimps, as men and women decided to make the best financial use of available resources. I discovered I was not so

94

much jealous as rather hoping for evidence of Milena's infidelity, which would let me off whatever vague hook it was I found myself upon. Not so difficult a hook. She and I had always been discreet: I had not mentioned our relationship to a soul back home. Milena was in another country; she did not really count: her high bouncing bosom, her narrow rib cage and fleshless hips vanished from my erotic imagination as the plane reached the far side of the mountain tops—the turbulence serving as some rite of passage—to re-imprint itself only as it passed over them once again, on my return.

The cleaning processes had not yet reached the bridge, I was glad to see. The stone saints who lined it were still black with the accumulated grime of the past.

"Who are these saints?" I asked, but Milena didn't know. Some hold books, others candles; noses are weather-flattened. Milena apologised for her ignorance. She had not, she said, had the opportunity of a religious education: she hoped her son Milo would. Her son lived with Milena's mother, who was a good Catholic, in the Southern province—a place about to secede, to become independent, to ethnic-cleanse in its own time, in its own way. "I didn't know you had a son," I said. I was surprised, and ashamed at myself for being so uncurious about her. "Why didn't you tell me?"

"It's my problem," Milena said. "I don't want to burden you. He's ten now. When he was born I was not well, and times were hard. It seemed better that he go to my mother. But she's getting old now and there's trouble in the Southern province. They are not nice people down there."

Once the city's dislike and suspicion had been reserved for the Russians. Now it had been unleashed and spread everywhere. The day the Berlin Wall fell Milena and I had been sitting next to each other in the small Institute cinema, watching the show reels of politically sound directors on the Institute's books, in the strange, flickering half-dark of such places. Her small white hand had strayed unexpectedly on to my thigh, unashamedly direct in its approach. But then exhilaration and expectation, mixed with fear, was in the air. Sex seemed the natural expression of such emotions, such events. And perhaps that was why I never quite trusted her, never quite loved her, found it so easy to forget her when she wasn't under my nose—I despised her because it was she who had approached me, not I her. If Joanna and I are apart it's because, or so she says, I'm so conditioned in the old, pre-feminist ways of thinking I'm impossible for a civilised woman to live with. I am honest, that is to say, and scrupulous in the investigation of my feelings and opinions.

"Why didn't you put the child into a crèche?" I asked.

It shocked me that Milena, that any woman, could give a child away so easily.

"I was in a crèche," she said bleakly. "It's the same for nearly everyone in this city under forty. The crèche was our real home, our parents were strangers. I didn't want it to happen to Milo. He was better with my mother, though there are too many Muslims down there. More and more of them. It's like a disease."

I caught the stony eye of baby Jesus on St. Joseph's shoulder—that one at least I knew—and one or the other sent me a vision, not that I believed in such things, as I looked down at the greeny, sickly waters of the river. I saw, ranked and rippling, row upon row of infants, small, pale children, institutionalised, deprived, pasty-faced from the atrocious city food—meat, starch, fat, no fruit, no vegetables—and understood that I was looking at the destruction of a people. They turned their little faces to me in despair, and I looked quickly up and away and back at Milena to shake off the vision; but there behind her, where the river met the sky, saw that nation grown up, marching towards me into the mists of its future, a sad mockery of those sunny early Social Realist posters which decked my local once-Marxist, now Leftish bookshop back home: the proletariat marching square-jawed and determined into the new dawn, scythes and spanners at the ready, only here there were no square jaws, only wretchedness; the quivering lip of the English ex-public schoolboy, wrenched from his home at a tender age, now made general; the same profound puzzled sorrow spread through an entire young population, male and female. See it in the easy surface emotion, the facile sexuality, the rush of tears to the eyes, uncontrolled and uncontrollable, pleading for a recognition that never comes, a comfort that is unavailable. Pity me, the unspoken words upon a nation's lips, because I am indeed pitiable. I have been deprived of freedom, yes, of course, all that. And of proper food and of fancy things, consumer durables and material wealth of every kind, all that; but mostly I have been robbed of my birthright, my mother, my father, my home. And how can I ever recover from that? Murmur as a last despairing cry the latest prayer, market forces, market forces, say it over and over as once the Hail Mary was said, to ward off all ills and rescue the soul, but we know in our hearts it won't work. There is no magic here contained. Wasted lives, lost souls, unfixable. Pity me, pity me, pity me.

"I think the fog's coming down," said Milena, and so it was. The new dawn faded into it. A young man on the bridge was selling black rubber spiders: you hurled them against a board and they crept down, leg over leg, stillness alternating with sudden movement. No one was buying.

"Well," I said, "I expect you made the right decision about Milo. What happened to his father?" I turned to button her cardigan. I wanted her warmed. This much at least I could do. Perhaps if she

was warm, she would not feel so much hate for the Southern province and its people.

"We are divorced," she said. "I am free to marry again. Look,
there's Jesus crucified. Hanging from nails in his hands. At least
the communists took down the crosses. Why should we have
to think about torture all the time? It was the Russians taught our
secret police their tricks: we would never have come to it on our
own."

I commented on the contradiction between her wanting her son
to have a Catholic upbringing, and her dislike of the Christian
symbol, the tortured man upon the cross, but she shrugged it off:
she did not want the point pursued. She was not interested in it.
She saw no virtue in consistency. First you had this feeling, then
that: that was all there was to it. No parent had ever intervened
between the tantrum and its cause; no doubt Milena along with
her generation had been slapped into silence, when protesting
frustration and outrage. She was wounded: she was damaged: not
her fault, but there it was. What I'd seen as childlike, as charming, in the early stages of a relationship, was in the end merely
irritating. I could not stir myself to become interested in her son
or in a marriage which had ended in divorce. I could not take her
initial commitment seriously.

"I'm pregnant," Milena now says. "Last time you were here we
made a baby. Isn't that wonderful? Now you will marry me, and
take me to London, and we will live happily ever after."
Fiends come surging up the river through the mist, past me, gaunt,
thin, soundlessly shrieking. These are the ghosts of the insulted,
the injured, the wronged and tortured, whose efforts have been
in vain. Those whose language has been taken away, whose bodies have been starved: they are the wrongfully dead. All the great

rivers of the world carry these images with them; over time they have infected me by their existence. They breathe all around me. I take in their exhalations. I am their persecutor, their ruler, the origin of their woes: the one who despises. They shake their ghoul-ish locks at me; they mock me with their sightless eyes, snap-ping to attention as they pass. Eyes right! Blind eyes, forever staring. They honour me, the living.

"Is something the matter?" asks Milena. "Aren't you happy? You told me you loved me."

Did I? Probably. I remind her that I've also told her that I'm married.

"But you will divorce her," she says. "Why not? Your children are grown. She doesn't need you any more. I do." Her eyes are large in their hollows: she fears disaster. Of course she does. It so often happens. I can hardly tell whether she is alive or dead. To bear a child by a ghost!

Milena is perfectly right. Joanna doesn't need me. Milena does. The first night I went with Milena she was wearing a purple vel-vet bra. It fired me sexually, it was so extraordinary, but put too great an element of pity into what otherwise could have been love. There seemed something more valuable in my wife Joanna's white Marks & Spencer bra with its valiant label, 40A. Broad-backed, that is, and flat-chested. I supposed Milena's to be a 36C. English women lean towards the pear-shaped; the city women towards the top-heavy. It's unfashionable, dangerous even, to make comparisons between the characteristics of the peoples of the world, this tribe, that tribe, this religion or that. The ghouls that people the river, who send their dying breath back, day after day, in the form of the fog that blights the place, mists up the new Disney facades with mystery droplets, met their end because people like me whispered, nudged and made odious comparisons, and the odium grew and grew and ended up in torture, murder, slaughter, genocide. Nevertheless, I must insist: it is true. Pear-shaped that lot, top-heavy this. And if I suspected Milena's purple velvet bra of being some kind of secret police state issue, or part of the Film Institute's plan to attract hard currency and Western business, an end to which their young female staff were encouraged, even paid, it is not surprising. Had I been of her nationality, I knew well enough, her hand would not have strayed across my thigh in the film-flickering dark. I was offended that the Gods of Freedom, good health, good teeth, good nourishment, prosperity and market forces, whom I myself did not worship, endowed me with this wondrous capacity to attract. I could snap my fingers and all the girls in Eastern Europe would come trotting, and fall on their knees.

"Milena," I said, and I was only temporising, "I have no way of knowing this baby is mine, if baby there be."

Milena threw her hands into the air, and cried aloud, a thin, horrid squeal, chin to the heavens, lips drawn back in a harsh grimace. There were few people left on the bridge. The fog had driven them away. The seller of rubber spiders had given up and gone home. Milena ran towards the parapet, and wriggled and crawled until she lay along its top on the cold stone, and then she simply rolled off and fell into the water below; this in the most casual way possible. From my straightforward question to this dramatic answer only fifteen seconds can have intervened. I was too stunned to feel alarm. I found myself leaning over the parapet to look downwards; the fog was patchy. I saw a police launch veer off course and make for the spot where Milena fell. No doubt she had seen it coming or she would not have done what she did, launched herself into thick air, thin, swirling water. I had confidence in her ability to survive. Authorities of one kind or another, as merciful in succour as they were cruel in the detection of sedition, would pull her out of the wet murk, dry her, wrap her in blankets, warm her, return her to her apartment. She would be all right.

I walked to the end of the bridge, unsure as to whether I would then turn left to the police pier and Milena or to the right and the taxi rank. Why had the woman done it? Hysteria, despair, or some convenient social way of terminating unwanted pregnancies? I could take a flight back home, if I chose, forty-eight hours earlier than I had intended. The flights were full, but I would get a priority booking, as befitted my status, however whimsical, as a provider of hard currency. The powerful are indeed whimsical: they leave their elegant droppings where they choose—be they Milena's baby, Benetton, the Marlboro ads which now dominate the city: no end even now to the wheezing, the coughing, the death rattling along the river.

I turned to the right, where the taxis stood waiting for stray foreigners, anxious to get out of the fog, back to their hotels.
"The airport," I said. He understood. "To the airport" are golden words to taxi drivers all over the world. This way at least I created a smile. To have turned left would have meant endless trouble. I was thoroughly out of love with Milena. I wanted to help, of course I did, but the child in the Southern provinces would have had to be fetched by the Catholic mother, taken in. There would be no end to it. My children would not accept a new family: Joanna would have been made thoroughly miserable. To do good to one is to do bad to another. But you don't need to hear my excuses. They are the same that everyone makes to themselves when faced with the misery of others, and though they would like to do the right thing, simply fail to do so, but look after themselves instead.

LOVE AMONGST THE ARTISTS

"Happy Christmas, my own true love," said Lucy to Pierre, on the morning of December 25, 1899. She woke amongst a flurry of white sheets and feather pillows and this was the nearest she would get to seasonal and romantic snow, for the day was mild and they were in the South of France, not Connecticut, which was Lucy's home, or Paris, which was Pierre's.

Pierre stirred but did not wake. Lucy whispered in his ear again. "Happy Christmas, my own true love," and this time he murmured a reply.

"If you and I are to be free souls, Lucy," said Pierre with a clarity apparently quite undiminished by slumber, "we must put all such religious cant behind us," and closed his eyes again and slept on. His arms lay brown and young amongst the sheets and his dark hair was wild and curly on the pillow and she loved him. But she loved Christmas too, and always had.

Morning sun shone in through the little square window and bounced back from the whitewashed walls. She smoothed down her white cambric nightgown and wound her hair back around her head and pinned it up, and climbed down from the high bed, and crossed the bare wooden floor and looked out of the undraped window. She could see across a river valley to vineyards which marched across hills like soldiers going to their death. She put the image from her mind. And if there was a smell of rottenness in the air, as if all the grapes which should have been gathered in the autumn to make wine had been allowed to fall and fester on the ground instead, that was nothing worse than French plumbing. Some things had to be bad, Pierre said, so bad there was nothing left for them to do but get better.

"Religion is the opiate of the people," said Pierre from his pillow. "God is a drug fed by the masters to the poor and hungry, so they are content with poverty and hunger. Jesus was never born: heaven does not exist. Blind belief is a thorn in the side of mankind and we will pluck it out."

In one more week it would be 1900, the dawn of the twentieth century, and into that dawn would strike through the light of new hope and new liberty, and all the energy of free thought and free love, untrammelled by convention, and Lucy's soul soared at the thought that Pierre and she were part of it: that he and she were one step ahead of that new dawn. They would be in Paris by New Year's Eve to be amongst the anarchists; they would gather there together to drink to the future: the passionate brotherhood of the enlightened, and their sisters in that passion.

What a different stroke of midnight it would be from the one she would have envisaged just a few months back: a single glass of wine raised solemnly at the first stroke, in the parlour, in the company of Edwin her husband and Joseph her brother, and then to bed. And each stroke sounding its annual dirge to lost hope and failing passion: its welcome to the triumph of boredom and the death of the soul.

* * *

Pierre left the bed and stood beside her. He was naked. Lucy could not become accustomed to it. She had been married to Edwin for fourteen years and had never caught more than a flash of white limb in the bathroom, a movement of bare flesh above her in the bed. Now Pierre unpinned her hair so it flowed around her shoulders.

"So never name that day again," said Pierre, "or it will drag you back to the Lord of the Dark Domain," and they both laughed. Lord of the Dark Domain was their name for Edwin. Lucy's husband wrote novels for a living; once every five years or so, to the acclaim of serious critics, he would publish an extremely melancholy book, the text so closely printed that Lucy had no patience with it, but then she was not expected to. Edwin loved Lucy for her folly; she was his child bride, his pretty wife: now he would see how he had misjudged her! Now he would find out: now that another man understood her talent, her intelligence, her quality, her passion.

"All the same," said Lucy, "it comes as a shock! No mince pies, no gifts and ribbons and best dresses? Never more?"

"Never more," said Pierre, "or you will be dragged back into the Hell of Domesticity, which is the Death of Art."

Pierre was a composer of fine if difficult song cycles which so few people in the world could understand that when Pierre came to New York from Paris to perform, the concert hall was all but empty, the tour was cancelled and Pierre left penniless and stranded in a strange land. Edwin, as an act of kindness, had offered him work for the summer, teaching Bessie and Bertie the piano. Bessie was twelve and Bertie was ten. They would wake this Christmas morning to a house which lacked a mother. Lucy put that image from her too. Bessie had Edwin's beetling brows; Bertie aped Edwin's clipped, dry manner of speech. They were Edwin's children more than Lucy's. Pierre saw it. Edwin claimed it. The law acknowledged it: let the law have its way.

* * *

"An artist needs freedom, not a family," said Pierre; he could so easily read her mind. She felt his warm breath on her cheek. "The artist's duty is to all mankind; he must break free of the chains of convention. And women can be artists too, as you are, Lucy, remember that!"

The first time Pierre had heard Lucy sing, in her sweet, clear, untrained voice, helping Bessie's fumbling notes along, he had claimed her as an artist, the one he had been waiting for, the one who could truly bring his music to life. Poor Bessie was forgotten: she could hardly get to the piano: Lucy and Pierre were always there, as she worked to catch the notes between notes he found so significant he could make them include the whole universe. Edwin was on the last chapter of a novel: a time he found particularly tense. There was to be piano-playing only between two and four o'clock of an afternoon. He said so with some force. The house trembled. People wept.

"He has you in prison," said Pierre of Edwin then. "For what is a home but a man's prison for a woman, and what is a wife but an unpaid whore? She lies on her back for her keep, bears children and cooks dinner likewise." And when Lucy had recovered from her shock, the more she thought of it the more she perceived that what Pierre said was true. Lucy understood now that the sapphire necklace she wore round her neck was the symbol of her imprisonment: that her ruby earrings marked her as an instrument of lust, that the gold charms on her bracelet were for Edwin's benefit, not her own; for is not a willing slave more useful than one who is unwilling?

"You would not be my slave," said Pierre, "you would be my love."

Lucy's eyes went to the suitcase, and she wondered whether she should check that they were still there, in the suitcase, tucked in tissue in a dancing shoe: the sapphire, the rubies and the gold. But of course they were. Why should they not be? And they were hers by right, every one, payment for years of servitude. In the new world women would have equal dignity with men. When the workers of the world rose up, they would lift up women with them.

"All the same," said Lucy, "on this day of all days, allow me to feel like a mother, not an artist, and cry just a little."

"You should be ashamed to even consider such a betrayal," said Pierre. "Weeping is something which women of the *haute bourgeoisie* do, the better to control men," and Lucy was glad to understand that he was joking, for Edwin had scolded her and chided her and made her feel foolish from the day he had met her, and never ever joked about anything.

Pierre called down to the landlady to bring breakfast up to the room. He stood naked at the top of the stairs and dodged behind the door when the woman arrived with the tray: she seemed to Lucy too small and old to carry such a weight. The servants at home were stout and strong.

"Don't upset her too much," said Lucy when she had stopped laughing. "We owe her too much rent for that. I don't know why you put off paying her."

But Pierre said they would wait for dark and then slip away unnoticed and pick up the Paris train before anyone realised, and he didn't want any silly nonsense from Lucy: the landlady was an old witch who took advantage of travellers and overcharged, and deserved what she got.

Lucy said nothing, but after she'd eaten the breakfast the landlady brought—hot coffee and fresh frothy milk, long crisp bread, and farm butter and apricot preserve—she said, "I'd really rather pay her, Pierre."

"What with?" asked Pierre. "We have no francs left. The journey across France is costing more than I thought. An artist shouldn't be bothered by such sordid things as money: I don't want to talk about it any more. We'll send her some from Paris if you insist when we've sold your jewellery, but she doesn't deserve it. She is a lackey of the masters, that's all she is."

Lucy felt her eyes mist with tears: she couldn't tell the difference between the frothy milk and the thick white china jug. They merged together. At home the milk jugs were of fine porcelain, and had little flowers upon them. One of them came from Limoges. She wondered where Limoges was, and if she'd ever go there. She could see such an event was more likely now that she was Pierre's lover, no longer Edwin's wife; on the other hand, any such journey would be accomplished in less comfort. She did not understand money: it seemed necessary for all kinds of things she had thought just happened—such as being warm, or welcomed, or treated with politeness by porters, and gendarmes, shopkeepers and landladies. But money did not buy love, or freedom, or truth, or hope, or any of the important things in life.

"Don't cry," said Pierre. "You're homesick, that's all it is," and he leaned towards her and removed a crumb from her lip, and her heart melted; the act was so tender and true. Edwin would have mentioned the crumb, not removed it. Pierre put on his shirt and she was glad, though she knew she shouldn't be.

"I'm not homesick," Lucy said, "not one bit. You've no idea how dank and drear the woods around the house are at this time of year. How they drip and drizzle!"

"Worse than Bessie on a bad day," murmured Pierre, nuzzling into her hair, and she thought why is he allowed to mention Bessie's name and I am not, but Lucy laughed too, to keep Pierre company, to be of one accord in mind, as they were in body.

Bessie was a plain girl and had not been blessed with a musical ear, so Pierre could not take her seriously, and that made it hard for Lucy, now Bessie was at a distance, to do so either. Lucy could see that love unconfined, love outside convention, might well make a woman an unfit mother; you were one kind of woman or another: you were good or you were bad, as the world saw it, and no stations in between. They allowed you to choose; you could be the maternal or the erotic, but not a bit of both. The latter made you forget the former. Men married the maternal and then longed for the erotic. Or they married the erotic by mistake, and set about making it into the maternal, and then were just as disappointed. Edwin had married a child and tried to stop her choosing, but now thanks to Pierre she had grown up and made her own choice.

She hoped Edwin would keep Christmas without her. She hoped he would remember, when he brought in the Christmas Tree, the little fir which had grown in its pot on the step since the first year of the marriage, that it had to be watered well. She hoped he knew the boxes in the attic where the decorations were. Lucy added a new one every year—would he remember that? Would he realise you had to balance the golden horses with their silver riders? And part of her hoped he'd get it all wrong. Part of her hoped that now she was not there, he would have no heart for any of it, he would be so sorry she had gone. She would find a letter from him in Paris, forgiving her, asking her to go home. Of course she would not go.

"A penny for your thoughts," said Pierre, but he wouldn't have liked them if he heard them so Lucy said, "I'm really glad I'm not at home, Pierre. This time of year. When the days are really short, and winter hasn't quite caught up with them and the skies just seem to sulk. Why, they sulk even worse than Bertie on a bad day," and she laughed again, betraying her other child, for the sake of love. "And the rooms of the house are so crowded and sad," said Lucy, "and here everything is simple and graceful and plain. I promise you I don't miss a thing. You make up for it all, Pierre."

Lucy's brother Joseph would have arrived on Christmas Eve, as was his custom, bearing gifts. They would be the wrong gifts: an impossible doll, an unworkable cannon, a scarf she hated, the kind of pen Edwin never used. Joseph's talent for the wrong gifts was a marvel: it was a joke she and Edwin shared: a look between them every year, no more: that much they had at least: this equality of shared experience, which grew every year as the Christmas Tree grew, so slowly you could never see it, soil never quite right, too wet or too dry, so you feared for it; but every Christmas an inch or so higher. This year it would have to go on its side to get through the front door, and could only stand in the window arch— would Edwin and Joseph talk about Lucy, or would her name not be mentioned? An impossible subject, an inexplicable situation: a woman lost to duty, lost to honour, lost to motherhood: a woman altogether vanished away, erased from the mind, nameless. A subdued source of sorrow, of better-never-born-dom.

"No children to tug at my skirts," said Lucy, "no brother at my sympathy, no husband at my conscience. A day like any other, dawning bright and fair on our new life together. Just you and I, and art, and beauty, and love, and music. All the things that passed poor stuffy old Edwin by!"
"I pity Edwin," said Pierre. "He had no ear. A man who rations music to two hours a day has no ear and a man who locks a piano has no soul!"

The better to enforce his ruling, Edwin had kept the piano closed; unlocking it at two o'clock after lunch: emerging from his study at four o'clock to close it once again. In the mornings, thus freed from practice, Lucy and Pierre had walked in the woods, and talked about

music, and presently love, and then more than talked, and Pierre
had explained to Lucy how unhappy she was, and how her way of
life stifled her, and how he could not be a great artist without her,
and Bessie had seen them in the woods and Lucy had forged one
of Edwin's cheques and paid both their passages over; and left
Edwin a note and was gone, taking her jewellery because Pierre
said she must, and the way not to think about any of it was to be in
bed with Pierre. They had scarcely left the cabin on the way over:
they had been the talk of the ship and she hadn't cared. To fly in
the face of all things respectable intensified the pleasure she had
with Pierre: what was forbidden was sweet: she hoped they would
never reach Paris, where everyone felt as she and Pierre did, but of
course that was silly of her: what was forbidden could not be kept
up for long and in any case had to be sandwiched between the permitted in order to count—why had there been no one to stop her?
If you were a child wasn't that what happened? That someone
stopped you? She'd relied on Edwin for that all her grown life, but
since she couldn't tell him about Pierre how could he have helped
her? But she blamed him because he hadn't, because he'd been so
busy with his book he hadn't even noticed the time she was spending with Pierre: it was Edwin's fault she had left.

She wondered what she and Pierre would do all day. When they
were out of bed there seemed not very much to do, except wait for
other days to arrive, or messages to come which didn't come from
friends she had only heard of, never seen. If she was at home on
this day she would be so busy—it would be all best clothes and
mince pies and the gifts beneath the Christmas Tree, and a formal
kiss from Edwin before the unwrapping ceremony began—

Pierre said, "We'll smuggle the suitcase out after lunch, when
Madame takes her nap. She sleeps well: she doesn't care how

the rest of the world toils for her profit! Then in the evening you dress as me and I'll dress as you, and that will be the best disguise in the world, and we'll escape. We'll be so clever!"

Lucy thought it was probably better as an idea than it would be as an actuality—she could get into his coat but her jacket would never stretch over his shoulders—but didn't say so. It was the kind of prank Bertie would think of. Pierre had explained to her how Edwin was a father/husband, but what did she have now instead—a son/lover? Was such a thing possible?

"I could offer her a gold charm from my bracelet," said Lucy. "In fact I think I'll do that."

And to her astonishment Pierre hit her, or she thought that was what had happened, since there was a sudden kind of stinging blackness around her head, but how could she know; no one had ever hit her before. For a second or so she couldn't see, and was perhaps suffering from amnesia, for she couldn't quite remember where she was; but yes, it wasn't home, it was indeed an inn somewhere in the South of France, and she was leaning against a whitewashed wall, while a strange man rather younger than herself apologised for something rather trivial, and she could hear a kind of *knock, knock, knock,* which she thought was Edwin chopping down the Christmas Tree, the one that had started little and grown deep and strong. Edwin divided it root from branch, because it spoke of a celebration Lucy could no longer name, and anyway it spoke a lie. But of course the sound was only the *knock, knock, knock* of the landlady at the door, demanding money she and Pierre didn't have, speaking in a language Lucy didn't understand, but who knew them better than they knew themselves. She could see that to look after yourself you would have to know yourself, but who was there in that land, in that time, to hear such a thing if it were said?

LEDA AND THE SWAN

When Gosling was two, his body was smooth, plump and bronzed. He ran in and out of the waves at the water's edge and was happy. "He's a real water baby," his mother would say fondly. But she carried his little brother in her arms, and her eyes were even softer and kinder for the baby than they were for the little boy, and Gosling noticed.

She called the older one Gosling in pure affection, and the younger one Duckling, which was even more affectionate. Gosling once pushed Duckling under the bath water, but fortunately help came in time: for Duckling, that is, not Gosling.

"Did your mother hope you'd grow up to be a swan?" asked Gosling's wife, interested.

"I don't know what she thought," was all he said. He would volunteer information about his past, but did not like his wife to be too inquisitive. His past was a private planet, full of unscalable heights and hopeless depths where he alone was brave enough to wander. "Anyway," Gosling added, "it's ugly ducklings, not goslings, who grow up to be swans. My little brother was the one she had hopes for."

"Well, I think you grew up to be a swan," she said. They had been married for a year when she said that. She was proud of him: his fine dark eyes, his smooth skin, his sexual confidence; the gregarious fits which interrupted his more sombre moods. She felt she was very ordinary, compared to him. Her name was Eileen, but he called her Leda, and this gratified her very much.

Eileen met Gosling in a London park at the edge of a swimming pool. He was a Sunday father; he took his little daughter Nadine swimming while, he complained, his ex-wife entertained her lover. Nadine did not share her father's enthusiasm for the water; no, but she endured it with patience and polite smiles. She was a good girl. Eileen, that Sunday afternoon, splashed about in the water happily enough, though she did complain of its coldness. But then her parents kept a hotel in Bermuda: Eileen had spent her youth in warm water, chasing sailboats. English water was hard and bitter with chlorine: why did so many people want to go in it? The pool was crowded.

Gosling and Eileen collided underwater: he had to help her to the surface. His hand, firm upon her arm, seemed to transmit some kind of magnetic current: at any rate his touch acted like an electric shock. She squealed aloud and snatched her arm away in alarm; nearly sank. They touched again, tentatively. Again she let out a little yelp. That made him laugh. "We are seriously attracted to each other," he said as they surfaced, and she had to agree. She was eighteen: he was thirty.

* * *

When she pulled herself out of the pool, she felt awkward and unattractive; she regretted her freckled, friendly face, her strong, muscular body: men liked her, but that was all. She worried at once about her epileptic brother: she would have to confess to it. Then who would want her? Her brother's existence spoiled everything. Her eyes were pink and smarting. She wished she were not a swimmer: she would like to be Diana the Huntress, chaste and fair, icy and cool like the moon, not goose-pimpled.

"I like swimming," Gosling said.

"I love it," she said, and forgot about Diana and thought his brown eyes grew troubled for a minute, and then he dived back into the water and swam lazily and confidently up and down the pool, knowing quite well she was waiting for him.

"You could be a champion if you tried," said Eileen, as they drank hot chocolate from the drink-dispenser. Her mother had told her the way to win a man was to flatter him, and Eileen wanted to win Gosling as never before had she wanted to win a man.

"I don't want to be a champion," he said. "I just enjoy the water."

"Oh, so do I!" And so she did: she loved the buoyancy of her body in this murderous liquid, which healed and soothed when it didn't kill. Water was both adversary and friend: it parted in front of her, closed behind her. How powerful she was when she cleaved the water. Eileen cleaved unto Gosling the day they met, and after that they never wanted to part. Not really. She didn't tell him all the things that swimming meant to her, partly because she didn't know she was unusual and thought most people felt the same, and partly because she did not want to love what he only liked. While Eileen had an intense relationship with water, Gosling just swam. He'd swum, he said, in the Atlantic, the Pacific, the Mediterranean, the Black Sea, the North Sea, the English Channel; even in the Dead Sea.

"But the Dead Sea isn't really water," Gosling said. "It's just a chemical soup." The Dead Sea had brought tears to his eyes. He hadn't liked that. He was an engineer and travelled the world, bringing back to Eileen, who became Leda on their wedding day, all kinds of strange presents.

Leda stayed home and looked after her stepdaughter Nadine, and presently her own baby Europa, and joined a swimming club and won a race or two.

Leda told Gosling about her victories when he returned from abroad and he raised an eyebrow. "Swimming is something to enjoy," he said, "it shouldn't be something competitive," and she was obliged to agree. He told her about the ocean rollers of Florida and the surfing there, so they thought about these natural wonders instead of victories at the local swimming club.

The family went for an excursion to the seaside: Gosling and Leda and Nadine and Europa; they pottered about rock-pools and avoided the patches of oil on the sand, and Leda tried not to wonder how far was the coast of France and just how fast she could swim there.

Gosling swam and dived and ducked and lashed about. He was, oh yes he was, the real water baby his mother had defined; he was the gosling who was never quite the duckling who never quite became a swan. He was passed over for promotion. Perhaps he had spent too much time on foreign beaches, and not enough in foreign offices. But he was the man who liked swimming: he thought the world well lost for that. His mother had died of cancer, painfully, when he was a young man, at the time when it seemed important for him to renounce and defy her: at the wrong time.

He felt his mother had given him contrary instructions. She had named him Gosling, in the hope of his becoming a swan: she had called him water baby, and water babies surely did not grow up.

When he was on foreign trips he was unfaithful to Leda. He stayed in hotels where there were swimming pools, and always some girl, who did not swim but splashed about, who would admire Gosling's prowess, his lazy confidence in the water, his wet, rippling muscles which gave promise of excitement to come.

"It doesn't mean anything," Gosling would say to Leda. "I like them, I don't love them." Gosling did not believe in lying. "We must be honest with each other," he'd say.

Leda started training in earnest. Her times startled the trainer at the local swimming club.

"You're four seconds off the Olympic crawl record," he said.

"Four seconds is a long time," said Leda.

But she talked about it to Gosling when he returned from New Zealand, where the beaches are long, white and clean, and the girls likewise.

"Crawl is not a swimmer's stroke," he said. "It's the competitor's stroke. An antagonistic, angry sort of swimming. Nothing to do with water, just with doing down your fellow human beings. At best see crawl as the getting-somewhere stroke, not the being-someone stroke."

* * *

Leda thereafter swam breast-stroke instead of crawl, to her trainer's annoyance, but soon excelled in that as well. She swam for the County team and won a cup or two. And then rather a lot of cups. They began to line the walls.

"Of course back-stroke is the one that requires real swimming talent," said Gosling. It was his own best stroke, and Leda's weakest. They swam a jokey sort of race, one day, back-stroke, and he won, and after that they were happy for a time. But she knew she had not really tried to win, just been polite: won time and his favour, just for a little.

Gosling was good company, liked good food, good drink and bad women; he could tell a good story. For some reason, friends who liked sport faded away, or perhaps they were gently mocked out of the house. Presently there was no one to ask exactly what the silver cups on the sideboard were, or to care, or admire. The task of polishing them became oppressive; there was so much else to do. Gosling referred to them in any case as "Leda's ego-trip" and she began to be embarrassed for them, and of them. The cups went into the spare room cupboard in the end; the surfboard came out of it, and they went on family weekends to Cornwall, where they all surfed.

Surfing made Leda impatient: she did not like waiting about for the waves, or the messy rough and tumble of the water in their wake. She wanted to conquer the water, cleave it, and enlist its help to do so: as a man about to be shot might be induced to dig his own grave. It was a horrible simile, but one which came to mind, and made her ashamed.

* * *

Gosling loved the surf and the thrashing water. "You have to abandon yourself to the sea," he said. "And then you reap its benefits. How anyone can waste their time in swimming pools, I can't imagine. You know why your eyes hurt when you've been in them? It's other people's piss does the damage—not chlorine, as is commonly supposed."

When Leda came home from the swimming pool her eyes would be pink and swollen. When Gosling admired other women—not unkindly or over-frequently—he would always refer to their bright, wide, young eyes.

Sometimes Leda's heart ached so much she thought she was having some kind of seizure. She could not distinguish physical from mental pain. Still she swam.

One evening, when Leda was eight years married, and within a year or two of being past her swimming prime—which Gosling would mention in passing from time to time—and actually in the running for the English Olympic team—a fact which Leda did not mention to Gosling at all—Leda made her usual excuses and left for the pool. This was the evening when the final Olympic selection was to be made. Evenings were family time and it was Leda's practice to stay home if she possibly could, but tonight she had to go.

As Leda walked out of the house, a young woman walked up to it. "Someone called Gosling live round here?" asked the bright, clear-eyed young girl. "He wrote the number on a cigarette paper, but I lost it. You know what parties are."

"Not really," said Leda. "I'm usually looking after the children."

"God save me from children," observed the girl, "and, after children, from husbands. This one's mother should have called him Jack Rabbit."

And the girl walked one way and Leda walked the other, and that night Leda knocked two seconds off her best and was selected for the England team. Pain in the muscles alleviated pain in the heart: concentration on the matter in hand lessened the bite of jealousy. There was no pleasure in the victory, the record, the selection, the smiles of those who'd trained her, believed in her, and now saw their faith justified. All Leda felt after the race, as she smiled and chatted, and accepted adulation modestly and graciously, was the return of pain.

When Leda got home that night, the bedroom smelt of someone else's scent, but Gosling made love to her sweetly and power-fully, and the electricity glanced from them and round them and seemed to embrace the universe and she knew he loved her, in spite of everything; in spite of her annoying habit of winning, coming first, competing. "She was only here," he said when Leda commented on the smell of scent, "because you weren't. You were swimming."

The word had become bad, somewhere between sinning and shamming. Gosling hardly ever swam himself, these days. It was as if she had stolen his birthright. He, who should have been a water baby, should have gambolled for ever on the water's edge, was now forced by Leda onto dry, arid land. She was his mother's enemy.

Photographers took pictures of Leda. Her body, once so unluminous, prosaic, now seemed something remarkable and beautiful. With it went the nation's hopes.

* * *

"I can't have Europa exposed to this kind of thing," said Gosling. "It's one step up from skin-flicks. Surely the least you could do is allow them to photograph you *clothed*."

"But I'm a swimmer," said Leda. "They have to take me in a swimsuit."

"You hardly have the figure for it," he said.

He looked at her body without affection, without admiration, and raised his eyebrows at the folly of the nation.

But always, when the time came and the flag dropped and the water embraced her in its deathly, lovely clasp, Leda would fight it back with its own weapons; she would make it her servant. She would say, vaguely, when people asked her if she was tired or cold or nervous, that she was used to hardship. No one quite understood what she meant by this, for a friendly engineer husband and a little daughter significantly named Europa could hardly count as hardship.

Oh faster, faster: concentrate the will. In the last resort it is not the muscles, not the training, that counts; not up there at the extremity of physical achievement: no, it is the will; it is the pulling down from the sky of a strength that belongs to someone else, in some other world where fish fly and birds swim and human beings are happy.

Swimming, sinning, shamming. Water blinding eyes, deafening ears, to sights that should not be seen and sounds that should not be heard.

On the night of the European Championships, Leda's mother rang from Bermuda: her brother was dying.

"You must fly out at once," said Gosling. "Not even you, surely, can put a competition above life itself."

But Leda did. At seven forty-five she was not on a Boeing 747 on her way to Bermuda, but at the pool's edge at Wembley. She took half a second off her best time, came in first, and only then did she fly out, and her brother was dead when she arrived.
"But you're glad he's dead," observed Gosling when she cried. "Don't be so hypocritical," and he was right, she was, because the epileptic fits had frightened her when she was a child. The writhing, the jerking, the foaming; somewhere in her mind between sex and swimming; something to be ashamed of: something to be admitted to boyfriends, and be ashamed of being ashamed.

Swimming, sinning, shamming. Something held between the teeth to stop the tongue being bitten off. Or was that boxing?

Leda had loved her brother, all the same, as she loved Gosling. Part of her, part of life.

"And you thought winning a race more important than seeing him alive for the last time!" he marvelled.
"I don't want to win," she said. "I can't help winning. You make me win."

He didn't understand her. Leda cried. The more she cried by night, the faster she swam by day, eyes tightly closed against water out, or water in.

"It must be difficult for Gosling," people began to say, "being married to someone as famous as you."

* * *

Famous? Did that count as fame? Her picture on the back page, the sports page, not even the front? The Olympics were coming up. Gosling certainly found that difficult.

"Europa needs a natural life," he'd say. "You should never have had a child."

Leda cried. Naiad, child of tears, creature of mythology. If you wandered round Mount Olympus, you could always find a Naiad weeping in the corner of some pool, half tree, half water, all female: creating the tears that filled the pool, that gave you enough to swim in.

Europa went off to boarding school to be out of the glare of publicity. Gosling insisted. Poor little girl, her mother an Olympic swimmer! How could a child develop normally, in such a home?

Tears gave Leda an ethereal look, added eroticism to her body. Her freckles faded, as if the kisses of the sun were of no avail against the embraces of the night. And how they embraced! Leda and her Gosling, Gosling and his Leda: the music of the spheres sang around their bed. By night, in the forgetful dark, all was well. By day Leda remembered Europa, whom she should never have conceived, and missed her.

"In a way," said Gosling, "I suppose you could see something epileptic about winning swimming races, swimming faster than anyone else. It has to be done in a kind of fit. It certainly lacks grace. A matter of frothing and jerks. I can see it runs in the family." And he laughed. It was a joke. "I hope Europa is spared."

* * *

Europa, aged six, home for the holidays, ran a very high temperature on the eve of the next Olympic trials; she had convulsions.

"Of course she doesn't have epilepsy," said the doctor, surprised.

"Of course she has epilepsy," said Gosling. "He's only trying to comfort you. But drugs control it very well, don't worry."

"Next time her temperature gets as high as that," said the doctor, leaving, "sponge her down, don't wrap her up."

Leda was chosen for the final team. Flashbulbs clicked. Gosling shut the door in the face of newspaper people.

"This is unendurable," he said, and slept on his side of the bed, not touching. When she put down an ashtray or a vase of flowers he would move it at once to a different place, as if to signify she did not exist. He would sprinkle condiments lavishly upon the food she cooked, as if to change its nature; or would push away the plate entirely, and say he was not hungry, and go out and come back with fish and chips, and eat them silently. Gosling was increasingly silent. When she went out training, he did not raise his head: nor did he when she returned.

Europa's illness returned. The doctor remained puzzled.

Europa's fever rose. Now it was one hundred and six degrees. Gosling wrapped her in blankets.
"Don't, don't," cried Leda. "We must cool her down, not heat her up."
"That's nonsense," cried Gosling. "When I was ill as a child my

mother always wrapped me up well. Don't fuss. It's your fussing makes her ill."

Leda seized Europa up, hailed a taxi, and ran with her into the hospital. Here staff put the burning scrap in ice-packs and her fever fell at once. In the morning she was perfectly well, nor did the fever return. Leda missed an eve-of-tour practice, but that was all. She did not go back to Gosling. She stayed at the hospital that night and the next morning her mother flew in from Bermuda to take care of Europa, and said of course Europa should go to Moscow to watch her mother win a gold medal: anything else was not just absurd but nasty.

The next night they all stayed in an hotel; grandmother, mother and daughter; and laughed and talked and cracked jokes and ate chips while photographers clicked and reporters asked questions which she did not answer. Finally she drove them out, and had her family to herself.

Gosling rang Leda just before she left for Moscow to say he could not face life without Europa; he had taken an overdose of sleeping pills.

"Die then," said Leda, and went on to win the Gold.

TALES OF
WICKED
CHILDREN

TALE OF TIMOTHY BAGSHOTT

Picture the scene. Frame it in your mind's eye. We are looking at a great new development to the east of the City, with the eye of a TV cameraman (we will call him Les) who loves the very idea of it, who sees beauty in a tower block slanting cool and clean into a windy sky, and in the blossom drifting from the instant trees of the Garden Centres, and in the majesty of a great steel and glass pyramid so vast he can hardly lose it from his frame, even if he wanted to, even if he was paid to, which you may be sure he isn't: symbol of the city's wealth and busy-ness. Les sees no point in dwelling on the TO LET or FOR SALE signs, or the homeless who drift like the blossom up against the concrete walls, already stained by soot, weather and urine, or on the rats which nose up out of the flooding sewers; Les prefers to focus his lens on the beautiful faces of the PR women and the gently crumpled Armani suits of their employers, and who wouldn't? His shots are disciplined, beautifully framed. He's one of the best around.

But what's this? We're into fiction now? Thank God for that. We need no longer take anything seriously. We know all that other bad news, don't we; indeed, we're pleased, to know it so well.

How are the mighty fallen, we rejoice! Serve them right, we cry—the bastards, the property developers, sticky fingers in the pension fund: serve them right for being richer than us, for sending their useless unecological spires into the godless sky. Forget all that. We have a story to tell. Let's turn our cameras west a little, while we consider our children, all our victims. Let's turn our minds to the tale of young Timothy Bagshott, son of Jim Bagshott, property developer, swindler, charmer. Les, are you on line? Sound-man; are you there? Paul, are you happy? (Most sound-men are called Paul, and directors always say, "Paul, are you happy?" and Paul always replies, "Yes." So I have a vision of all Pauls as happy men or liars, take your pick.)

Paul is giving us the sound of schoolchildren singing, a little further to the west of the great city development to which we have been referring. Paul has located a school of the new regime: they're singing a Christian song as recommended by an Act of Parliament at morning assembly. Their innocent voices carol: this is what they sing:

> *"So here hath been dawning*
> *Another blue day,*
> *Think, wilt thou let it*
> *Fly useless away?"*

So far so good; the Protestant work ethic still about its perfectly decent business. But what is this? What are they singing now?

> *"Or wilt thou use it*
> *For profit, and say*
> *Hasten the dawn*
> *Of another blue day?"*

What has got into their voices, their hearts, their souls? What view is this of their own existences? Do they no longer want to go to heaven? Do they want heaven on earth, these kids? Do they want their oats now, not later? Good God, how will we keep our youth in order, if they have adopted the hopes and aspirations of their elders and betters, Mr. Maxwell, Mrs. Thatcher and her fine son Mark, all those City folk whose names we have already forgotten, stabbed in the back by their colleagues, the insider dealers, the fraudsters, the goers to sea in sleazy yachts? The new robber barons. Weep, children, weep for your lost souls. Trust Les to be hot on Paul's heels, getting them into shot. What's happened is that Paul and Les have a new master now: the stern director Angus, and a commission from the BBC, though it scrapes its barrel for funds. Oh yes, we're into fiction now. We're allowed a glimpse of the terrors of reality.

Here, little sister to Canary Wharf, we see Bagshott Towers, an unfinished development complex striving to survive recession. Once it was the little river port of Parrot Pier: a pretty place: a miniature Greenwich, albeit on the wrong side of the river. Parrot Pier boasted a Georgian house or so, and an old playhouse, some bonded warehouses, a host of railway cottages and navy dwellings. Gone, all gone: in their place a cluster of concrete structures rise out of a river of mud. If Les will only point his camera where Angus requires, we can see what can only be a group of anxious structural engineers teetering on the still unfinished thirteenth floor of a residential block, wondering whether or not it's entirely safe. Too late, in any case—from the ground floor up to the twelfth the habitation units are already occupied; here now dwell the desperate human overflow from the Inner City (the local council hires in homeless from other city boroughs for a substantial fee, hires out its own homeless to others for a lesser one, and so mysteriously makes a profit: it has something to do with the river view and Poll Tax levels).

Listen hard, and hear the hurrying feet of Rupert Oates, the social worker, driven by pressure of overwork to speak his thoughts aloud, at our expense. "Les, where are you? Paul, Paul, pick up Mr. Oates' thought patterns, if you please. Paul, are you happy?" "More than happy, Mr. Angus, sir. I call you 'sir' because you as my director are equipped to take an overview, earn more than I do, are not staff but work freelance, and can engage the bosses in conversation. I, who do not have the benefits of your education, your background, your capacity for chutzpah, am only fit to lick your boots, be told what to do and develop biceps, which my girlfriend hates, by swinging the sound boom overhead. She does not like me to be muscly, macho. More than happy, sir! What option do I have? The thoughts in Mr. Rupert Oates' head run thus:
'Listen, folks, I have a tale to tell of Bagshott Towers, I know it well. Being the welfare man round here: kept sadly busy too, I fear. Here, where once stood Parrot Pier and village pond and willows dear, now soars the height of Bagshott Towers, stressed concrete takes the place of bowers—'
"You live in a flowery house called The Bowers, I believe, Mr. Director Angus, over on Hampstead Hill, next door to 'The Cot' where Mr. Bagshott used to live, before he was carted away for corruption. Bagshott tore down his dovecote, according to the gutter press, and put in a swimming pool and re-named The Cot 'Amanda' after his girlfriend—and why not, Mr. Director? Mr. Bagshott was a vulgarian, as am I: happy Paul the sound-man. Mr. Oates has a word or two to say on that. They go like this:
'The grass of course is greener on the other side, where the gentry of the world reside. But listen, folks, we have a tale to tell, of

how the rich and mighty fell. The property speculators' bubble produced this land of mud and rubble. And Timothy Bagshott's dad, I fear, is much to blame for all that's here, and now he languishes in jail, so let Jim himself take up the tale.'"

"Les," says Angus, "that's more than enough of Paul. Can we reconstruct Amanda three months ago, when the fraud squad swooped at five that summer morning, and eased Jim Bagshott out of bed, and put him in a police car and sped him off to meet his just deserts? And can we do it within budget?"

You, the viewer, will have seen similar scenes on TV many times. The camera, following the vanishing car, seldom turns back to the house to see the forlorn figures of those left behind, waving goodbye on the step: in this case it's young Timothy Bagshott and his dismal Aunt Annie. Or, as Rupert Oates observes, "My tale's of Timothy Bagshott, son of Jim, and how misfortune came to him, and how the lad faced up to perils great, and how at least he conquered cruel fate."

Paul the sound-man swears this is what goes on in Rupert Oates' head, and Paul has the acuity of the really happy to be believed now. "Paul, are you happy?" "Happy as Larry, Angus." There is hope, you see: there is always some underlying happy refrain, if only we can hear it. Let's for God's sake get on before the light goes.

"I'll have something to say to my solicitor," says Jim, and who should he find sharing his open prison cell, of course, but Clive his solicitor, so this is how the word or two went:
"What are you doing here?" asked Jim.
"Six years," said Clive. "For fraud. And you?"
"Twenty years," said Jim, "for bribery and corruption."

"Last time we met," said Clive, "we had champagne and chips for breakfast. Remember that."

"And now," said Jim, "we are reduced to porridge. But, knowing us, we'll soon have cream on it. My only worry is the boy. Poor Timothy, poor motherless boy. The house sold over his head; his school fees left unpaid. Nothing between him and destitution but my sister, his Aunt Annie, and all she cares about is herself, but then who doesn't?"

"But he's got the Welfare, Jim," said Clive. "Let us not forget the Welfare. It's what we paid our Poll Tax for, or failed to, as the case may be."

"What's to become of the boy?" asked Jim again. A tear or two fell from his eyes.

"The criminal classes often weep for the sorrows of children," Angus the director says in a note to the actor playing Jim, "although they have caused the sorrows themselves." The actor yawns.

Ripple-dissolve to a month ago—Angus favours ripple dissolves: they remind him of his childhood and save re-writes—when on the step of the shuttered Amanda, Timothy Bagshott stood alone, his smart pigskin suitcase by his side, the very model of a smart City gent in uniform, only slightly miniatured by virtue of his lack of years. And zooming up is a battered mini-van, with DEPART-MENT OF YOUTH writ large upon its rusty side—nothing rustier than the Welfare, these days, in any city in the world—and in the van our good friend Rupert Oates himself. Paul, happy Paul, pick up his thoughts!

"See, here I come, the Welfare Man, in the County Council van, though Bagshott is a cursed name round here, still Timothy does deserve my care."

* * *

And Timothy and his poor Aunt Annie, a nervous, plain, unmarried lady in her middle years, much burdened by black plastic sacks into which are crammed all her worldly belongings and such of Timothy's as she could be bothered to bring, step into the van. The boy would not be seen in public, even on the steps of a disgraced and shuttered house, with a black plastic sack. He would rather die than lose his dignity. This is what private education does to a lad.

And off the van goes, through the dilapidation of poor Parrot Pier, to the slightly less broken structures of the new estate. Here removal vans abound: the hopeful and the hopeless, the repossessed and unpossessed: have you got them in shot, Les? You're not doing a promotional video now: this is real life.
"Till Timothy's fortunes we decide," thinks Rupert Oates, "it's been judged best that he reside, for such are fate's ironic powers, with his aunt in Bagshott Towers. A Council rent book! Oh, what shame, to those with Bagshott as a name."

Les captures the faces of Timothy and his Auntie Annie, as they stare up the soaring, if truncated, face of Audrey Tower, their future home. Twelve floors finished and twenty-five hoped for. "Most of us," observes Rupert, "of course are glad to take what there is to be had, but Audrey Tower I have to tell is where the problem families dwell, and as a pleasant place to live is quite the worst the Council has to give."

The arrival of the Bagshott aunt and nephew and Mr. Oates in Council towers is observed by one Jon-Jon Ooster, a sixteen-year-old punk of some charm and intelligence, albeit white-faced, grimy and hung with leather, chains and nose rings. Jon-Jon, a vegetarian, smokes a cigar in the corridor he is to share with the

Bagshotts (and a dozen others, of course, but they're too in terror of Jon-Jon to leave their apartments to put in an appearance). Paul, a snatch of conversation, please. Are you dreaming? We have to hear as well as look.

"I'm certain there'll be a shortage of oxygen this high up," said Aunt Annie. "If Timothy's asthma returns I shall hold you responsible, Mr. Oates."

"I didn't know you had asthma, Timothy," says Mr. Oates.

"I haven't," says Timothy.

"Yes, he has," declares Aunt Annie. "It started the day his mother left home. He was only seven. Do you remember that day, Timothy?"

"Not if I can help it," observes Timothy.

"See? How he suffers!" says Aunt Annie. "Poor little Timothy! Poor wee boy!"

Aunt Annie has decided that the mercy directed at Timothy, by virtue of his childish state, shall include her too, by reason of the sympathy and concern she clearly shows for her nephew. Aunt Annie is not without a soupçon of her brother Jim's self-interested genes.

Into the flat they go, gene sharers both, sister and child of brother Jim, and find it bleak, and sparse and grim. The view's terrific, even so.

"Is this really how the workers live?" asks Annie. "Come away from the window, Timothy, it isn't safe. Timothy suffers from vertigo. Don't you, Timothy?"

"No," says Timothy.

"You must understand, Mr. Oates," says Aunt Annie, "that it's impossible for us to live here."

"All flats on the Bagshott Estate are of standard size and shape, Miss Bagshott," observes Mr. Oates. "You are very lucky indeed to have anywhere at all to live. Bed and breakfast is the best that you could have reasonably hoped for. I had to plead your case most strongly at the last Council meeting to get you even this."

"But my brother built the place," says Aunt Annie.

"Exactly," says Rupert Oates.

"Ingratitude!" exclaims Aunt Annie. "And how are we expected to live? I am penniless, you understand. All my money was in my brother's companies."

"So was the Council's," says Mr. Oates. "The Social Security office is not far. Try to attend early, otherwise a queue builds up."

"I must live on charity?" asks Annie.

"It's that or work," says Rupert Oates. "The same for you as it is for everyone. Nor can the Council continue Timothy at his private school: last term's incidentals, we notice, came to £1,500. Timothy must say goodbye to riding lessons, stables for his mounts, music and fencing tuition, and a log fire in his study. Timothy must go to the local comprehensive, like anybody else. To Bagshott School."

Les, turn your camera to the comprehensive school, a structure twenty-five years old, once pride of Parrot Pier, now in excessive disrepair, except that a recent Council grant of £150,000 paid through Jim Bagshott's companies has recently effected some meagre improvement. Graffiti sour the walls, the scuttle of cockroaches unnerves the listening ear.

"A boy with Bagshott as a name at Bagshott School? It seems unkind but that's the rule," muses our friend and Timothy's, Rupert Oates, who now uses his mobile phone to get in touch with Mr. Korn, headmaster of Bagshott School.

Picture Mr. Korn, frame him in shot: a good man, the hope of the nation, of middle class origin and working class aspirations: he has children's art upon his walls: night and day he fights for the rights of his pupils and the survival of civilisation, in the face of finance cuts, the irrationality of the parent classes and the original sin of his pupils. He's tired but he won't give up. What's he saying, Paul?

"I'd like to oblige but I can't. The second year's full and I'm understaffed as it is. I know, Mr. Oates, that it's my happy duty to educate all the kids in this area regardless of race, colour, creed and handicap. If there were only something special about him. There is? What is it? His dad's in prison? So are all the dads in prison. What's that you say? Jim Bagshott's boy? Impossible! I won't be responsible. He'll be lynched, and I'll be blamed."

But Mr. Oates puts the pressure on and so the second years squeeze over to make room for Timothy Bagshott. On his way down twelve flights of stairs—the lift is broken—Mr. Oates has a word or two with Jon-Jon Ooster, who keeps him company.

"I had a letter from your headmaster, Jon-Jon."

"Two thousand pupils and Mr. Korn writes about little me! *Quel honneur!*"

"You can hardly count as a pupil, Jon-Jon, since it seems you seldom attend."

"They go on at you if you're there," says Jon-Jon, "and they go on at you if you aren't. So what does it matter one way or another?"

"Tell you what, Jon-Jon," says Mr. Oates, "since we're all in this together, how about you keep a helpful eye on young Timothy Bagshott, your new neighbour. You're a good boy at heart. Help him settle in."

And Jon-Jon laughs and says, "Yes, me and my mates, we'll help settle any Bagshott in."

"Ingratitude, complaints," thinks Rupert Oates, "what else can be expected? We have so far from nature's way defected, the Bagshott lift in Bagshott Towers is often stuck for hours and hours; they piss into the shaft and rust soon turns all moving parts to dust."

"I say," said Timothy Bagshott to his Aunt Annie as dirty water from the loo bubbled up into the sink, "I'm sure the Pater never imagined his own family would end up here or he'd have seen to everything very differently. Tell you what, try running the bath: sometimes it's a simple matter of an airlock," but both are distracted by cries of help from the Ooster household and a sudden blow is directed upon the thin front door, which splinters, and there stands Jon-Jon.

"My mum," says Jon-Jon, "cannot abide it no more. Every time you empty your bath her loo fills up."

"Too bad, old chap," says Timothy, and shuts the door in Jon-Jon's face.

"People like that having the nerve to complain!" remarks Annie. "Why, they're nothing but a Problem Family!"

Another blow upon the door: a burst of splinters in the room: Jon-Jon enters in unasked, and with him brothers both older and younger.

"Ooster's the name," says Jon-Jon, "and this is Joe-Joe and this is little Ripper, and as for me, I'm Jon-Jon."

"What quaint names you have round here," says Timothy.

"None so quaint as Bagshott," observes the middle Ooster lad. "Ripper's called Ripper for a reason, and Joe-Joe's back from Borstal where they taught him love of animals and how to have a cold shower every day. We Oosters get about, enjoy life: they suspend our sentences more often than not, to save the prison service aggro."

"How fascinating," observes Timothy.

"I am reliably informed," says Jon-Jon, "that you are about to attend Bagshott Comprehensive. I am a pupil there myself. If I were you, I'd get your Auntie Annie not to take a bath from now on, because my mum don't like it when she does."

"I'll think about it," says Timothy, and closes what's left of the door and tries not to tremble.

News of his family's predicament flies fast to big bad Jim, but how can he help his little son?

"Lovely piece of renovation we did on that school," observes Jim. "He shouldn't have too hard a time. Re-named in my honour. A deal of asbestos in the assembly hall walls and high aluminium joists as well; not too good at stress-bearing but economical. Perhaps I should mention it? What do you think, Clive? Imprisonment makes me indecisive. I blame the Courts!"

"*Quieta non movere,*" replies Clive, which, being translated, is "Let sleeping dogs lie."

"A lot of glass in that assembly hall," muses Jim. "What with the roof. They may have had the impression it was anti-ultraviolet glass, but the contractors let me down. What could I do?"

"*Quieta non movere,*" says Clive.

"A fuss about nothing, a scare, this ozone layer," says Jim. "If a boy gets skin cancer it's easily cured. I blame his mother; she had no business walking out on me. Everything a woman could want—a fur, a chauffeur, nannies, holidays. Ingratitude! The boy takes after his mother, Clive, and that's the truth of it. All that money spent on his education, and not a flicker of gratitude: has he been to visit me? No! He thinks himself a cut above me: always did. Sneered at me from behind the bars of his cot. I hope his Aunt Annie's coping. Perhaps I should get in touch with his mother?"

"*Quieta non movere,*" is all Clive says, and Jim fears his friend means to sleep the years of his sentence away. . . .

* * *

An evening or two later (Angus deals with the passage of time on screen by flicking over the days in a calendar; that simple nostalgic device) and there's Auntie Annie removing soup stains and ironing a secondhand school uniform for Timothy to put on in the morning for his first day.

"Black, grey and navy blue," observes Timothy. "How dreary; necessary, I daresay, amongst the great unwashed or why would those in charge choose it? And supposing I get head lice, or impetigo? What then? Perhaps I should aim for a quick medical discharge?"

"Timothy dear," says Auntie Annie. "Try to be sensible. Co-operate. Don't put on airs. Be like the others. If you ever want to escape from Bagshott Estate you must work hard and pass exams, and I must be here to help you. There is some talk of a cut in our subsistence allowance, of my going out to work; but my work is here with you, helping you get an education. You look on me as a mother, don't you, Timothy dear?"

"Of course I do, dear Aunt," says Timothy. "Never let it be said that a Bagshott worked from nine to five."

"Or seven to midnight," said Auntie Annie, "now the Shop Act is cancelled and a crust is so very hard to earn."

"I will do what I can for you, Aunt," says Timothy. "I will aim for suspension rather than expulsion. Needs must and all that. But I will not willingly keep the company of the Oosters of this world."

Even as he spoke, a great convulsion shook the corridor; indeed the very structure of the dwelling block, the elevator, quivered between its rusty girders and fell an inch or so: Maisie Ooster was rounding up her boys. Maisie Ooster was twenty-four stone and perfect with it, if loud. Annie stuck her head out of her splintered front door.

"Take no notice of me," cried Maisie Ooster. "I washed these lads last night and I can't do a thing with them today," and she laughed so loud and heartily that Annie joined in, but not Timothy, and so night fell, and the full moon arose over Bagshott Towers, and made all things so boldly brilliant and beautiful even the rats and the cockroaches paused in their rustling, and the human scavengers lifted up their hearts, and even the muggers paused to consider the nature of creation, and the wild creatures of the night slept, thinking it was day: and those who normally slept by night awoke, including Rupert Oates; in the morning Paul had his thoughts on tape ready for playback to Angus. Paul's tapes are like some film, really sensitive, and just as film will pick up scenes that never were, so Paul's tapes pick up sound. He is always in employment. Perhaps that's why he's so happy.

"Night falls on Bagshott Towers," mused Rupert Oates that moonlit night, "on good and bad and in between, as most of us are seen to be. And who's to blame? Your poor old mum? No. She had a mum herself, you know, and is what she was made, as are we all. Moon on Bagshott Towers! And there's a fox, and there the night owl flies. Listen; the wild life of the city cries—and morning breaks, and unreality breaks in, on this strange world we're living in."

The moon set. The sun arose. Cameraman Les, up bright and early, uninstructed by Angus, who has a hangover, is filming the kids of Bagshott Comprehensive arriving—some on crack and some still clutching teddy bears, some pregnant and some virtuous still, and all shockable one way or another, either at the innocence of some, or the knowingness of others.

"Children of Bagshott Towers," says Rupert in his heart, "school's not so bad. It's warm and there is dinner to be had. Your teachers want to help you, honestly they do. I've asked them and they say it's true."

* * *

Angus arrives, apologetic, and the film crew sets up in the corridor outside Mr. Korn's office, where Timothy stands disdainful and alone. The headmaster appears—"Please, sir," says Timothy—but Mr. Korn is already inside and the door is shut. Even the best of teachers develop deafness to the pleas of the pupils: it is not the teachers' fault. Children are no different from adults, other than in scale and lack of experience; their clamour, their tugging at the conscience and coatstrings of those they see as powerful, render dazed, punch drunk and rude those who are paid to suffer it.

And coming down the corridor, framed by Les, observed by Timothy, a smallish, pimply, owlish child called Twitcher, son of an optician.

"I've had enough," says Twitcher, "of this day."

"Already?" enquires Timothy, quite alarmed.

"Ten minutes in this place is always enough. Already my eye is twitching. My mother said if it happened I was to go home."

"Well!" say Jon-Jon, Joe-Joe and Ripper, fast approaching, "Well, well, well. If it isn't little Twitcher: off home are we, darlint, nice back home with Mummy? Twitcher wears an undershirt," they say, and so on, and then, "Tell you what, Twitcher, give us a dance and show us how happy you are!"

"I don't know how to dance," says Twitcher.

"Then we'll jump on your toes," says Jon-Jon, "and teach you, unless by any chance you have dinner money to spare. Just a borrow, of course, until tomorrow."

"I don't take school dinners," says Twitcher, "because someone always takes the money. I bring packed lunch instead, with egg and curry filling that nobody likes, not even me. But at least I don't starve."

"Better than what our mum gives us," says Ripper.

"A biff on the communal ear hole. If you got no money, you gotta dance. If you can't dance, then we gotta stamp."

"Now look here, you fellows," says Timothy Bagshott, "bullying a little fellow like this. It simply isn't on."

Six cold eyes focus in upon Timothy Bagshott; Twitcher dodges away and who can blame him.

"If it isn't my neighbour Timothy Bagshott," says Jon-Jon.

"Fairdos. You let Twitcher go so it's up to you to see us right."

"You'll get nothing from me," says Timothy Bagshott.

"We will," says Jon-Jon, "cos we'll smash your face in or else. All you've got and more; your dad dines on champagne and chips, you've got a lot to spare."

"But he's in clink," says Timothy boldly.

"We know his sort," say the Ooster boys. "Some men are born to champagne and chips as the sparks fly upwards," says Jon-Jon, who'd been in Mr. Korn's high-flyers special English class until his thirteenth birthday, the day he went on mental and moral strike and they let him into the cinema without his parents. The porn he takes home for the video and the subtleties of the PAUSE button on the VCR.

"Hand over what you've got and we'll have your trainers too, unless you want to dance."

"I wish you boys wouldn't dance in the corridor," says Mr. Korn, emerging from his room. "Just stand quiet, boy, until I've time for you."

In post-production, we are allowed merciful release from scenes of teenage torture; Angus tactfully intercuts a scene between Maisie and Annie which, according to Paul's sound tape, carried above even the sound of Bagshott plumbing. The two women had got together with a book called *Plumbing Made Easy* to solve the bath/loo problem.

"A wire like this, Miss Bagshott," Maisie said, "must have a dozen uses. Say you had a dress shop with a fair size letterbox, you could pull it through and hook your winter outfit out in no time at all."

"You have a lively mind, Mrs. Ooster," said Miss Bagshott.

"If you were married to my Barley," said Mrs. Ooster kindly, "no doubt you'd have the same. A wife contrives as best she must."

And with a gurgle and a splodge the blockage was cleared; that the water supply and the sewage now intermingled on the floor below was no concern of theirs.

Annie thanked Maisie and Maisie remarked, "My Gawd, you could do with a thing or two in here. Telly, video, three-piece, cocktail cabinet. My Barley can get things cheap."

"Thank you," said Annie primly, "but we Bagshotts don't like to be indebted. We're cosy as we are."

"Don't put on airs," said Maisie. "Your brother's doing time, like anyone else."

"That's rather different," said Annie. "My brother is no criminal."

"I call it criminal," said Maisie Ooster outright, "when other people's drains come up my sink, and who's doing that but your brother?"

"I accept your censure, Mrs. Ooster," said Annie, "or may I call you Maisie? The fact of the matter is, I used to live a lonely life up at Amanda; my brother always away on business, and Timothy learning to be a little gent at boarding school. But here! Why, even the dole queue is quite jolly. And I packed little Timothy his favourite lunch: egg and curry sandwiches."

"My boys never bother with lunch," said Maisie. "They pick something up on the way, they say. They're such good boys. We believe in discipline, Barley and me. Take the stick to them often and hard, they grow up good as gold."

* * *

"Sir," says Timothy the while, entering Mr. Korn's office unasked and unabashed, "I will not continue to wait outside; it was you who wished to see me, not I you. In the circumstances, I'd be glad if you said what you had to, and let me begin the education the State so kindly provides, and not waste the taxpayers' money, nor my valuable time, keeping me waiting."

"You'll be Timothy Bagshott," murmured Mr. Korn.

"And you'll be Mr. Korn," replied Timothy.

"I was only going to welcome you to the school, Timothy," said Mr. Korn.

"I'd rather you called me Bagshott," said Timothy. "We are not friends."

"Boy," said Mr. Korn, "is it your intention that I suspend you?"

"It is, sir."

"Then you will have to do better than that, Timothy. My threshold of natural indignation is high. Are you perhaps having trouble with the Ooster boys, Joe-Joe, Jon-Jon and Ripper? The family is not easy, but they are all our responsibility, and yours perhaps more than anyone, your name being Bagshott."

"Guilt by association, sir?"

"A matter of cultural, family and communal guilt. Your father and his like are responsible for many social ills round here: bad housing for a start; the breakdown of family life in general; the squalor of our streets and schools."

"So the sins of the father are to be visited on the children?"

"I think you'll find they are, my boy, whenever you enter the toilet block. The sewers leak: the plastic pipes are all too permeable. There you are, Mr. Hobbs!"

Enter Mr. Hobbs, the PE teacher: a karate expert, shaven-headed with an evil mien, as are too many of his ilk.

"Mr. Hobbs," said Mr. Korn, "we have a problem or two to deal with today. When the indoor swimming pool overflowed because of the stuck ball cock, electrical damage was clearly done. The fire alarms have rung six times already—"

"I thought that was your little joke, sir," said Mr. Hobbs, "to keep us on our toes."

"My sense of humour is quite, quite gone," said Mr. Korn. "And the automatic doors to the assembly hall are working in reverse. They close when anyone approaches."

Timothy laughed.

"I'm glad you find that funny, Timothy," said Mr. Korn. "Trust a Bagshott! Let me introduce you to your head of year, our Mr. Hobbs. Mr. Hobbs doubles as caretaker at this, your father's school, in order to pay his mortgage. Timothy, if I might give you a word of advice: a slight note of diffidence, even of apology, might help you get along with pupils and with staff."

"I have nothing of which I need be ashamed," said Timothy. "I am proud of my father, as any son might be."

"He's a lucky lad," said Mr. Hobbs. "I'll let him be first on the wall-bars since he's new. They carry quite an electric charge; the wiring in the gym being what it is, after the flooding, and even before."

"Perhaps I am just a little ashamed," said Timothy. "Sir."

Now what of Timothy's mother? Doesn't she care? Surely she's read of Jim Bagshott's disgrace, arrest and imprisonment in the press; surely she'll care, do something to rescue the flesh of her flesh, love of her love?

"Meanwhile the Welfare, ever tender-hearted," observes Rupert Oates, "seeks to trace our Timothy's mum, long departed, and finds her—what surprise!—not so far away though feeling unmaternal, sad to say."

* * *

Audrey, for such is her name, works as the barmaid at the local pub, the Bagshott Arms—the landlord is in trouble with Equal Opportunities for describing her as barmaid, when it should be barperson. No one has yet got round to insisting that he be called the landnoble, which presumably is the non-gender specific of landlord. But who cares about that? On with the story. Are you happy, Les? Paul? Angus? Happy, happy, happy, in the execution of our craft. What other happiness can there be?

"Rhubarb, rhubarb, rhubarb," says Rupert now, for although Paul swore he was happy, his boom proved faulty. Let it just be said Rupert Oates put the child's plight to the mother and the mother denied all knowledge of the child. Some mothers are like that and a lot of fathers too. Children are plentiful, since parents must opt out of parenthood, not opt in: the former is a boring, expensive, time-consuming thing to do. But Rupert Oates persevered, and finally Audrey grudgingly acknowledged she had borne a child to a property developer of note and criminality, Jim Bagshott of Bagshott Towers and Bagshott School.

Where Mr. Hobbs now addressed his class in language vile, insulting and persuasive, as was his custom.
"First one to talk gets a detention," said Mr. Hobbs, "and the one sitting next to him. Both sides. Anyone who thinks my bark is worse than my bite is mistaken. My little darlings, my sensitive children, welcome back. How many walls did you deface in the holidays? How many old ladies did you mug, cars did you joyride, reefers did you inhale and raves attend? I've brought an extra little playmate for you today: young Timothy Bagshott. He's son of Jim, perpetrator of your fate. Once you lived in squalor in slums upon the ground, now you live up on high, in half-completed

tower blocks. The rest of Europe gave up the habit years ago, of housing its riff-raff in the sky, but Jim Bagshott told your elected representatives the old ways were the best, that is to say the cheapest, and your elected representatives, mesmerised like the snakes they are—"

"Sir," said Timothy, "isn't it the snakes who do the mesmerising, and the rabbits who get mesmerised?"

"Take a detention, lad," said Mr. Hobbs. "Have it your own way. Your father is a snake and the Council are rabbits. And it is thanks to your snake of a father that the PE wing is flooded and I am teaching History to Form 13, a class well known throughout the school to be composed of spastics and pygmies."

"Sir," said Timothy, "I really must protest. You shouldn't call people pygmies. Say rather people of restricted growth, or the vertically challenged."

"Another detention, boy," said Mr. Hobbs. "I call you lot what I like and so long as it's not racist and I don't lay a finger on you, no one can say me nay. Spastics and pygmies, the lot of you!" Mr. Hobbs left the class to check the basement's pumps in case the central heating blew.

"If you tear Timothy Bagshott limb from limb, class," said Mr. Hobbs, "you'll only get probation. Why don't you have a go?"

Form 13, so familiarly called because it was understood to be unlucky in that its members had Mr. Hobbs as year tutor, personal counsellor and careers officer, turned to stare at Timothy, undecided as to its group response. The toilets in both school and home were so often out of order that even the young ones had noticed—it is one thing to defecate in lifts and corridors out of choice, in a spirit of defiance, quite another to have nowhere else to go. And there always has to be someone to blame, and how seldom is that person not just in the room with you, but on the same scale? Mr. Hobbs had given permission to hate, and to not a few in the class Mr. Hobbs was a hero. The oppressed soon learn to lick the oppressor's boot. It was, in other words, a tense moment.

"I expect," said Timothy, "you get quite a few days off because of the structural difficulties inherent in the rehabilitation of any educational institution."

Jaws dropped.

"That is to say," said Timothy, "if you ask me, my dad cocked up this sodding school on purpose. My dad hates schools."

The moment passed. Ordinary mayhem broke out, and Twitcher was its target, not our Timothy. Twitcher got his glasses broken but that was nothing unusual. All knew Twitcher's father was an optician, the only dad not in prison, and could easily acquire more. Form 13, the other side of their culture and conditioning, were quite reasonable and thoughtful lads, whose habit it was to take justice into their own hands, since society afforded so little evidence of it. And pleasure likewise, since so much of what they did was frowned upon.

Up at the Bagshott Arms the while, Rupert Oates wrestled with the soul of Audrey Bagshott.

"So what if I ran off with the chauffeur?" cried Audrey. "I chose love, not money, didn't I? Isn't that what a girl is supposed to do? And don't tell me Jim turned criminal when I left; he was born like that: devious, greedy and grungy. And he always did the plumbing himself, liked to turn his hand to a real man's job, so Amanda was always awash with water. My built-in cupboards filled up with the stuff. Drip, drip, drip, off my shoes and my furs. And I couldn't take Timothy with me: the chauffeur didn't like kids. You know what kids are like in cars, never at their best."

"He's thirteen now," said Mr. Oates. "I had him in my own car. He made no trouble."

"But I'm with the landlord now," said Audrey, "and you have to be eighteen to get in for a drink. And I know those boys from Bagshott Comprehensive. Nasty, thieving little hooligans, lacing their Cokes with rum if you so much as look the other way."

It is always hard to reason with the not altogether reasonable, but on the other hand the least reasonable make the warmest mothers, so Mr. Oates persisted, and on hearing that the lad lived in a block of flats named in her memory, and perceiving that Jim Bagshott's heart was still tender towards her, she consented to visit both her child and her husband.

And Mr. Oates was relieved, because he knew only too well for any child to be in Mr. Hobbs' class was a strain upon that child's source of cheerfulness, and cheerfulness in Bagshott Towers was the rarest and most precious of all commodities.

"Sticks and stones," said Rupert Oates in his heart, "may break my bones, and words can always hurt me. And who it is who says they don't can only mean to bruise me. Flesh and bones will heal at last, but insults past stay with me."

Mr. Oates did not like Mr. Hobbs. Neither did Mr. Korn, but Mr. Hobbs was on a fixed contract, and could not be fired other than for gross professional negligence, which he took care not to show. And, besides, Mr. Hobbs was a dab hand at keeping the boilers going. Disgraceful people often develop very rare and precise skills, so that others will be obliged to put up with them.

Mrs. Ooster, in spite of the wild and aggressive mien of her very large sons, was an agreeable person indeed. Angus cuts gratefully away from Rupert Oates' light verse musings—which Angus feels are somehow happy Paul's fault, and totally out of order, considering the overall style of the piece—to Aunt Annie's new home and the arrival of Mrs. Ooster with a daintily pale pink TV set with a built-in aerial like a leaping dolphin.

"So kind of you, Maisie," Aunt Annie is saying. "The only people who ever came up to Amanda were those bearing writs and solicitors' letters. No one ever seemed to like us, for all Jim was forever throwing parties. Why did you say the TV didn't have a back, Maisie? It seems to me to have a back. I imagine one could get quite a shock if it didn't. All those nasty wires."

"Things which fall off lorries," said Mrs. Ooster enigmatically, "don't have backs. Never mind. You'll learn, now you live in Audrey Tower. Would you care to come to Bingo with me tonight?"

"I've never gambled in my life," said Auntie Annie.

"It's not a gamble," said Mrs. Ooster. "The Caller is a very good friend of mine."

And Aunt Annie was glad that Mrs. Ooster had a very good friend, because she'd had a glimpse of Mr. Ooster and thought him a surly and miserable fellow indeed.

Angus prefers to look through his viewfinder at Audrey, who, although into her forties, is blonde, well-bosomed and high-heeled, rather than at staid (so far) Auntie Annie and vast Mrs. Ooster—agreeableness is a quality that can get you lost on the cutting room floor, but sexiness keeps anyone in shot. So visiting hours at the open prison are here and Audrey's sitting opposite Jim, who doesn't seem one bit pleased to see her. The Rupert Oateses of this world, in spite of the harmonies inside their heads, can be naive, believing that others are as they are: that is to say, really nice if a trifle power-hungry.

"I've come all this way," says Audrey, "and you aren't one bit pleased to see me."

"Because I know what you want," says Jim. "And it's the same as everyone else wants."

"What's that?" asks Audrey.

"Money," says Jim. "The only thing I've ever had to offer. So now you come running to me for the fees, so your boy can go to boarding school and be a little gent."

"Such a thing never crossed my heart, Jim," says Audrey.

"Then it should have," says Jim. "What sort of mother are you? Running out on your own child. That boy's going to spend the rest of his life searching for an absent mother figure."

"What's got into you, Jim?" asks Audrey.

"Psychology classes," says Jim. "There's nothing else to do round here. I wasn't much of a father myself. He'll be searching for an absent father figure too. Not much of a husband either. A workaholic like me leaves a trail of personal disasters behind."

"You go on saying things like that, Jim," says Audrey, "and I'll be on the step waiting when you come out."

"As to the fees," says Jim, "I'll see what I can do. I haven't been fair to him. Bringing him up posh, then pushing him in the deep end."

Audrey expresses admiration that a man in prison could still get his hands on money; Jim expresses his anxiety about the swimming pool at Bagshott School—chlorine might eat away at the new-style insulation of the underwater electrics—and suggests Timothy be warned not to take a dip. And so love, affection and trust is re-established between the two. Angus makes a note to establish a heart-shape frame around the pair in post-production.

Aunt Annie has packed a very special lunch for Timothy today. He eats it in the safety of the Art Room. Twitcher is there, together with a small group of boys in need of quiet and protection. The Art Room door affords some protection against the clanging and banging, the shouting and screaming, the pushing and shoving in the corridors outside.

"Anyone care for a chicken leg?" enquires Timothy. "Seasoned with salt, and lemon, roasted in butter and basil. Only 40p the piece, and a bargain at the price."

"Sounds foreign to me," says Twitcher.

"Then how about a cigarette?" asks Timothy. "Twenty-five pence each or three for a pound."

"Why are three more expensive than one?" asks Twitcher.

"Because I have my father's blood in me," says Timothy.

"He's inside, isn't he?" says Boy 1.

"He is indeed," says Timothy. "Left to rot by a corrupt authority, a society indifferent to the rightness of his case."

"Open prison?" asks Boy 2.

"Of course," says Timothy.

"Then it doesn't count," says Boy 3. "My dad's doing thirty years in high security, and not even a political."

Boys 1, 2 and 3 will have to double as prison attendants (trainees, of course; they will have to age down for the one, age up for the other). This is not a lavish production, and extras are expensive. The producer can see no merit in having Boys 1, 2 and 3: the dialogue could have been accomplished with just the one bit part player. But Angus says the way to look lavish is to be lavish.

"Besides," says Boy 2, "it's not fathers that count in here, it's mothers. How's yours?"

"Run off," says Timothy.

"That's nothing," says Boy 2.

"It was to me," says Timothy sadly.

All contemplate the truth of this. Angus studies each face at some length to get the value of their hiring and keep the producers in their place. The Ooster boys at this point lean on the Art Room door so it collapses inward, being made none too solidly, and deprive the already dismal group of their dinner: chicken legs, ham rolls, crisps, Ryvita and cheese slices, and a bottle of Montrachet Cadet which Timothy has been keeping to himself. Well, the Ooster boys have to live too, and Mrs. Ooster is too busy keeping Mr. Ooster happy in the mornings to do much in the way of providing lunch, nor does their father see why he should provide men younger, bigger and more energetic than he with funds simply because they are his sons. Rupert Oates' voice shivers over the scene: "Children remember this, that childhood ends. When you grow up, at least you'll choose your friends."

Mr. Oates then appears in conversation with Aunt Annie, offering her a change of residence: he has organised it so that she and Timothy can exchange dwellings with a family living on the outskirts of town, almost in the country; Timothy can be taken out of Bagshott School and go to Parrot High, a smaller and altogether milder institution in a better area, so much so that it is soon to become a Direct Grant School. But Aunt Annie, to Rupert Oates' surprise, will have none of it. She is happy, she says, as Mrs. Ooster's neighbour: she's on her way to Bingo and, besides, she's come to fancy the view from the twelfth floor and Timothy no longer suffers from vertigo.

"But I'm offering you a thatched cottage," says Rupert Oates, and all Aunt Annie says, pushing past, is, "Nasty, germy things, thatches." Mr. Oates inhales the fetid air of the Ooster level, as it's known at the Council offices, and marvels. The Ooster boys are active and healthy eaters and drinkers and seldom make it inside their home before being overtaken by the call of nature. The lift is so often out of order, their own door so seldom opened promptly to them (Mr. Ooster has the lock changed frequently) they can hardly be blamed for this lack of control. So far one can get, no farther. Requests to the Council by Mr. Oates that common lavatory provision should be made at the entrance to Audrey Tower convulsed the Supplies and Facilities Department with mirth. How many hours would such constructs survive the vandals? Let the corridors stink; there was nothing to be done about it.

Angus decided against attempting to dramatise this sorry state of affairs. Producers, viewers and indeed Les would resist anything too graphic, so Mr. Oates was merely left sniffing the air and wincing; Angus then cut away to a scene at Bagshott School, where the French class was in process, cheerful enough, if punctuated by cheers, jeers, Kung Fu kicks and the sound of breaking windows. A student teacher, pretty and eighteen, and in her first year at college, stood weeping in front of the class, who thought it best to tactfully ignore her distress. The lads were not unkind but no doubt thought the sooner she toughened up the happier everyone would be. That, or get out of teaching. Timothy sat at the back of the class, reading.

"Tim," muttered the boy next to him, "what are you reading?"
"A book called *Teach Yourself French,*" said Timothy. At which point Mr. Hobbs erupted into the room, shouting, swearing, thwacking everyone in sight. "Dregs and rabble!" he shouted. "Form 13, the dross of the streets: what's the point of teaching them French; they can't even speak their native tongue. The sooner they're out on the streets and on crack the better. Their mothers are, *et tes grand'mères.*" The class fell silent, shocked and stunned, and the student teacher ran from the room and out of the profession altogether. Had it not been for Mr. Hobbs, she would have toughened up perfectly well in her own good time.

* * *

It was this particular scene which causes the TV critic of *The Times,* who later became editor of *Punch*—a humorous magazine, now deceased—to become almost incoherent in his outrage: the film, he complained, was a vicious attack against the educational system of the nation. Schools such as Bagshott Comprehensive did not exist. A foul fabrication! Everyone knew schools were places where calm and kindly teachers, in an organised fashion, set about the business of teaching and socialising the docile and grateful young. Else what were the taxpayers paying their taxes for? But that is by the by. Just why *The Tale of Timothy Bagshott,* a play for TV, was never repeated and wiped from the BBC archives. Just as Les could not bring himself to turn his camera on what we had better call defecatory matter, nor could the critic of *The Times* face truth. Why should he be expected to do better than Les?

The cookery class at the Open Prison was doing rather better: Clive and Jim were baking £50 notes into a cake tin. Clive extracted them from between the pages of a cookery book called *Easy Steps to Home Baking* and handed them to Jim, who dipped them one by one into a rather over-vanillaed mix before laying them in the tin. He sang as he dipped. He was in love, and for a man to fall in love with his own wife is a happy experience. Can electrified fences a prison make, or cookery classes a cage?

And because new love flies through the universe, turning all things rosy, tipping the spires of the Bagshott Development—and even the poor, unfinished, stunted growth of Audrey Tower itself—with gold, Aunt Annie looking out over what to many was the debris of a ruined city and a languid slime of murky river and seeing only charm, progress and infinite possibility, said to Timothy, "Oh, by the way, a postcard came for you. It's from your mother." She'd meant just to forget its arrival. She'd never liked Audrey, even before she ran off with the chauffeur and so upset Jim.

The postcard was what's known as a Sixteenth Century Dutch interior, a woman sweeping clean a yard, forget the yard's outside, not inside. *See ya soon, kid,* the message on the back said in its enchantingly quivery red-biroed writing. The hand of his mother. Timothy rejoiced in his heart, felt his father's blood surge more strongly in his veins, and his mother's too, and the very next day took Mr. Hobbs aside and offered him and his wife a free holiday for two in the Bahamas, through certain travel agencies known personally to the Bagshott family, in return for Mr. Hobbs desisting from libelling Form 13.

"Schedule flight or charter?" asked Mr. Hobbs.

"Schedule," replied Timothy.

"Club Class or Economy?" asked Mr. Hobbs.

"Club," said Timothy, and so the deal was done. That Mr. Hobbs knew his time was up in teaching, that Mr. Korn—following a doctor's report relating to the traumas suffered by the pretty student teacher (I'm not saying her prettiness had anything to do with the advent of natural justice: merely that it helps) which she had the courage to attribute to Mr. Hobbs and not the pupils—finally had sufficient evidence to apply to the Council for Mr. Hobbs' dismissal, was neither here nor there. One thing to be said for Mr. Hobbs was that he was not proud, and another was that he knew which side his bread was buttered. It is important to keep looking for good in people, otherwise one might succumb to despair.

We next see Rupert Oates visiting Audrey Tower with a cake, a gift for Annie, baked by her brother Jim in prison. A nice scene

this: Annie's surprise and gratification at her brother's thought-
fulness: her mixed pleasure (once Mr. Oates was gone—no
Bagshott was born yesterday) and disappointment at finding her
mouth more full of money than cake: the internal struggle as to
whether or not to just swallow the note that said the money was
to take Timothy out of Bagshott School and pay for his private
education, or just keep the money herself, and the eventual triumph of good. Aunt Annie decided to act unselfishly and do as
her brother wished. People make this kind of decision all the time,
though cynics think they don't. The assumption that the great men
of the people act only in their own interest is a plague of our time.

Meanwhile, it's packed lunch time in the Art Room, and Timothy stands on a chair and exhorts fans and doubters both to direct
action. The power of the union, the will of the workers, so fast
fading in the adult world, will find its revival in our schools: it is
a prophecy: not a difficult one, if you consider the state of our
schools. Rather like a Western scientist impressing a native tribe
by predicting an eclipse.
"Fellow pupils," cries Timothy. "Comrades! Have you no courage, no common sense? Are you sheep or are you men? Packed
lunchers all, have you no pride? Daily we are subjected to these
Ooster raids: it is too much. We must unite against these bullies:
singly we are powerless; united and organised, who can stand
against us? The formation of the Bagshott Protection Agency is
under way—membership 50p, payable to me. Twitcher here will
make a note of it. An offence against one is from now on an offence against all. The Teamsters Union was better than none. Ask
any U.S. baggage handler."
"We'll get found out," said Boy 1.
"We'll get into trouble," said Boy 2.
"We'll get sent to Mr. Korn," said Boy 3.

"But you'll get to eat your dinner," said Timothy Bagshott, and as the faces of Boys 1, 2 and 3 broke into smiles, Les lingered long upon them, at Angus' request.

Happy Paul took care to record the conversation of the Ooster boys as they approached the Art Room, the dinner of others on their minds. It went like this:
Ripper: "Jon-Jon, big brother, there's something I want to know."
"What's that?" asked Jon-Jon.
Ripper: "If our mum ever won at Bingo, instead of always losing, would we get chicken legs for dinner, like Timothy Bagshott?"
"Spastic," said Jon-Jon, "you are a spastic. Our mum always wins at Bingo. She just tells us she doesn't."
Tears came into Ripper's eyes. Boys depend dreadfully upon their mother's love, no matter how much taller than their mothers they become. Joe-Joe said nothing. He was a silent lad, and had spoken very little since the day his pet rabbit produced a litter of twelve and Barley Ooster flushed the lot down the toilet. It had been a miracle birth: how can a single pet rabbit produce a litter without divine intervention? And indeed, the problems with Audrey Tower plumbing dated from that traumatic day, though the tenants preferred to blame Jim Bagshott.

As the Ooster boys leaned heavily through the Art Room door and splintered it for the third time that term, they were set upon by the Bagshott Protection Society, in united and organised protest, and forcibly thrown out again into the corridor, bruised, surprised, and without their trainers.
"It's a madhouse, this school," said Jon-Jon.
"You can't even get dinner when you're hungry," said Ripper.
But Joe-Joe said, he who had been silent for so long, "If we asked Mr. Oates, he'd get us free cooked dinners every day."

* * *

Money, time and patience ran out for Angus at this stage. There was trouble with the crew. Paul had another job to go to; Les lost interest once he had perceived there was nowhere for the story to go but to a happy ending, and began to frame his shots sloppily and forgot to renew the batteries before they ran out, thus holding everybody up intolerably, and to the detriment of the shooting schedule.

Angus was obliged to forgo the dramatic—well, fairly dramatic—scenes in which Timothy Bagshott gave the cake money back to his Aunt Annie, and told Mr. Korn he wanted to stay on at Bagshott School, which, now he had organised a little, he had come to love. He was certainly finding it profitable. Viewers never got to see how Jim confessed to the Parent Governors that the school swimming pool was potentially dangerous and how in return, and for health reasons, he was let out on parole. How Audrey and Jim (reformed by love) and Timothy returned to Amanda, to run a centre for the homeless. How Aunt Annie ran off with Barley Ooster—why do you think she wouldn't move to a thatched cottage?—to Mrs. Ooster's great relief. Mrs. Ooster had come to dislike sex and Annie had all her years of celibacy to make up for, which suited everyone. Mrs. Ooster was now able to give all her love and affection to her boys, who became model members of society. How Twitcher's father paid for him to have his short-sightedness cured by the new Soviet method of paring away the cornea, so the lad was no longer obliged to wear glasses. How Joe-Joe's rabbit gave birth to another set of miraculous young, which Joe-Joe, now his father was happy with Aunt Annie, was allowed to raise: how a vandal-proof toilet was installed at the entrance to Audrey Tower and its remaining seven floors constructed without undue torment to those already living there, and so forth. All these happy occurrences were left drifting in the hopeful air—too expensive to be nailed on film and, besides, as everyone knows, good news is no news. So forget it. Who cares about dramatic form?

"Paul, are you happy?" enquired Angus for the last time, and Paul replied, "Yes" with some sincerity, for with the end of filming he was at least free to return to the arms of his girlfriend, and as his parting shot gave Angus a few more lines from Rupert Oates' head.

> *"Though socialism's dead and gone, they say,*
> *Yet still shall justice and compassion win the day.*
> *How else can man (and woman too) live with him*
> *(her) self?*
> *Only with understanding, empathy, good management*
> *these three,*
> *Shall come the proper sharing out of wealth,*
> *The best will, not the worst will, of the people be*
> *set free.*
> *No one's a villain, but the world has made him so.*
> *No one's a villain, but if you ask him won't say no.*
> *Who, me?"*

Thank you, Rupert Oates, you'll be late for your meeting.

VALEDICTION

"Some things are held in common by all of us," I tell Ed.

"Like what?" he asks.

"The way a young woman looks in a mirror," I say, "and pats her hair as she passes. A tilt of the chin, a twisting of profile. Love me, love me, how loveable I am! How perfect!"

The way a man straightens his tie, takes a breath and squares his jaw before going into a room full of strangers who make him nervous: gestures held in common, I say; species behaviour, no matter how individual we believe them to be: your Aunt Sally, my nephew Bill; you name them, they do it: or did it when young. And indeed these are gestures which can trigger love, if observed at the right time, at the right place, and thereby work to the furtherance of the species. Women are more fertile when they love their partners, did you know that? Orgasm—researchers equate orgasm with love, for some reason—enables women to retain sperm. That's what all that excitement's about, apparently. It would be easy enough for Ed to agree with me: he does. He nods. I am accustomed to sweeping a generalisation or so through his head; he not too resisting. The "men do this; women do that" stuff goes on sounding reasonable enough, but the times catch up with us and overwhelm us, and what I could once say now turns out to be, when I think about it a little longer—how can I put it?— gender deceptive.

That is to say, these days a young man will pat his hair as he passes a mirror, with an equal tilt of his chin, a misting of exhaled breath, just as if he were Marilyn Monroe, and a career woman will pause and square her shoulder-pads before going into her meeting to convince and impress the foe. Nor will either activity be indicative of any dilution of—and here I search for the new language and come up with—"appropriate gender energy." The man who admires his hair in the mirror is as likely to relate to the "opposite" sex as his own, or as likely as he ever was: and it's the same for women. You can be as female as you like or don't like, in your big clumping boots; as male as you like in your crushed velvet trews. Or at least in the great cities of the world this is so; in country areas the sexes remain "opposite" in their forced polarity, the better to reproduce the species.

These thoughts come to me as we wait for the next batch of prospective house-buyers to come up the drive. We sit in the front garden in the sun and watch for a car to turn in from the main road, down the dip, past the duck pond, and up the drive to the yard. This is an old farmhouse; the yard is still partly cobbled. City drivers hate it: they fear for their suspension. Naively, I once believed a partly cobbled yard would be a selling point. The Estate Agent tells me otherwise.

Edward and I can no longer live here at Grazecot. We are too old, the children tell us, and we agree. Our knees creak. We lose the energy for gardening, though Edward can still prune the roses, and I still cry, "Not so hard, not so deep!" and he makes his annual reply: "The harsher the better: no gain without pain!" The children describe us as "rattling round in that great house like peas in a pod," but I never noticed peas rattling in a pod—broad beans will do it sometimes, if they're accidentally left on the stalks through the winter: the pods turn brown and brittle and the beans inside shrivel a little and lose their attaching strings as their housing shakes in the wind. But peas don't rattle: especially modern peas, with their almost edible, tender pods, genetically engineered turning into *mange-tout*. Eat everything!

But the children were never interested in the garden. There was too much of it around to arouse their interest. Hetty disconcerted me the other day—she had come to stay, bringing the children: she had had another quarrel with Rory: it is time they stopped it: she is my youngest and nearly forty—Hetty, as I say, disconcerted me by calling a dahlia a poppy. I looked at her aghast and she said, "Oh, Mom, you know they all look alike to me. I'm not a visual person, never was." And all I said was, as I always say: the familiar rhetoric "Don't call me Mom." And Hetty, of course, took not the slightest notice. The protests of mothers blow like a mild, familiar wind round the ears of children, fit only to be ignored.

When Guy, my oldest, was twelve, he brought an American friend home for the school holidays, and the poor boy's mother died suddenly in the States while he was with us, and I rashly said, "Look on me as your mother, Al"—the kind of sentimental, silly thing one says *in extremis*—and the wretched child did. He took to calling me "Mom." His father was already dead, and he was a whole two years with us at Grazecot, waiting to be claimed, by which time all the children called me that: Mom. Al left and simply vanished from our lives: he didn't even write a thank-you letter: some wealthy uncle had finally turned up to fetch him, as if he were out of a Dickens novel. All Al left as legacy was "Mom." He was nearly fifteen by the time he left—I don't blame him for his discourtesy—fifteen is a self-conscious age, when one is only too anxious to forget the past, and Al, given the opportunity to disconnect the young man from the child, no doubt simply took it. And I was busy enough with my own three, and working too—Supermom, Al called me—up and down to the city on the train, forever trying to catch up with myself, with never quite enough time to feel the pleasure of simply living.

Now the house is up for sale, and I refuse to feel melancholy about it. Edward and myself are by no means finished. We are to buy a small cottage on the seafront at Hastings, on the south-east coast. Hetty's youngest, Ira, aged ten, advises against it. "The South-East is tilting into the sea," he claims. "The North-West is rising. It's madness to go south-east. The tide will be rising inside your house before you know it." He is a precocious lad: he looks like Edward's father, and behaves like him too. Ira is a natural collector. He collects CDs: his great grandfather collected butterflies, and stuck them on pins. Ira's collection is more expensive but more humane.

Edward once explained to Hetty that "Ira" meant "rage" in Latin; why was she calling his grandchild "rage"? But Hetty just laughed and said Ira was the Hebraic for "watcher" anyway, and she thought it sounded nice; who cared what it meant; and Rory said it was a Po-Mo name.
"Po-Mo?" I asked.
"Post-modern," Rory replied. "A post-modernist is someone who knows the meaning of everything and the value of nothing."

"In that case," I said, "Hetty was saying Ira isn't a Po-Mo name; in fact, the opposite."

But they weren't listening to me. They like to talk to each other, to tie each other up in knots, and if sometimes they tie in the fringes of someone like me, by mistake, they take no notice. One has to struggle free without help. Hetty and Rory would have fewer rows if they were each less clever at the other's expense, it's obvious, but who wants their mother to say a thing like that, let alone notice? Hetty walks out on Rory at least twice a year, usually waiting for the school holidays to do so, so the kids' schooling isn't interrupted. Then she comes to us, bringing them too. She and Rory have long, long, wrangling phone calls, on our bill, before they are finally reconciled, amid tears and laughter; and fortunately the walls and floors at Grazecot are thick, so the bedspring twanging is muted. Once their rows would agitate and distress me, if only for the children's sake, but in the end the little ones knew the pattern well enough for themselves, and appeared unconcerned. Their mother's sudden stays gave me time to inculcate at least some semblance of table manners in my grandchildren, and to get them into the habit of washing night and morning. A woman who can't tell a dahlia from a poppy because she's so busy with the inside of her head needs her mother around to help her with her children. Hetty tells me so herself, half-demanding, half-apologising. I don't think Hetty ever got beyond sixteen. She'll say so herself. How is she going to cope without this place to come to? Without Grazecot? She says she's glad the place is going; she says if the family home doesn't exist, she'll just have to grow up. Ira says, "Mum, you're a Professor of Economics at King's. You want to grow up *too*?"

And Ed says "no pain, no gain." Lettice gave me a Jane Fonda tape one Christmas—most of the kids come home for Christmas most of the time; though life, time and partners sometimes of course intervene—and the "no pain, no gain" concept really appealed to Ed. It seemed to explain a lot about life: why pleasure now so seldom leads to pleasure later. But then Ed likes a slogan. He once joined Alcoholics Anonymous, I'll swear, in order to be able to hear himself saying, "I am an alcoholic." His drinking was not in truth excessive; he just loved drama. I think Ed sees the selling of Grazecot as some kind of verbal, rather than real, activity. "They were rattling round like peas in a pod, so of course they had to sell" sounds somehow right. As if "selling" were some kind of species activity, not something made up of a series of small events: an initial wayward speculation, hardening into decision, leading to a phone call to an Estate Agent; and then the hell as teams of professionals move in, to make their point and make their money and make you feel ignorant and not as good as the next person. While they get rich and you get poor.

My grandfather the butterfly-collector left me Grazecot when I was eighteen, thus circumscribing and defining my life, driving a pin through my middle, trapping me here. Now the pin is being withdrawn. The wound will be severe, but the edges clean. It's what I want, the sensible thing. I will heal quickly. Obviously there is no sense in Ed and myself staying rattling in a winter wind. Let some other family take the place over: Grazecot needs young energy, new money, new standards. Dimmer switches: on and off has apparently become too simple for a source of light. Remote control for the curtains. Forget closing them by hand, with nothing to go wrong.

I will live happily with Ira's tides lapping through my living room. I love the sea. I love storms. I love the excitements of the ocean. Sometimes I have really hated Grazecot: it's altogether in the wrong place, I have complained: stuck on a hillside miles from anywhere: it swallows money. If it hasn't needed re-roofing, it's needed new plumbing: the septic tank has always seeped: there's no main water: no gas, come to that. The Gas Board say they'll bring in a supply for £8,000 approx. Oh, thanks, we say. The Electricity Board say, if we complain about power cuts, we're lucky to have electricity at all. The wiring needs to be modernised: it's a fire risk. Falling branches carry our telephone wires with them. And the Estate Agent raises his eyebrows—Grazecot has all the disadvantages of a country house, apparently, but few of the advantages. A four-lane link road was recently driven through along the path of the old drovers' track up on the ridge, within sight of the house—which is apparently bad news—and within hearing distance as well—which is worse—if the wind's from the north, and it often is. Apparently the house is too exposed: certainly all the trees in any position to do so fell through the roof over the decades. Yes, you really get to feel the weather here at Grazecot. I hate Estate Agents. My house, my beloved house: my home, my history, my children, my family, my life.

The local amenity planners propose a golf course on the fields at the back of the house, the Estate Agent tells us. The farmer who owns the fields is being paid by the EU to keep them out of food production. At least that means no more insecticide-spraying from the air, I say brightly, but the Estate Agent just shakes his head and clucks his tongue and says, "If you can see cars if you look one way, and people if you look another, it hardly counts as country living," and asks us to drop our price. There's no demand for properties like ours, he says: neither one thing nor the other. Not grand enough for the gentry; too large and rambling for young families. "It's a vicarage type of dwelling," he says. "There's no demand for them any more. 'Rambling' is no longer a selling plus."

* * *

I have come to see Grazecot as a symbol of a changing world. What happens here is happening everywhere. When it comes to it, myself and Ed, and Guy, and Lettice and Hetty are helpless. The real world stampedes in. We just have to dodge out of the way: creep into our little shelter by the sea and hope the new reality doesn't come after us. We've been subject to forces we may not understand but have come to realise that there's no avoiding them. We're not daft. As above, so below.

We had a dreadful time five years ago when Lettice's cruise ship was hijacked by terrorists. She had a job as Entertainments Officer. We read about it first in the newspapers: no one informed us. Eight people had been killed. No names were given. I sat where I'm sitting now, on the lawn, in the evening sun, in frozen panic. I could not act. I had not realised until then that fear could paralyse. I could not even answer the phone. How was it possible to sit in this familiar place, amongst this familiar green, while madmen ran amok for a cause hitherto plausible, and threatened your child? Why should pretty Lettice, whose greatest crime was to be silly (to be as wilfully ignorant of politics as Hetty was of gardens), who liked to take her life day by day—"Who cares about gain," she'd say, "so long as there's no pain"—why should Lettice be the one to get swatted like this by the flailing of real life? I wished then I had never had children: never held these hostages to fortune: had not been trapped by Grazecot, by my affection for it, by my sense of what my forbears require. I had never seen beyond my own nose, never recognised responsibility other than to my nearest and dearest, and was now being punished for it.

Hetty had been trouble enough. At twenty-one, mid-college, she started a sexual relationship with a girlfriend, and made me go to consciousness-raising classes for the parents of lesbians. We parents looked at each other aghast—not because our daughters were lesbians but because they insisted on making such a song and dance about it: because they assumed their decision to come out would be a significant enough event-in-common for us parents to need to form a support group. I went along twice; then Hetty met Rory and that was the end of her lesbian phase and I was let off the meetings. When I cook dinner for their children, trying to ignore the hysteria, I sometimes wish she'd stayed firm in her principle. I do not see the bearing of children as of any particular value: I don't even want my children to be happy: I just want them to keep out of my hair, which I suppose is more or less the same thing.

I certainly did not want to find myself paralysed by fear because Lettice, usually so good at looking after her own interests, her own comfort, was marooned on a hijacked liner in the middle of the Indian Ocean. Ed looked it up for me. A blue flat patch on a map criss-crossed by squares. Truly the world is an insane place: even the way we picture it is peculiar, if traditional. Flat, on paper: an abstract rather than an actual truth. As it was, Lettice was just fine: not even shocked: awed by the physical beauty of the hijackers, finding their particular type of murderousness attractive: the tourists they had killed—inadvertently, Lettice claimed—ugly and worthless by comparison. Hetty was made furious by the way Lettice spoke.

Guy said that was why Lettice said it in the first place: to annoy Hetty. Lettice spent most of her life, said Guy, annoying her family one way or another. Bringing us down, or so she believed, by dropping out of school young, being actively anti-intellectual, taking hopeless jobs, bringing home homophobic boyfriends to

meet Guy. Guy just laughed. Guy was not exactly gay: but people
assumed he was. He was attractive to, and attracted by, persons
rather than bodies of any particular gender, let me put it like that.
"Bi-sexual, you mean?" people would say if you tried to explain.
City people, that is. The neighbours did not seek explanations,
nor were they judgemental. If Guy helped chase a straying heifer,
or rescued a cat from a tree, spent his money at the village shop
when he came home for weekends and was generally helpful,
what did they care what our son's sexual orientation was?

Guy was finely built, soft-voiced, sweet. He was my oldest child
and only after the girls came along did I wonder whether there
shouldn't be more difference between the male and the female
child. He never wanted guns, or motor cars. He always loved
dolls. When he got to his teens he had first girlfriends, then boyfriends. Later, it occurred to me he had been conceived as a girl,
but one who then, by some carelessness of nature, developed male
genitalia; when I had this in my mind, it was easier to define my
son. He was, as they say, well-hung, but never particularly sexually active. Now he is married to the most extraordinarily beautiful transsexual, sufficiently female to allow a marriage between
them to take place. They seem very happy: companionable,
exotic, a trifle camp but witty and lively. They run an interior
design firm in Brighton. It has been a strange fate for Ed and me,
here at Grazecot, to produce this new version of person, for so it
seems to me Guy is. Fit for a new race, whose purpose is not so
much to multiply, but to see the importance of themselves in the
here and now. Ed and myself belong, with our "no pain, no gain"
philosophy, to a generation who never lived now, but who were
always, with our preoccupation with family, children, bricks and
mortar, security, keeping our powder dry; somewhere in the
future, seldom now. We were anxious, as they are not—apart from

whether a dye takes properly, curtains hang smoothly, that Christmas will be fun. And it does, they do, it is: Guy and his Staria make sure of it. They work hard, but without anxiety. I am proud of them, my Guy and his Staria; so is Ed, though at first he was disconcerted. It is strange enough for a woman to give birth to a man; how can the female produce the male? It seems to go against both reason and nature, but a woman learns to get used to the notion. A man has never even had this simple lesson in accepting the unlikely. He has to start from scratch, dealing with not quite the unthinkable, but the so far unthought.

The world must move on, with its motorways and its wind machines (they are threatened, too, as an alternative to the golf course) and its new genders, and Ed and I must step aside. Neither Guy nor Hetty nor Lettice are interested in living here at Grazecot. It is too far from the city. Who would they talk to? How would they get to work? The countryside itself has become irrelevant: fit only for parents.

I find this resignation dreadful.

We will put most of the furniture into auction when the house is sold. It will not fetch a good price. The pieces are too large to suit small, modern houses, where central heating radiators take up most of the wall space anyway.

Ed fell in love with one of Lettice's girlfriends. She passed the gilt-framed mirror, and paused and patted her corn-silk hair—she had one of those other-worldly, translucent faces you get sometimes on sixteen-year-old girls, as if they were composed of two beams of light meeting and accidentally sustaining life. By eighteen she was just an ordinary pretty girl, but at sixteen she was amazing. I could see why he loved her, but it was painful. I felt ordinary and heavy, a plain domestic creature, painfully and point-lessly rushing here and there to no apparent purpose, long past my sell-by date. I have never liked the mirror since: it showed me what I did not want to see. The eternal gesture of the seduc-tive girl, the response of the man, the pain of the woman passed over, left behind; and that stricken woman in the mirror was myself: my own wall, my own mirror, me. The mirror will go to auction. I don't want it.

She rejected him, of course, and he stayed home, grateful for my comfort. It was never a role I wanted—comforter—but better than none. I think I forgot it all sooner than Ed did. The tides of fam-ily swept us on. Now we are that rare thing: a well-suited couple who have survived well enough to rattle around in an empty house, to hold hands together like Darby and Joan as we go into the twilight of our years.

But this is specious twaddle. Even as I murmur these familiar words I realise the house is far from empty. Guy and Staria have left us two cabinet-makers working in the barn; Ira is in the attic with the old train set; a friend of Lettice's is in the guest room recovering from what I suspect is an OD of acid.

"I don't want to sell this house at all," I say to Ed. A car is turn-ing into the drive.
"Too late to turn back now," he says. "It wouldn't be fair."
"Fair to whom?" I ask. He doesn't reply.
"I thought you were set on moving house," he said. "You told me you couldn't cope any more."
"Only to keep you in face," I said, "because you're too proud to get a gardener in, and the nettles are taking over."

* * *

The car's a Mercedes. Whoever it is looks as if they have money.
A man driving, not a couple. Couples are the worst. You hear
them picking holes in the best and most well-loved features with
your home, despising your efforts.

"God, how can people live with a kitchen like that?"

"It's too inconvenient, darling. We'd have to rip the whole place
apart."

"I suppose if the colours weren't so dreadful, this bedroom would
just about do."

"What, only two bathrooms?"

Single people are not so critical or, if they are, don't have the
opportunity of displaying it. And at least you're not dealing with
the hidden agendas of other people's relationships.

"I simply don't know what to do," admits Ed. "I look at it one
way, and look at it another, and the advantage of staying balances
the disadvantages of going. But now we've got this far just let's
carry on."

It was like this with all three pregnancies. Because they'd got so
far, we just carried on. Guy, Hetty, Lettice. I was fed up with it.
"We'll leave it to chance," I said. "If this guy actually buys it,
we sell. If he doesn't, we take it off the market."

"Okay," said Ed.

Chance came up trumps. The potential buyer was an American,
was Al, Guy's original friend. Al apologised for his long absence,
his lack of a thank-you note, which had been bothering him all
his life. He embraced me; he called me Mom. I shuddered. He
was doing well; he was gay; he lived in San Francisco; his busi-

ness now brought him over to England frequently; he had come looking for properties in areas he knew; had found Grazecot for sale; was horrified. It was his happy childhood; it could not be sold. He needed to keep the place in his head, and with us in it, growing old gracefully.

Guy, Lettice and Hetty had never said anything so bold or so simple. They'd seemed happy enough to see their childhood obliterated, their parents shipped off into nowhere anyone would ever visit. Ungrateful bastard, bitches, thought I, with unusual fervour: or all three bitches, to give Guy his proper due for once.

Al, it seemed, had overcome the embarrassment of his early social gaffe sufficiently to call. It seemed churlish to reject so plain a message from Destiny.

"We changed our minds about selling," said Ed, "as it happens," and I went to the telephone to call the Estate Agent before minds could change again. The Agent was furious, and I didn't care. We would rattle around in Grazecot till the end of our days, till we rattled around to death, till they carried us out feet-first. Let the kids deal with the problem of what to do with a changing world, since it was beyond us. That was what we'd had them for.

FROM THE
OTHER
SIDE

THROUGH A DUSTBIN, DARKLY

"Oh, Serena," they said. "Serena! Serena was quite mad, you know. She would have made the finest surrealist painter of the twentieth century, only she ended up in a dustbin."

And the little circle of ex-art students filled up their glasses and rolled a smidgen more dope and stared exhausted and melancholy into their mutual past. They wore sandals although it was cold outside.

"You mean," said Philly, "her paintings ended up in a dustbin?" "Oh no," they said, whichever one of them it was, Harold or Perse or Don or Steve—Philly found them hard to tell apart, so information about Basil's past seemed to come from some communal centre—"Serena ended up in the dustbin. She left Basil when she found him upstairs in the studio in bed with Ruthy Franklyn, and shacked up with some frame-maker she met in a hostel, who then committed suicide. She must have gone completely bonkers after that because she broke into Basil's studio upstairs: burned all her own paintings in the stove—five years' work gone in five hours—and had begun on Basil's when luckily Ruthy came by and stopped her.

* * *

"So poor Basil changed the locks and Serena went and lived in the alley at the back of the house for a week or so, shouting and screaming, selling herself to passers-by, and then OD'd on heroin. She fell headfirst into a dustbin from whence she was carted off to the booby hatch, where she died. That was four years ago."

"Poor Basil," they chorused.

Philly envisaged Serena's thin, white legs waving out of a big, black, plastic bin: a rag doll thrown away.

"He'd married her to calm her down and help her paint, but it didn't work," said Harold, Perse, Don or Steve. "Serena was always completely mad, perhaps even because she was so talented. More talented even than Basil."

"Completely mad," agreed the Jean, Holly, Ryan and Olive who went with the men. Way, way over the top. OTT. Poor Basil. Better luck next time!"

They were all thirtyish: Basil was fortyish: Philly was twenty-one. In her family people only got married once. What did she know?

They were in Basil's house, which had been left him by his grand-mother. It had been designed in the thirties, and was made of functional and brutalist concrete: a long, low, expensive building with portholes where other people would have had windows. Philly had moved in a week ago. She was pregnant with Basil's baby. The house was cold because the gas bill had not been paid. No one seemed to mind. Philly could see she'd be the one who'd have to attend to such matters.

Basil came down from the studio to join his friends, to join Philly. He had worn out his talent for the day. Now they could all party.

He had a gentle manner, a sweet smile, and a reputation as a major painter. His father had been a Royal Academician; his grandmother had slept with Augustus John. Dark green foliage surged up against the portholes, as if the house was under water. A sudden wind must have got up outside. The place was crowded in by trees. Philly would have risen to turn on the lights, but there was no electricity. Those bills had not been paid either.

So many things about the house, Philly could see, glamorous though it was, more exciting than anything she had ever known, which needed seeing to, organising, fixing, changing, cheering up. Then it could be a home. But not yet, not yet: better to offer no judgements. Philly knew the friends accepted her, or why would they talk about Serena? But perhaps to Basil she was just another item of changing human scenery. Wait and see. She sat quiet in the half-dark.

"Let's not talk about Serena," Basil said, "ever again. This is Philly's home now. A new life starts for her and me. Let's forget Serena."

So everyone forgot Serena, including Philly.

That was in September. Philly set about making the house her own.

The kitchen door was stuck. It had not been opened for years. But since the back garden had at some time been sold off to keep creditors at bay, and the door led almost directly into the loading bays and alleys which backed a shopping complex, who would want to open it anyway? Better, Basil said, to use the front door, walk up the garden path and go round to the shops. Philly did. How did you unstick a door, anyway? It seemed better closed.

The back of the complex was sunless by day, poorly lit by night. It always seemed deserted, but if ever you opened the windows at the back you could smell stale urine and hear a scuttling sound—rats or cockroaches, no doubt startled by the noise. So Philly kept the back windows closed: she let fresh air blow in from the front. Hardly windows, anyway: hinged portholes. And you had to force foliage back in order to get them open.

By November the trees on windy days were bare and the portholes easier to open, although branches scratched up against the glass, and there was never silence. Philly's father came to visit her. Philly's mother had died that same month only a year ago, and left her daughter eleven thousand pounds. Perhaps Philly had got pregnant to forget the grief, sorrow and shock, to lose herself in a new life: the thought hung between father and daughter. "I'd have those trees cut down," said Philly's father. "They make the house dark and damp. Personally, I'd rather live in a bungalow. Shall I come over and get rid of a few branches for you?"

But Basil liked trees. The worst offender, when it came to opening the studio window, was an elm which had escaped Dutch elm disease, and was apparently as rare as it was beautiful. Basil was shocked at the notion that there could be a leaf, a twig less of the tree than nature suggested. But what did Philly know? To Philly, according to Basil, one leaf was much like another. She was a barbarian: but hadn't they always known that: Harold, Perse, Don and Steve, Jean, Holly, Ryan and Olive, too? Philly was the new blank canvas on which Basil could imprint his taste, his knowledge, his guidance.

"But don't you need as much light as possible to paint?" asked Philly.

"This house is perfectly light and cheerful," Basil said, and discouraged her father from visiting thereafter, on the grounds that he made Philly gloomy.

Philly was six months pregnant and didn't like to argue with Basil, since she only got upset and never won. The fact was that it was a dark, cold house, no matter how much was spent on gas and electricity, how much wine was drunk by the friends. Basil encouraged her to put in new radiators: she'd turn them up full but the concrete walls seemed to swallow warmth and give none back. She put in wall lights to supplement the stark central bulbs; she washed the concrete walls with white: she brought halogen uplighters, but even by night, light seemed not to be doing its proper job of banishing gloom. A stubborn month. Well, November is never the brightest of months: just grey, grey.

Basil didn't like spending money on the house: she used her own, and was happy to. He was pleased with what she did.

"It's your home," he'd say. "Have it the way you want it." That encouraged her. She did what she could. She called in a carpenter to plane down the back door, and he freed it, but damp must have swelled the wood again, because within a week it was stuck once more. She had an electrician in to fix the oven, which had always either burned or cut out at the worst possible time, but its thermostat stayed unreliable. It was only five years old. Basil balked at the cost of a new one. Philly couldn't make the floors "come up," to use her mother's phrase. Over and over she'd washed wide stretches of dark green floor tiles, and polished them too, but some of the tiles must have been unusually porous: the result was always patchy. Unsightly lines of what seemed like white salt kept rising up to spoil the finish. The whole floor should by rights have gleamed and shone; perhaps it was something about the pattern of light from the porthole windows which managed to give it a ridged effect. Philly would scrub and polish on her hands and knees. It was comfortable so to do. When she was upright, pressure on her sciatic nerve gave her a continual pain. It was not an easy pregnancy.

When Philly was seven months pregnant, in December, Basil suggested they get married. Twelfth Night, he said, would be the right kind of day: a special day: one you wouldn't forget when it came to anniversaries.

January, and Philly was Basil's second wife. Harold and Perse, Don and Steve came to the party after the wedding, in the house, along with Jean, Holly, Ryan and Olive. One of them observed, "Serena's birthday was Twelfth Night," and Philly said, "Who's Serena?" a moment before she remembered. A rather strange thing happened. A box of indoor fireworks somehow caught fire inside its wrapping: blackish ash erupted from the box, swelled and burst the plastic: a series of tiny explosions then sent the ash flying and whirling through the air, so all the surfaces in the room were soon covered with a soft film of grey. It was not unpretty; and the event had not even been dangerous, just extraordinary, watching the box jump up and down as if of its own volition, puffing out ash. But when someone else said, "Philly, you forgot to take down the Christmas decorations: that's unlucky," she worried at once. She feared for her baby. Dear God, let me be lucky, prayed Philly. Babies got born with all kinds of things wrong with them. She vacuumed carefully every day, into every corner, and felt better. Cleaning was a kind of talisman. Amazing how Christmas tree needles hung around and got everywhere, no matter how sure you were you'd finally got rid of the last of them. But you could clean and clean in this house and it just never looked as if you'd done a thing. She couldn't understand it.

Basil laughed when she complained.
"It looks just fine to me," he said. "But thank God you have proper domestic ambition. You are the right wife for me, Philly."

Philly's father hadn't been invited to the wedding. He'd written to ask if Philly would hand back the eleven thousand pounds from her mother for his safekeeping. He'd invest it for her, to her advantage. Basil had understandably taken offence. Philly felt her loyalties were to her husband, not her father, and Harold, Perse, Don and Steve, Jean, Holly, Ryan and Mattie agreed.
"The thing to do with Basil," all agreed, "is not make waves. He can be ruthless if you do. Poor Olive!"
Olive had been taken on at the same gallery as Basil. She had had a one-person show and, instead of being a failure, was now a success. She was no longer in the group of friends. Steve had taken on Mattie instead: it was that, or be out of the circle too. Mattie was a pleasant, daft girl, good at the Benefit Game, and no one spoke much about Olive any more, and within weeks she, too, was forgotten.

February, and there were only four thousand pounds left of Philly's legacy. Basil needed better frames for his paintings than his gallery was prepared to provide: anything looks better, sells better, if surrounded by real gold leaf: that had been Olive's one trick, Basil had said, unfairly used. Nothing to do with talent. Then the roof had to be re-tiled. Rain had leaked down from the ceilings, corrugating the studio walls with lines of damp. The studio was where Basil and Philly slept, in the large brass bed which was there when Philly moved in. They slept surrounded by canvas, rags, easels, paints, brushes: his hand companionable on her thigh. The famous hand: how she loved it! Completed paintings were stacked against the walls. These days Basil painted, to the despair of his gallery, only swirls of grey and black: gold leaf helped, but not enough. Philly could get quite depressed, looking at the swirls. The smell of paint and turps lingered in the studio all night through, although tubes and jars were closed, sealed; she once tried wrapping them in plastic to stop the fumes, but it didn't help. Sometimes they made her feel quite sick. It was as if morning sickness, which she had not suffered from in early pregnancy, had stored itself up till now, when she had just a few weeks to go.

Basil's baby! Oh, she was lucky. So was he; he said so, lucky second time round. He'd always wanted a baby: someone to inherit the family's genes. A pity he had to be away so often now, in Edinburgh, commissioned to paint a mural on a town hall wall. But times were hard: an artist did what he could. If he had to be a man of the people, so he would be. Philly would be okay, polishing and scouring away. When he called on the phone, its ring sounded oddly echoey: his voice would babble, as if he were under water.

Eight and a half months pregnant and who should turn up for tea one day, while Basil was away, but someone who announced herself as Ruthy Franklyn, an old friend of Basil's. Ruthy just stood on the doorstep, a total stranger, and asked herself in for tea. She was fortyish, smart, small, thin and lively and made Philly feel bulky, stupid and slow. Ruthy wore a silk turban in green and had a yellowy chiffon scarf at her wiry neck. Ruthy owned a small gallery. She'd come to collect an early painting of Basil's for a show she was mounting. She looked a little death's headish to Philly, as if the Reaper had come calling. Ruthy drank Earl

Grey and took lemon: always a problem to provide. You had to use a teapot, not teabags, and slice the lemon thinly, and serve the whole thing properly.

"Nice rock cakes," said Ruthy, "if on the crispy side."

"It's one of those ovens," said Philly, "you can never quite get to understand. Always leaping out of control."

"Serena never had any trouble with it," said Ruthy.

Philly had not quite realised the oven had once been Serena's. Presumably Serena had slept in the brass bed with Basil. Philly cooked in Serena's kitchen: slept in Serena's bed: Philly replaced Serena. Ruthy had slept in the brass bed with Basil too, by all accounts.

"Did you use Serena's recipe?" asked Ruthy, yellowy teeth scraping away at the hard little cake, which seemed the best Philly could contrive. "She was hopeless at housework but always a wonderful cook. Just generally creative, I suppose."

"I'm not a very creative person," said Philly. "But I wish I could make the house look better."

"It looks perfect to me," said Ruthy Franklyn, surprised. "You must make Basil very happy. All this and pregnant too! The famous genes will survive. Serena only ever miscarried. Four times in five years. Basil thought she somehow did it on purpose to annoy, but he would, wouldn't he? Basil likes a woman to be a woman: simple and sweet and fertile; up to her elbows in soap suds. That's why he likes you so much, no doubt." And Ruthy laughed. Why does she dislike me so much? wondered Philly. What went on? Ruthy in Basil's bed while Serena, out in the rain, banged and pummelled at the back door, stuck forever, swelled in the damp.

White snow hit against the portholes and turned bitter black. It was a storm at sea: foam and black water. How could you tell earth from sea, plant from person? Even the baby seemed to be tossing inside her.

"Do you see much of Basil?" asked Philly. "I know you did in the past, but now?"

"From time to time," said Ruthy. "But only when he wants something. Right now he wants me to sell an early painting, and his current gallery not to know. Don't take any of it seriously. I don't any more. It's you and the baby he wants," and Ruthy Franklyn laughed. She went up to the studio, and took the painting she wanted. It was a nude: one of Basil's very early works: face to the wall for years, its plain wooden frame blackened by smoke. "Since he started swirling the greys and the blacks," said Ruthy as she left, "he's hardly sold a thing. Sometimes I think it's Serena's curse. I get myself checked over pretty carefully for cancer, I can tell you that. Serena might have been mad but she had a strong personality. She loved Basil. A pity he didn't love her. But then, he probably can't love anybody. Not really."

And she looked at Philly with the drop-dead look women sometimes do give pregnant women. You have what I don't. Die, then!

Ruthy left before the blizzard got worse. Philly felt, and was, alone in the world, and the washing machine, on its fast spin, tipped itself forward on to a loose tile which vibrated and made an echoing sound, worse than the phone, worse than anything she'd ever known, right inside Philly's head. She thought she'd go deaf. Presently it faded and she could think again. She called Basil at his hotel in Edinburgh but they said there was no guest checked in under that name, and she didn't have the strength or the will to argue. The walls of the room closed in to encircle her, ridged and streaked; ash filled her nostrils. It was an old tin dustbin she was in, she realised, not the black plastic one she'd somehow envisaged: she was head down in a bin half-filled with water, and what

Serena saw, Philly saw, and always would. What Serena heard, *clang, clang,* so would Philly, for ever. As for the first wife, so for her successors.

Philly took a couple of packets of firelighters up to the studio, placed them under the brass bed and fired them. The white valance caught; the mattress smouldered and flared; the turpentine went up satisfactorily: so did the paints. The wooden stretchers of a hundred canvases flickered merrily: the canvas itself puckered, blackened, shrivelled to nothing. Gold leaf, Philly discovered, burns in a series of little spurting explosions. When there seemed no possibility of bed or paintings surviving, Philly went downstairs; the fire came with her. Concrete would not burn; the house itself would survive. Philly watched while streaks of fire raced over the tiled floor, feeding themselves on layer after layer of polish: generations' worth, as woman after woman had tried to erase the gritty, salty patches of grief and anger that past and future met to create.

"Okay, Serena?" she said, leaving by the kitchen door, the one which led out into the alley, and which today opened perfectly easily: the alley where the old tin dustbins stood and the homeless lingered, and the lager louts peed, and Serena had howled and screamed, day after day, night after night, while Basil and Ruthy waited for her to just go away. "Okay now?" she asked.

A GOOD SOUND MARRIAGE

Carrie cried herself to sleep, and her grandmother appeared to her in a dream and spoke to her. At least Carrie supposed it to be her grandmother. The apparition, or phantom, or whatever it was, who spoke so lucidly, materialised as a pretty but elderly flat-chested woman with short, brown, carefully waved hair, who wore a straight grey soft dress, which came down to mid-calf level, rather thick stockings, and low-cut shoes with little heels and a strap across the top of the foot.

Carrie worked in the BBC's Costume Design department and, professional even in her sleep, placed the dress as being late nineteen twenties or possibly early thirties. Carrie estimated her grandmother's age at around sixty but trying for fifty; an age, at any rate, that predated Carrie's life on earth.

Her grandmother had died at the age of eighty-two, when Carrie was eleven; and Carrie's mother, Kate, had not allowed the child to go to the funeral. Carrie remembered being much put out. She liked to be where the action was, just as much as her mother seemed always to like her not to be. Trouble at home was one of the reasons why now, at twenty-six, and five months pregnant, Carrie cried herself to sleep. Carrie's mother, too, was as good as dead; that is to say Kate had scarcely a word to say to her now that Carrie had gone out and married Clive. Kate threw up her hands in horror and just left her alone to get on with her husband and her pregnancy, and Carrie, to her own surprise, felt the loss. She was the first of her friends to have a baby, and who was there to talk about it with, who knew anything about the subject whatsoever? Carrie, on a good day, was glad about the baby, and on a bad day was scared stiff, and the good days were further in between, and from time to time she could only deduce that she had done the wrong thing. She should never have married Clive, who was not lying in the bed beside her as he ought to be; she should never have gotten pregnant. Now Carrie wept, and slept, and dreamed.

"Cut out the crying and the carrying on," said Carrie's grandmother, Christabel, or whoever it was. "It's bad for the baby, and it's pointless: there's no grown-up around to hear you and make things better. Worse, you're one of the grown-ups yourself, not even a child any more. You weep, but now there's no one to hear, so you weep and weep and weep some more.

"When your mother, Kate, made me a grandmother by having you, I can tell you, I wept and wept and wept some more, because the transition of the generations is never properly or finally made. But I was careful not to let David, Kate's father, your grandfather, know that I was crying, or why, because some things, even in a good sound marriage, are better kept private. Your generation does too much sharing. To share grief is to double grief, not halve it; each spouse likes to believe in the other's strength, wants the other to stay the grown-up for the moments when he, she, becomes the weeping child again. Childish burdens are to be borne alone, not shared with a husband who himself is worrying because when he combed his hair that morning there was more hair left on his comb than on his head, and that, too, is the beginning of the end for him. And because the fear of growing old masks the real fear, the fear of death, which is as strong and inevitable as death, it is to be faced, not diminished by sharing, washed away by weeping. But you—you cried so long and hard, you forced me out of my grave to rise and speak to you myself. Dead as I am, I reckon I'm still kinder and more responsible than your mother ever is alive.

"Stop crying, Carrie. It's bad for the baby, which means it's bad for you, which is why I mention it. If you cry now, out of distrust of the future, regret for the past and fear of death, the baby will be in the habit of crying when it comes out and will give you hell and sleepless nights. I'm thinking of you, not so much of the baby—for there's another thing you resent: the way people now focus on the bright energy of new life inside you, as if you, the soft surrounding shell, were of no significance at all—that's the other reason you cry yourself to sleep."

"You talk very fancy for a ghost," said Carrie. "Are you just a projection of me telling me about myself, putting into words things I do vaguely feel, or are you *really* my grandmother?"
"Carrie!" said her grandmother. "A terrible name."
"I never liked it myself," said Carrie.

She sat up abruptly in bed and the apparition, instead of vanishing, as Carrie had rather hoped it would, sat down in the wicker chair as if to keep things in balance.

"I tried to get the better of the name she christened me," complained Carrie. "I know what she had in mind for me: she wanted a sporty, woolly-hat sort of daughter with no soul. But I refused to do sports, and I went to Art School and passed my exams and I got my career going, and now I'm having a baby, and I don't see how we're going to manage and I'm not sure I want to manage. I can't give up work. I'm not sure I want to give up work. And we need my salary. You hear such terrible things these days about child care: baby-sitters turn out to be murderers. I have married a man fourteen years older than me with two teenage children, and he says, 'Don't worry, they'll do the baby-sitting,' but he must be joking. Those kids really hate me."

"Men are given to wishful thinking, it's true," said Carrie's grandmother. "Not just about baby-sitters but about everything. Your grandfather believed our troubles would be solved when his uncle died and left him his fortune, but his uncle lived to be one hundred and one, and then taxes took it all anyway. But I believed with him, though two minutes' thought would have told me the prospect of sudden riches was highly unlikely. We had a good strong marriage."

"And what about all the men I'm never going to meet?" asked Carrie. "I've settled too early and too young and how am I going to get out of it?"

The vision quavered and wavered, but it was only the tears in Carrie's eyes that were doing it.

"I cried a lot, like you, in spite of the good strong marriage," said Christabel. "And, like you, I always wondered if I had done the right thing, and all my life I waited for the man I really loved to come along. But of course he was there in the bed already. There is no perfect love, there is no perfect man; there is only what you have, there in the bed."

"There isn't one in the bed," observed Carrie, somewhat acidly.

"That's one of the main reasons I'm in this state now. Clive went to a party. I didn't feel like going. How could I go? I've nothing to wear because my waist is gone. He said he had to go because it was work, not pleasure, so he'd be home before midnight, but now it's two o'clock and he isn't home, and I just stayed behind and baby-sat those two monsters created by his first wife, and they made me play Monopoly and fetch the Cokes because I was nearest the kitchen, and who is he with? Where is he? I have married a forty-year-old alcoholic—I don't care how he denies it—and got myself pregnant, and I wish I were dead. How can the absence of someone you hate so much hurt so much?"

Grandmother laughed, and she seemed to fade out a bit, so Carrie could see the window through her body, and only the shape of her breasts and the two round nipples were apparent. But then she recoalesced, as it were, and sat there, bold as brass.

"We had a good strong marriage, your grandfather and me," said this Christabel, "and I'm sure I felt like you do now at least once a week, but on average I reckon twice a week, for forty-five years, though rather more toward the beginning and rather less toward the end, he'd roll over me in bed or I'd roll over him and we'd forget our mistrust, and no doubt it will be the same for you."
"In forty-five years," said Carrie in horror, "he'll be eighty-five."
"And you'll be seventy-one. So what?"
"The world will have ended before then," said Carrie.
"No such luck," said the apparition smugly. And there was a kind of *click-click-click*, which might have been knitting needles, or a beetle in the beams of the old house thirty miles from London where Clive and Carrie lived. They had put the house on the market in order to raise some money and start afresh in a different home, but no one would buy it, thus making Carrie's stepchildren, Chrissie and Harry, Clive's children by Audrey, rejoice.

This house was where they'd always lived, and where their mother, Audrey, died. It was theirs. Forget Carrie.

"He only married me," said Carrie, "to have a mother for his children, to make use of me."

"If he'd wanted that," said the apparition, settling in to the knitting of a long, long scarf that seemed to run in and out the centuries, "he'd have chosen someone more naturally attuned to domesticity, a more practical sort, not a natural nibbler from delicatessens, a weeper in bed through the long lonely nights.

"Look at it like this," said the phantom, "nothing is ever perfect. The dangerous thing for a woman is to wait too long, so she ends with nothing. Time flows the wrong way, starts as a slow and mighty river, then it begins to race along, over shallows, narrower, faster; suddenly it disappears, dives underground and it's gone and if you don't look out you're alone. No baby is ever perfectly timed, no man exactly right. If man and baby offer themselves, accept them. The things in life you regret most are not what you do, but what you don't do. So you held your nose and jumped, Carrie, and good for you. You'll learn to swim.

"I predict for you a good strong marriage in which there will never be peace—for who wants peace?—but much gratification: this is only the first of your children. It will be the kind of marriage that attracts both saboteurs and hangers-on. See that as the sign of its strength. Clive-and-Carrie, people will say, as once they said David-and-Christabel, and the very words will be bound together. David-and-Christabel, Jim-and-Kate, Clive-and-Carrie. Those are the generations. Audrey-and-Clive turned out to be a mere hors d'oeuvre—you're the main course. That sometimes happens. But Jim-and-Kate became Jonathan and Kate and that was wrong, and you never forgave your mother for divorcing and remarrying, so she's dead to you, and you to her, because the new names simply didn't fit. You, Carrie, quite rightly, stayed loyal to the concept of Jim-and-Kate. As I daresay your stepchildren for the moment stay loyal to Audrey-and-Clive. But you'll win, Carrie. You're the second marriage, but it's the strong one, the long one. Clive and Carrie, sturdy and central."

"How do you know?" Carrie jeered.

"I know what I know," said the grandmother, darkly, as befitted a messenger from the other side. "And if you take my advice, you'll bring your mother, that naughty, selfish girl, back to life now that you're having a baby of your own. You will need her. It might even be good for her to think about something other than herself."

"I know everything I need to know about childbirth from books," said Carrie. "New knowledge. Modern knowledge. Not mid-wives' talk. What would you know?"

"Take my advice if you won't take hers," said the great-grandmother-to-be. "Just remember, nature kills. When it comes to the birth, go for least pain if you're given a choice, and may God have mercy on mother and child."

"It's only five months," said Carrie, "and already I don't see how it's ever going to get out."

"Exactly," said the grandmother.

The ghost of Christabel looked askance at the knitted scarf. "I don't knit," she said. "I swear I never knitted. My own grand-mother Frances Mary knitted, and I hated the clacking, the click-ing, while I lay awake at night, frightened of ghosts, wondering how babies ever got out."

"Now see what's happened," said Carrie. "You've turned into a ghost yourself."

"So will you," said Christabel shortly. Then the knitting was gone, and the phone on the bedside rang. Christabel remained where she was, to Carrie's surprise.

"So?" said Carrie snappily into the phone, assuming it was Clive. "What happened?"

A woman's voice replied. "Clive asked me to tell you he's on his way home. He'd drunk so much I didn't like to let him drive. I called a taxi and it took forever to come."

"Who are you?" asked Carrie, rudely.

"I'm Andrea," said the voice. "Tim and Andrea; we were Audrey and Clive's best friends. But now Tim and I are divorced. It's Tim and Valerie, and so far just Andrea and Andrea. Didn't Clive tell you?"

"No," said Carrie, pride forbidding more inquiry. "But thanks for not letting him drive." She put the phone down.

"A saboteur," said Christabel. "It's a good sign. They cluster round at the beginning. They see the oak tree's trunk thickening, swelling the graceful branches which mean children budding, just here, just so, and they don't like it; they want to shake it to bits; they resent it; all good strong marriages attract the saboteur. Women will creep up on him, sly and beckoning. Men will slip up your stairs while he's away. 'Try me,' they'll say. 'I'm better.' And so they might be, so reason may tell you; but all they are in truth are saboteurs. Turn the peaceful ones into hangers-on; ask them to baby-sit. They will, if only from guilt."

"What was he doing in this woman Andrea's house?" asked Carrie, and she felt the baby weigh her down, or she'd have gotten out of bed and broken things, in spite of her grandmother's presence. "I'll divorce him," she said, "that's what I'll do. I'll leave now before he gets home. I'll go and sleep on my friend

Vera's sofa. He doesn't love me, his children hate me. I should never have done it. I must have been mad. I could have married anyone and I married a middle-aged alcoholic widower who can't keep his productions under budget and will be fired any moment." "You're not listening to what I'm saying," said the apparition. "I suppose you will have to start from the beginning and work it all out for yourself, like everyone else. I'm wasting my time. I am your future as well as your past, and available for inspection, but try telling any young woman that. They would far rather weep, and shriek, and squirm in the present." And she vanished, the semi-circled outline of her meagre breasts fading last, and Carrie went back to sleep, or had never woken out of it.

WEB CENTRAL

The girl, Mandy Miller, aged twenty-three, had made an appointment to see Josie Toothpad, the well-known literary guru, at 11 a.m. But already it was six minutes past, and Mandy's face had not yet flashed up on Josie's screen. Six minutes late: six minutes' worth of ungratefulness, adding to the burden of Josie's day.

Mandy was privileged; Josie did not normally see aspiring writers: her time was considered better spent writing haikus. But the Authors' Guild saw promise in the girl, whose writing profile peaked at *lyricism* and fell to a disastrous trough around *compromise,* in a decade where such profiles usually ran as straight and flat as the heart trace of someone newly dead. So Josie had been generous.

Josie filled in the waiting minutes playing solitaire. She hadn't done that for ages. Click, click: cards flying, red and black slicing the screen. Then the familiar melancholy settled in, that stuffy sadness which so often accompanies any obsessional activity and in particular solitaire—so much chance, so little skill. Josie adjusted the dial of her drip feed as Dr. Owen her personal physician had so often asked her not, increasing the flow of uppers as opposed to downers. But now she just felt edgy. She stopped playing and put her drip feed back to normal. But the edginess wouldn't go away: it was moving into anxiety, foreboding. Josie turned up the voltage of the muscle contractors, the ones designed to keep her limbs viable and strong, but for once the tingling sensation didn't please her, but irritated. She turned the voltage down again. Personal monitors on the banks of screens around the room showed a steady, profound green. She should be in a state of tranquillity, but was not. The gap between what she felt and what the screen said she felt was unusually wide.

Josie punched in a query to Zelda, her personal therapist, and Zelda's sweet, reassuring face appeared instantly on the main screen and softly asked Josie to profile her current emotions, choosing four appropriate adjectives from the available selection. None applied. Josie felt bored and closed Zelda, but Zelda wouldn't be closed. Zelda just blanked out and reappeared before even a mouse had time to click. Zelda said, "I've been waiting for a call from you, Josie. It's your birthday, and it's your right and your privilege to consult me, as you come to terms with the downside of being 132 today."

The pause between the one, the three and the two were minute but discernible. It was crass of Web Central, Josie thought, to thus remind Heaven-on-Earthers that Zelda was a machine. And Zelda had got it wrong: Josie's birthday was six days past. What's more, Zelda once closed had not stayed closed, which could only mean Zelda was now operated directly from Nex Control. Since last week's acquisition of Web Central's main shareholding, Nex Control could over-ride the Web Central computer. Which meant, Josie supposed, Nex Control could break into a transmission any time they liked, as an aircraft captain would choose to break into the sound track of a film you were watching, with warnings of turbulence. An archaic image, which almost made Josie laugh, for who went anywhere, physically, any more? Space was in your head: vast quantities of it, as much as you wanted. You travelled the universe freely through the voices in your mind.

There was something wrong with the transmission: Zelda's whole face flickered so that her smile looked like a smirk. Then Zelda blanked out mid-sentence.

At the time of the takeover Nex Control had promised there'd be no changes in management style. Promises, promises. Josie remembered enough about pre-Web life to know that the State was never to be trusted: States dealt in lies, as Nietzsche had pointed out; they spoke in all tongues of good and evil, and in the end what was Nex Control but another State, gobbling up smaller territories, grabbing up Web Central, asset stripping.

When in doubt, keep your head down, don't make waves. Josie completed her mood profile, punching in "tranquil, reflective, industrious, confident." Central records were kept. Web Central had been created by a consensus of newly young idealists; their computer's mission, to keep Web Heaven non-political, pacific and angst-free for its subscribers. But that had been fifty years ago: language could have changed, the very words now have a different meaning.

Josie took off her helmet and at once felt less paranoic. She was both post-menopausal and pre-menstrual, that was the trouble. For a couple of days a month she suffered from both conditions. Today was one of the days. She knew too much and felt too much.

She was an original Heaven-on-Earther. Sixty years ago a daily dose of Ecstasy 3, which reversed the ageing process and settled the body at around twenty-five years old, combined with good old-fashioned oestrogen, had become available to any female who could afford it. Josie could, and did. Ageing, for Heaven-on-Earthers, need no longer be a cause of death, but there were drawbacks: one's personality remained cyclical.

Still no sign of Mandy: 11:12 a.m. Another of Josie's screens leapt into life. Traders were ingenious; they found ways of appearing on screen no matter what.

"Just punch D O N U T: revo @ efil," required the salesman. He was dressed like a butler, smiled like a fiend, and had a metronome—banned by Web Central as a hypnotic device, but perhaps Nex Control permitted them—ticking away in the background.

> *"Only punch and you will see*
> *Something long denied and free*
> *Stuffed with honey, fruit and rum*
> *Down your food-chute swift will come.*
> *DONUT!"*

Some things never changed. Josie obediently punched up DONUT: revo @ efil. She'd been losing weight recently, but Dr. Owen didn't seem worried. Her fingers looked just plain bony—but still pretty. She'd always liked her hands: loved their dextrous moving over keys, their flawless clicking of the mouse. If you liked yourself and loved being alive, what did your chronological age matter?

* * *

Josie steered her chair to the window and opened the blinds; she had to put her drip feed on hold to get so far. Alone of her friends, Josie still liked daylight, and a view. Down below the Underclass swarmed: the unfortunates who lived on earth, not in the space in their heads. Hardly anyone over twenty-five, the whole lot HIV positive, doomed to death ten years or so after their first sexual contact. So much noise, and dirt, and squalor. The Underclass lived their short lives intensely: they were even said to write naive poetry, novels, plays. Well, why not? Shelley, Keats: short lives, great poetry—for a moment Josie almost envied the wretched of the earth. The Underclass lived unobserved and uncounted, unnoticed, unfrightened: they'd make way only for the armed Delivery Squads who attended to the physical needs of an Overclass which lived decorously, individual unit by individual unit, stacked one above the other. AIDS-free. They had Zelda to keep them healthy in mind; Dr. Owen, healthy in body. Josie's friend from way back, Honour, had once said there was now political unrest in the Underclass: there was a growing sense that computer literacy—a capital offence for them—was a human right. That was absurd. The Underclass was too physical, too little given to logic, ever to cope happily with computers.

"They touch one another so much," said Josie aloud, and the sound bounced strangely off window and walls. She was accustomed to headphones. "All the time they fondle and embrace, push or hit or hug. Kiss and copulate. Flesh touches flesh." There was no one to answer her. Josie remembered that eight decades or so back, she had actually given birth, had shared a living space with a man. They'd slept touching, side by side. It seemed a strange thing to have done, let alone enjoyed. Her son, one of a generation of men who had declined to take up the Heaven-on-Earth project, being reluctant to give up their masculinity, had died of old age one decade back. She did not want to think about that. She went back to the console, readjusted her medication and changed the colours on all the screens for the fun of it.

Again Zelda's face appeared unsummoned on the screen. "Josie," she said, and her voice sounded cracked and strange, "I know you are troubled. Let's talk about it, dear. Together we'll work on it."

But Zelda's lips and nostrils were blurring. She was hideous. Zelda dissolved and vanished in a scramble of snow. Josie pressed the alarm for the emergency technician. "Your fault has been automatically recorded," the stand-by screen flashed. "Please do not block emergency lines, OK?" Josie clicked on OK, although it was far from okay. But what could you do? If you didn't ac-knowledge OK, the screen pinged back at you interminably. She tried to click to No-Sound, but couldn't. Was this what life was going to be like under Nex Control? It was intolerable. Perhaps 132 years of life was intolerable, full stop.

The whole point of age was the acquisition of wisdom; she could impart it, in haiku form, or in advice to the likes of Mandy Miller. But if Mandy Miller didn't turn up, what use was Josie Toothpad? A silly name, given to her by a computer. Anyway, she'd gone off haikus: recently she'd developed a liking for romantic verse. She wanted to be in love again. If she couldn't be in love she'd rather be dead. Right back in the beginning, she'd never wanted to live to be more than thirty. She'd outstayed her welcome by one hundred and two years.

How long since she'd ordered her doughnut? Six minutes? De-livery was meant to be within four. She'd complain, although that was a breach of good manners. The more reprehensible complaining was, the theory went, the more others would struggle to ensure no grounds for complaint existed. But Josie was allowed her eccentricities, as an original. "Your comment has been recorded," said the screen. "Please be patient. OK?" Okay, she clicked, lying in her teeth.

The Friendship Screen bleeped. It was Honour, her friend. These days Honour seldom called. Honour had got caught up in the Occult 'n' Oracle network; Josie had denied the existence of the paranormal. Honour and Josie had quarrelled. Zelda had advised them against patching it up. The two friends, she said, had outworn each other. It happened to Heaven-on-Earthers as the birthdays mounted up. There was always Zelda, for companionship and consolation. Zelda never fretted; Zelda always *knew*.

Honour looked lovely; about fourteen years old. Red hair tumbled round perfect features. Before you enrolled as a Heaven-on-Earther, you had cosmetic surgery to perfect any flaws blind Mother Nature had inflicted upon you. Not for the sake of attracting men—there weren't many around these days anyway; most who started male had foetal micro-surgery and a dose of oestrogen three weeks into conception and ended up female, or roughly so—but for the sake of self-esteem, self-image. You had to be comfortable with yourself.

Josie squealed and all but leapt up and down to see her friend. Her feet, oddly, had some difficulty reaching the ground. Josie thought, "But I've shrunk." Nor was there much life in her legs, for all the voltage she'd put through her muscles over the years. She didn't think she could get to the door. She just knew she didn't want to stay in her chair, though the chair it was which wrapped her, soothed her, stroked her, made love to her, sung to her—all of a sudden Josie just wanted not to be in it, couldn't bear to sit still a moment longer.

"Josie, what am I going to do?" asked Honour. "All my screens are on the blink, and Zelda's gone mad. She keeps giving me advice I haven't asked for. And my doughnut hasn't turned up."
"Mine either," said Josie. "But I know who I am and I'm perfect." It was their mantra from way back.
"You look about twelve," said Honour to Josie. "And I'm not much better. I guess what they're saying is true."
"Go on, tell," said Josie. "What are they saying?"
"Nex Control upped our Ecstasy 3 last week and our age reversal is now irreversible," said Honour. "We're all growing younger exponentially. Give us another fifteen minutes and we'll return to the womb and lapse into a coma; then we'll drift into nothingness; we'll be unconceived; we will not have existed. Funny thing is, I don't mind one bit."

Josie thought for a bit.

"Why would they do a thing like that?" asked Josie.

Curiosity survived, when little else did. Josie felt her chest and it was flat, flat, flat. She wailed a thin high wail. But cut it short for politeness' sake. Politeness lasted too.
"To make space," said Honour, "for themselves. The young want their turn too. The Underclass are tired of us."

Josie's central screen leapt into life. A girl of about seven looked out at her. "Hi, everyone," she said. "I'm ever so sorry. Honestly, I did my best. I called the technicians, but they were just toddlers and pooing all over the place—it was disgusting. So I told them to go away. What was I meant to do?"

Her place was taken by an ugly young woman in her early twenties. "My name's Mandy Miller," she said. "I am the death you have all been expecting."

Josie realised Mandy Miller wasn't ugly at all, merely human; that she, Josie, was so accustomed to seeing perfection on her screens, she'd forgotten what human was like.
"Nex Control has tried to make it easy for you," said Mandy Miller, "given you time to adjust. For DONUT read 'don't,' reverse Revo Efil and get Life Over. Not perfect, but the best I could do. Nex Control is an Underclass organisation. Time now for the young to march along your Highway, arm in arm, in glory."

At least that was what Josie thought she heard. But how could she know? She only knew she was 132 because Zelda had said so, and perhaps Zelda had got the decimal point wrong and she was 13.2. Really, one knew very little about anything. Words had begun to make little sense; now there were only shapes and sounds. Josie was conscious of a divine brilliance all around, and of wanting to be in the shade; then there was a sudden welcoming dark at the end of a tunnel, and she travelled through it, quite suddenly, to warmth and peace, safety and silence.

OF LOVE,
PAIN AND
GOOD CHEER

PAINS
A Story of
Most Contemporary Women, 1972

Paula lies amazed on the bed, like some poor butterfly with a pin driven through its middle. Can these be the contractions which indicate the beginning of labour? Or perhaps of false labour, or perhaps indeed, being more like pains than contractions, indigestion from the curry fetched in that evening by her kind, thoughtful and radically minded husband from the local take-away curry-in-a-hurry house. Who knows?

Paula, at the moment, feels she knows all too little. She does expect, however, soon to know more. The central heating has lately been repaired and there is a hole in the floor where the service engineers have carelessly removed a pipe. So Paula can now hear what is going on in the room below.

More has been going on down there, Paula suspects, than ought to have been.

At the moment her husband Deakey is opening the door to members of the local Women's Liberation Group. Paula has had an upsetting day, as Deakey has told her at least eight times this evening, and, being eight and a half months pregnant, has sensibly agreed to miss the meeting and has taken to her bed.

Outside, the moon rises.

"We live in an odd part of London," Paula and Deakey will explain at dinner parties. "Not exactly smart but it's a solid Edwardian house, with good soil for rose growing. We like roses. Well, who doesn't, but we especially like not those great modern, plastic-looking roses, but the little old-fashioned ones that smell. Yes, that kind of rose attracts greenfly, whitefly, aphids, slugs, and every invisible worm that ever flew in the night in the howling storm, but we think they do smell just wonderful."

Paula and Deakey like everything together, think everything together, change their views together, spray pests together, feel together, are together. We believe this, they say: we do that, we have found out the other. In and out of each other's apron pockets for a full seven years.

"Why shouldn't a man wear an apron just like a woman!" cried Deakey only last night, home at seven as usual from the Civil Service, wielding the garlic crusher like a man, slavering the meat-free roast with garlic slime.

"Careful the baby doesn't come out smelling of garlic," said a friend. There are usually friends about. Paula and Deakey are a very pleasant couple. Anyone would like them. Paula's contraceptive loop fell out one night, which is why she is pregnant. Paula and Deakey are not perfect, which makes them the more endearing.

* * *

The moon rises a little further and now shines in upon Paula. It is a full moon. Every full moon, regular as clockwork, Paula's curse has come upon her; until eight months ago, that is; until the un-planned slipping of the loop and the consequent stoppage of blood. What is this? This rusty red stuff? Why now? Merely the body's habit, thinks Paula, wriggling painfully on her contrac-tual pin; what a wonderful thing the body is! It carries its own remembrances.

Perhaps Deakey should be with his Paula at this moment of their joint life? When the moon shines and her body aches? No, thinks Paula. No need for that: Deakey is with me in spirit anyway and, besides, someone has to answer the door. If Paula lies quiet and still the pains will stop. The quieter she lies, the better she will hear. The rest she can imagine. Marta is arriving. Marta is always the last to come, snorting and jeering. Now they'll all be sitting down in the familiar conspiratorial ring.

"Male liberal," Marta will be sneering at Deakey's back as he goes to make coffee, and if she were black she would say, dis-paragingly, "White, white liberal!" and the others will be nod-ding their heads and appearing to agree, but thinking how nice to have a husband like Deakey; if only they had, instead of having to pacify their own, having to placate, lie, make coffee in advance, leave extra special dinners to warm up in the oven, if they want to be allowed out to attend. Well, a meeting such as this one is regarded as domestic treachery. Yes, it is treachery. Female com-plaints made public. All men do when they're together, every-one knows, is drink, tell funny stories and contemplate exercising their rights: there is no treachery inherent in this. But women shouldn't tell.

* * *

211

And what are the women doing now but telling? Do they not go fully conscious, hand in hand, where once they only went in dreams; one by one they return to that far back world of matriarchy and of Mother Right, and come back to tell the tale of it. Not so much a hen party, this, more a cosmic conspiracy. If it gets too powerful, delves too deep, the sun itself might go out. Don't forget your key when you go out, wife—you might not get back in again. He's serious.

Why hasn't Paula sealed the hole in the bedroom floor? Because Paula needs to know what's going on. Paula suspects that her husband Deakey sometimes has it off in the room below with Audrey, the woman next door. Audrey is married to an adulterous husband. For all anyone knows, the condition is catching. Who is to say what goes on when our eyes are closed and we sleep, as Paula would be sleeping now, if it were not that the Great Lasso-er in the sky keeps circling her round her middle and tugging tight, and has woken her. Listen now. Down below.

"That fact is," bejewelled Rachel is saying, her knees held tight together, "and as Engels was the first to point out, the nuclear family is founded on the open or concealed domestic slavery of the wife. Within the family, man is the bourgeois and the wife the proletariat. I think we could usefully examine the implications."

Oh Deakey. Deakey and Audrey. If it were true it would be more than mere adultery, it would be Treachery. Paula has said as much to Deakey. Deakey, however, maintains that if there is any treachery it lies in Paula's own paranoia, albeit made more pronounced than usual by her advanced state of pregnancy. So Deakey and Paula looked up paranoia as it relates to pregnancy in their various books on childbirth and human response and discovered only one mildly related reference, namely that acute womb envy in the male can predispose to destructive promiscuity. "Nonsense!" cried Deakey, dismissing the author as Freudian orientated, and Paula was obliged to agree. Nonsense! All the same, she consulted the midwife, who said she'd never heard of destructive promiscuity but did remark that all men were the same and told a sorry tale of how she once delivered a sixteen-year-old junkie girl of twins. The mother lay on a double bed between two men who, when asked, declined to move over, but lay just where they were while the midwife worked over and round them.

"Such a nicely spoken girl, too," said the midwife.

The midwife had taken the twins to hospital, she said, wrapped in her raincoat, but the girl never called to collect them.

What can Paula hear now? Is that Audrey's voice amongst the others? It is. It is. Why is Audrey here? She doesn't belong to the group. What is being plotted? A soft little female voice. Audrey's.

"Deakey said come and I know Paula's keen so I did, but I mean I *like* being a woman," says Audrey. "I mean, what's wrong with it? I mean, it's all a bit ridiculous, isn't it, all this bra-burning and why do they make themselves so *plain*. Present company excepted, of course. A woman has a duty to make herself look attractive. I'm happy as I am. I love being feminine and looked after by my husband."

"Adulteress," cries Paula in her heart. "Hypocrite!"

Whoosh and *wheesh* and there's water everywhere and the Abyssinian or wherever bedcover from Liberty's, with an embroidered Tree of Life upon it, embedded with little pieces of mirror, is not just probably ruined but is rendered cold and

uncomfortable to lie upon. What, is Paula now incontinent?
Has rage made her thus? Was it like this when she was a little
child?

"Little girls don't wet the bed," said Paula's mama, "only nasty
little boys." And she washed and cleaned and ironed on, saying,
"I sacrificed everything for you, my Paula—my career, my fame,
my fortune—your father didn't want a working wife and mother,
so now I'll grit my teeth for ever as I smile at you, my little bed-
wetting Paula." *Whoosh* and *wheesh.*

"But is the paternalistic society a function of only capitalism, or
of civilisation itself?" Dandy is asking, in her blue-chip voice.
Everyone hates it when Dandy speaks.

To a butterfly, thinks Paula, a pin must feel like an RSJ. A rolled-
steel joist, the kind you support whole houses on, from within.

"Do you mean function or symptom?" snaps Sybil. "Make up
your mind. If you're a revolutionary not a radical, you're in the
wrong group—"
"Oh dear," simpers Audrey, "oh dear, it's much too deep for me."

And now Deakey can be heard opening the door and saying more
coffee anyone? "Paula's still lying down," says Deakey. "She
went to a relaxation class this evening and it's exhausted her,
ha ha."

It did. It did. Paula hurried home early from the Clinic, wondering what she would find. But when she passed Audrey's house,
there was Audrey just ordinarily at her kitchen window. She even
smiled as Paula went by, waving her wooden spoon. Making jam,

her usual strawberry jam no doubt, and that was when Paula suddenly felt exhausted. Paula found Deakey calmly smoking a herbal cigarette in the living room, but such a sense of sudden departure in the air, such a scent of passion spent, that the baby kicked its heels in the pelvic what-have-you as an ostrich might bury its head in the sand, and shock ran through poor paranoid Paula, and she'd never in all her life felt so tired.

Why was Audrey smiling so at her window? Audrey's adulterous husband was away on business with his PA. Why should Audrey smile? Only one thing can make a betrayed wife smile, and that's betrayal on her own account.

Why should Deakey be smoking last year's Christmas-present herbal cigarette at six in the evening, if not to cover something up, fog the scent of betrayal?

"A plot," cried Paula.
"Paranoia," cried Deakey. "You insult me!"
"But we always think alike," pleaded Paula. "You know we do!" and Deakey buried his face in his hands.

"Do men have feelings the same way as women do?" asks Rachel now, down below. "That's what I always want to know."

"No," says Sybil. "They don't. Oh no! Or if they do, they invalidate them in relation to the degree of their involvement with male institutions. The nicest men will murder, sacrifice, betray, die in the name of patriotism, religion, efficiency, progress and even the Civil Service." Or that's what Paula supposes Sybil says. It is usually something like that.

* * *

A very small, rare butterfly flutters hopelessly in Paula's belly: a very large RSJ, one fit to keep up Centrepoint, pins it to the bed.

What I need, thinks Paula presently, is to consult one of the many books on the shelf which will tell me what the symptoms of labour are. Though I'm sure this is far, far worse than labour, which is a perfectly natural process, could possibly be. Paula sits up, falls off the bed, lies where she falls. If she moves, she feels she will do herself an injury. It is not comfortable being eight months plus pregnant at the best of times, as Deakey has lately said to Paula when she gets into bed. He keeps himself carefully and considerately to the far side of it, away from her—why?

"Nursery schools," says Phyllis. "That's the answer to all our problems. How I hate and despise Dr. Bowlby and his myth of mother-care! If hell were not a male institution I should wish him there. I suggest we lobby the Council, Monday."

"For lobby read lob," mutters Dandy. "A few broken windows should work wonders."

"We are not an extremist group. Go join the Maoists," shouts Sybil.

Deakey, where are you, Deakey? No, no, these can't be contractions. They're pains. This beautiful red rose opening inside, bursting from bud to bloom, thrusting everything aside to make room for it. Why can't you be here to admire it?

An ear to the ground. Well, it's there already. Paula still lies where she fell: the voices from below are louder now.

* * *

"Segregated toilets in infant schools," Phyllis is saying. "That's where the whole thing starts."

"Deakey," Paula had said earlier that evening, finding her husband smoking last year's herbal cigarette, "Audrey's been here, with you. You and she are having a sexual relationship."

"What nonsense," said Deakey. "Audrey's at home making jam. She wouldn't leave the jam on the cooker to burn. Our marriage is founded on truth. You and I are equal partners in it."

"You're laughing at me," said Paula. "And you know I have no sense of humour."

"I have enough for both of us," said Deakey. "That's why we have this perfect marriage."

"It's happened because I'm having the Women's Lib meeting here tonight," said Paula. "It's your revenge. If I cancel it, will you stop seeing Audrey?"

"For one thing," elaborated Deakey a little later as he washed up the plates after the take-away curry, "I am all for Women's Liberation. We both agree that women are a persecuted majority. For another, I am not having a sexual relationship with Audrey. She's half-witted and wouldn't understand the term. Would you like me to bring your slippers? You must be tired, back from your relaxation class."

"I don't like the way you keep saying 'I,'" said Paula. "It always used to be 'we.'"

* * *

"There are two of you now," Deakey had said. "It makes all the difference," and Paula had lumbered up the stairs and started to cry—why is it always Paula who cries, never Deakey?—fallen asleep, woke to what cannot be labour, for in labour one does not have pains, only contractions, all the books agree—and to hear Deakey opening the door to the Liberation Group, including tonight, for no apparent reason, Audrey.

Another red rose bursts into flower. A whole bush of vulgar floribunda blooms inside, forcing even the RSJ to bend and buckle.

"You are more than me, double what you were. I must look after myself," Deakey said to Paula. Yes he did, and baby buried his ostrich head further in the sand which is now growing these amazing flowers.

Downstairs the ladies' slips are showing. The slips are made of barbed wire, worn like hair shirts, excoriating—all women have them, apparently, keep them in their bottom drawers, in readiness.

Marta throws her wedding ring across the room. Tomorrow it will slip beneath one damp-raised lino tile and be lost for ever. Paula can envisage it.

"Why should I have to come home from work and cook and clean," cries Marta, "while he sits watching the ads on the telly and says why aren't you like the one on the screen who's wiping paint?"

He, he, he.

* * *

"The pill made me so depressed I had to have shock treatment," whispers Phyllis, "and the loop made me flood, all month, and the cap gives me nervous eczema, and he won't wear anything— what shall I do? If I say no, he'll be off."

"Well, we're Jewish," murmurs Rachel. "I only had daughters, so he made this other woman pregnant, and you know my youngest son Benjamin—well, he's hers, not mine. I've never told anyone till now."

"Oh God, oh God," says Sybil, "I'm not all that pretty, am I? I met this man, I thought it was true love. He took me to his flat, all night we made love, I told him I loved him. He left the room, he said for cigarettes, and when he got back into bed, it was another man. His flatmate. He'd had a good lay, he must have said, and passed the news on. Well, so I am. Who cares?"

"What I want to know," says Dandy darkly, "is why do they show female orgasm on the media and never male?"

"Women's Lib, Housebound Wives, Group Therapy, what's the difference?" says Audrey, bright and trite as ever. "It always sounds the same."

They go. Paula hears them depart. Doors open and close. There is silence. Then:
"Stay a little, Audrey," says Deakey. Paula hears. Audrey stays.

"Consider the tapeworm," Paula hears Deakey saying to Audrey. "Accord it all virtue. A complete set of male and female organs in each of its 50 to 200 proglottides: it spends its entire life copulating in all its sections with itself." It's the kind of thing Paula would love Deakey to say to her but, of course, Deakey only says it to Audrey, who doesn't understand a word of it. "Let me be your tapeworm, Audrey," says Deakey now.

"Thank you, Deakey, but what would Paula think? What would she say?" asks Audrey.
"Paula is in no position to say anything," says Deakey. "Paula's too pregnant to think and asleep upstairs in any case."

Do they kiss, do they copulate? Does Deakey tie Audrey's centre even tighter to her cosy fate, wrapping his 200 proglottides around her? Paula scarcely cares.

Pain. Quite definite pain. What is that noise? Is it Paula? A volcano? Addition or subtraction? The beginning of everything, wrenching more matter out of less? Division, multiplication? Strain and push: don't tear the sheets either, you naughty girl.

Push, rend, slither, pop, baby's here. Baby cries.

"Dear God, what's that?" says Deakey.

It's a boy.

A QUESTION OF TIMING

"Hi, it's me," said Philippa.

"Is that you, Philippa?" asked Paul.

"Of course it's me, Paul," said Philippa. "Who else says hi, it's me, in the middle of the night?"

"I'm sorry, Philippa darling," said Paul. "There's a kind of delay on the line. I think I spoke before the 'it's me' arrived. And your voice is distorted."

"Oh well," said Philippa, "I suppose it would be since the sound has to travel right across the globe to get to you."

"The sound waves aren't travelling across," said Paul. "They bounce up to a satellite and down again. It's a shorter distance, if you take the curvature of the earth into account."

"I take it everything's okay your end," said Philippa, "or you wouldn't be concerned with the curvature of the earth."

"But why shouldn't everything be okay?" asked Paul.

"I thought you might be missing me," said Philippa.

"Of course I'm missing you," said Paul. Was the pause longer than the distance merited? Either both spoke at once or waited for the other to speak. It was awkward.

"But I expect you're too busy to miss me," said Paul, while Philippa said, "Though I expect the children keep you busy enough," and both remarks sounded insincere to her, each plaiting into the other as they did. Distance made for remoteness, not closeness. Absence, combined with distance, was not the continuation of presence by other means, as she had affectionately and consolingly assured her husband only ten days earlier—it was a kind of blinking out of existence, and all you could do was hope it was a temporary situation. The silence had fallen again. Now neither spoke.

Paul coughed and Philippa had a vision of the sound bursting up and out of the wintry London fog into the night sky, to reach a satellite half-way to the moon before pouring down again here in Auckland, New Zealand, where the sun shone brightly through an ozone-thin sky onto blue, sparkling water. Christmas was nearly upon them. Philippa and Paul had been married for six years and this was the first Christmas they had spent apart.

The hotel where Philippa stayed looked out over a wide harbour: fine lines of white sand marked out a pattern of beaches on its other side: yachts, their coloured sails like halves of party balloons, lost and regained energy, clustered and dispersed in the foreground. Philippa had no idea how that kind of thing—sailing—was done; she had never had any desire to do it, or anything like it. People here seemed to be happy doing outdoor things, but outdoor things made Philippa feel desolate and awkward. She missed her house, her home, her children, Paul. She missed the winter. If the weather was cold you could put on a jersey to keep warm; but if you were hot all you could do was turn up the air-conditioning and contribute another nail in the planet's coffin. In London, to dislike outdoors was a perfectly natural state of

affairs: here in New Zealand it seemed an offence against a hos-
pitable and benign deity. Climate was something to be relished,
to be grateful for. To murmur here about loss of ozone and the
dangers of sunbathing was simply not in good taste; as mention-
ing insanity or cancer had not been in her grandmother's day.
Philippa wished she could tell Paul this, but how could she? It
would go on too long and words cost money.

Philippa could hear one of the Boondock Boys moving in the next
room. It was something that they were stirring. Four of them lived
in a suite with three bathrooms and only just enough space in
which to stretch their embryo personalities and their squalor: their
blackish shirts, their jewellery, hairsprays, overstretched tights,
cigarette papers, bondage gear, the knickers of their groupies
which they kept as souvenirs, the instruments which they claimed
they never let out of their sight but frequently did. Philippa would
somehow have to get them to their photo call by two o'clock. They
were pleasant enough lads, not very bright, who felt it commer-
cially prudent to act drunk, high and rude. They made her feel
like some solicitous and bourgeois grandmother, not the young
whiz kid she'd believed she was.

"So how's the tour going?" Paul was asking. "Everything okay?"
Philippa counted one, two, three, before saying, "It's a nightmare."
Her mother had once told her it was unwise to let the man in your
life know you were having a good time without him. But since
Philippa wasn't having a good time perhaps she should say she
was? Was that how it worked?
"Well," said Paul, "you would take it on, leaving us here to have
Christmas alone," just as Philippa said, "Actually, it's quite a lark
quite a lot of the time, and the weather's glorious."
It was like being killed by friendly fire.

Paul said, "Tell you what, you speak, and wait, and then I'll speak." Except that he went on talking and she thought he'd stopped, so there they were, speaking together again.

"I thought it would be ten times easier organising four people than it would be forty. But a pop group and a philharmonic are very different animals. At least classical musicians turn up where and when they say they will. And they can read schedules. They may be elderly and boring, most of them, but at least they're reliable."

When Philippa met Paul she had been working for the Avon Philharmonic for eight years. She was thirty-three. At an astoundingly young age, she had seized the languid orchestra by its vocal chords, as it were, and shaken it into life. Philippa, the young tyro, the bringer of life and energy, her name in all the papers. This was the role she was accustomed to: now she was the wet blanket, the damper down of creative fires; the one who had to flush the drugs down the loo, empty the whisky into the hotel pot plants.

None of it had been of her desiring, she now realised. Perhaps the timing had been wrong, had pushed her into this situation or that. Marriage to Paul, a first child within the year; handing in her notice when Paul, a consultant architect, got moved on to the Board of Entier Enterprises; thinking it would all work out. Then pregnant again: one baby she could have coped with; two she couldn't. Entier Enterprises went down the tubes, and where was the family income then? The timing had indeed been always wrong. Not very wrong, but wrong enough.

And the "if onlys." If only Philippa had hung on to her job just a month longer, which she could have if baby Pauline hadn't been born six weeks early; if Entier Enterprises had only gone bust three months earlier than it did, so that Paul hadn't had to go to law disclaiming liability for the company's debts. If only she and Paul had met six months later, so his first wife hadn't sued for divorce: if only, if only, if only, and all of it to do with faulty timing. If only Philippa hadn't stopped breastfeeding in order to get back to organise the Avon Phil's French tour, she wouldn't have got pregnant with Peter. Peter might have been an easier baby if he'd had a different set of genes. And he could have. Everything was chance and timing, and the two-second pause as their voices bounced across the world confirmed this fact. Apart they were lucky: together they were unlucky. If Philippa had called the Agency a day earlier she'd have got the Ardeche Quartet's tour in Northern Europe in January: as it was, the Boondock Boys' Christmas tour of Australia and New Zealand was the only opening left. How could she refuse? Together they needed the money. Paul would house-husband. Philippa would earn. They were lucky to be able to do it. There were many they knew who couldn't—who'd lost jobs or outlets and slid down the ranks from earning, intellectual, productive artist to non-employed, over-educated dole-taker in three months flat. Women she knew who'd been stay-at-home wives with Volvos were now taking nursing or teaching courses and setting about earning the family's living, or had gone home to mother while their husbands fell into depressions, left with mistresses, did voluntary work; who spent their time boringly nurturing any redundancy money that was about, working out which was cheaper, split peas or lentils. The Recession of the early nineties had hit the educated classes as none other had.

If it took the Boondock Boys' Christmas tour, it did, and that was that. Forget Christmas. If only one could. By rights, at this time of year the days were short, and Yuletide hysteria was mounting; but here yachts just scudded about on the harbour and people with black sweatsuit bottoms with a single white stripe up the outside of each leg jogged along special running tracks, and what gender they were seemed unimportant and what they were spending on Christmas worried no one. Philippa was homesick and jet-lagged and wanted to cry, but the timing was wrong.

"Pauline's running a bit of a temperature," Paul was saying, "but I'm sure it's okay. She's just missing you. And Peter got sent home from nursery for biting but it's the end of term anyway. They couldn't miss a trick of course; they're using it as an excuse to say he's not mature enough to be at nursery. I explained that you were away and they condescended to accept his biting as a temporary behaviourial problem due to maternal deprivation." Pause, two, three, four.

"Paul," said Philippa from the other side of the world, "if Pauline has a fever, you ought to call the doctor." Pause, two, three, four. "You have to take the fever to the doctor these days," said Paul. "The doctor won't come to the child. Don't worry. I asked Rosa-next-door to take a look at her. She said she thought it was just the kind of thing children got." Pause, two, three, four.

"I thought Rosa-next-door was seeing her family in the U.S.," said Philippa, as Paul said, "Rosa came back early from seeing her mother in the States; she got there and found no mother, because her mother had run off with a truck driver, a leading member of the Teamsters Union. Here, speak to Rosa. Rosa, come and speak to Philippa and tell her all about it."

Rosa Wheelwright had found Paul and Philippa their apartment. It just so happened to be next door to her own. Once she'd been Paul's assistant. It just so happened: everything just so happens, thought Philippa, and failed to wait for the sound to bounce.

"Don't bother, Paul," said Philippa. "I know someone else is paying for the call, but even so. Whatever Rosa has to say can wait. I was only calling to see if everything was okay, and I'm glad it is." Pause, two, three, four.

"Yes," said Paul. "I'm okay, but I'm not happy without you," and the "I'm okay" had an after-echo now, as if he were speaking to her from another universe, not just across the world, and she was left both consoled and forlorn as she heard her own answer, "Neither am I," echo as well, so the mixture of their voices were saying, "I'm okay and neither are you," which seemed to just about sum it all up.

RED ON BLACK

"I will not be defeated by a funeral," said Maria to her mother. "I will not."

But her mother just blinked and smiled and went on playing Patience, red on black, black on red, on the shiny mahogany table. Black the colour of death, red the colour of blood: that is to say life. Blood streamed monthly to prove your youth. Yellow sun shone on cream pile carpet; pink papered walls were lively with bursts of pale refracted light, as ocean waves beat against rocks below. The other side of the French windows, double-glazed to keep out the weather, the lawn which stretched to meet the sea cliff was acid Easter green.

My mother did not even hear me, thought Maria. Black on red. Red on black. The black Knave moved up to be on the red Queen. "I need a King," said Maria's mother. "An empty space, and no King. Please, St. Anthony, bring me a King!" And there the next card was, black King of Spades, St. Anthony's doing. Up went the Queen, and a train of dependents of lesser moment after her.

* * *

Maria's mother wore a dress splodged deep purple and bright mauve. Expensive imagined flowers clung to a body once slim, now bony. She's nearly seventy-five, thought Maria. But even as the colours bleach out of this one life, see how they reassert themselves all around.

Maria pulled the chintzy curtains to dull the glare from outside. Maria's mother went on playing cards. Maria was silent, sulking. "Who did you say had died?" asked Maria's mother, eventually, when it became evident that this particular game would remain unresolved, and she'd swept up the cards, swiftly and certainly, the sooner to shuffle, deal, and begin again.

She will live out the rest of her life like this, thought Maria, proving to herself over and over again that resolution of any kind is a rare event indeed, and there is nothing to any of it other than luck. And if there is only luck, there can be no blame. Black on red, red on black, in a beautiful room by the edge of the sea.

"I didn't say," said Maria. "And put the black four on the red five," said Maria, but her mother's hand had already moved. "It was Bernard's father who died. He was eighty-nine, and it was expected. It's not so bad in itself. I saw him just a week ago. We parted on good terms. All the same it's a shock and I don't like funerals."

Maria's mother studied the cards, to make sure she'd missed nothing. "Little Maria!" she observed absently, not even looking up. "Always trying to see the best in everything. Your father could never look a fact in the face either."
"I'm forty-two," said Maria. "I think I have my own nature by now."

"I expect so," agreed Maria's mother, and found the three she'd hoped for. Red on black, black on red. And there's the Ace. Good luck, bad luck, which will it be? Three coins in a fountain. Which one will the waters bless? Mother, father, Maria? Mother, when it comes to it. The one who leaves, not the ones who are left.

Mother left Maria with her father when Maria was fifteen to run off with a rich, rich man so that, now widowed, she can play Patience for ever at the edge of a sea. Today the weather was wild and bright, which was why the walls were so lively with shifting patches of light. You could search for a pattern and not find one; the wind-whipped waves broke out of proper sequence against their cliffs. Maria's car had been drenched in spray as she took the sea road up to her mother's house. Maria hated driving. Maria's car was cheap and old; Maria's mother's car was new and expensive and properly garaged, though seldom used. Maria was always constrained by money, by necessity, by proper feeling. Maria had to argue with her boss in order to take a couple of days off work to visit her mother, to go to a funeral. She had to go to her mother; her mother never came to her.

Maria had been exultant when her mother left home. It was the first and last illicit emotion she could remember. Sorry that Father was upset but exultant all the same, able at last to look after him. Mother gone! Now I can stop Father's ears forever to the sound of bitchery and complaint; only nice things will sound through this house from now on; at last I am in charge. Why should the world be all discord, when it can be harmony? Mother gone, so what? If a man has a daughter who loves him, what can he need with a wife? All his wife did was deny and deride him. Now we, the proper people, father and daughter, can start again. This gentle, kindly man deserves no less.

* * *

Only within the year Maria's father invited into his bed a woman called Eleanor; so Maria began to hear her mother's voice in her own, mocking and dispirited, carping and mean, whenever she spoke to her father, and it was so disagreeable a sound Maria married Bernard rather than stay home a second longer than she need.

Maria's mother came to Maria's wedding with her new husband, Victor. Maria's father came with his new wife, Eleanor. Eleanor had lent Maria a dress—Maria lived on a student grant, Maria's father had no money to spare: talk of money distressed him—and Eleanor had posted off the invitations. Maria's mother hadn't helped at all: she just said Maria was too young to get married; she'd have nothing to do with any of it, and hadn't. Eleanor had done everything, had been wonderful.

Except that at the wedding Maria's mother said, "I left because of Eleanor. I found her suspender belt in the marital bed. And you, Maria, didn't have the guts to stop her coming today. You want everything to be nice. You can never see why everyone shouldn't just be happy. But they can't be."
Maria had said, "You're spoiling my wedding, please go away, like you did before," and Maria's mother had done just that. Walking away down the path through the bright green grass, in a beige shantung suit and a little blue hat, next to grey-suited, solid Victor. In those days Maria's mother had dressed quietly.
"Never mind," said Eleanor. "We did what we could. At least we invited her."
"Good riddance," said Maria's father.

When family angels turn to demons, when the worm in the apple is healthier than the apple, what's a girl to do? Except marry

Bernard, forget the whole thing: quarrel with your mother, remember never to forgive her for abandoning you; make a friend of your stepmother, see her through a pregnancy more troubled than your own: gain a half-sister the day you gain a son. Watch Father wander through the house, in this marriage as in the last, but happier. Watch for and iron out the note in your own voice that reminds you of your mother: eradicate it. Make things good, as your mother made things bad. Get on with loving Bernard.

Red on black. Black on red. Maria's mother is stuck on a nine. Not an eight anywhere in sight. Maria's hungry. But not till a game comes out will Maria's mother ring the bell, call the maid, ask her to serve lunch. When it comes it will be frugal.

Eleanor's table was always extravagant. Stepmother came with a ready-made family: brothers, sisters, aunts, uncles, cousins; peopling a world, filling it with conversation and event. Maria's father gave up his job on a matter of principle. Eleanor's earnings eventually kept everyone: even subsidised Bernard, Maria and little Maurice. Superwoman Eleanor! Bernard was getting a PhD. Maria tried to repay Eleanor by looking after little Winnie, her half-sister, when Eleanor's child-care arrangements broke down.

Another game. Red on black, black on red. She's polite, but she never really speaks to me. Can she really not forgive me because Eleanor asked her to my wedding, because on that one day I spoke out of turn? Eleanor, whose suspender belt had induced Maria's mother to leave home. Except it wasn't like that. Maria's mother had been mercenary, after Victor's money. That was the only reason she'd left home, abandoned everyone. It was because Maria's mother had done such a dreadful thing that Maria's father had needed the consolation of Eleanor. Everyone knew that. Maria's mother was the villain of the piece.

Perhaps I can't forgive my mother, thought Maria, not because she abandoned me, but because in leaving us she let me think my father could be mine, gave credence to my illicit fantasies. Didn't I once hate Eleanor? I can hardly remember. Eleanor and my father, rising as one from the evening's television, hand in hand, going off into the bedroom together, where he'd been with my mother since the beginning of time, that is to say the beginning of my life? Leaving me shut out and excluded, to listen out for the sounds of gasps and moans, not the plaintive rise and fall of marital reproaches. When did I stop hating Eleanor? I can't remember that. Perhaps the day I married Bernard, and my mother saw Eleanor there, and I had to choose between Eleanor and her, and I chose Eleanor. Is not-hating-Eleanor the price I pay for not-hating my father?

"All you women," Bernard would say, "squabbling over one poor man." Such passions as we had, Bernard would reduce to nonsense.

"You shouldn't wear grey," said Maria's mother, clearing away the cards. "And shouldn't you do something about your hair?" "Bernard's father is dead," Maria wanted to say, "and I am in a state of distress. I am not entitled to official mourning: I have been disinherited from grief by divorce, along with everything else. I like grey. I will wear my hair as I want." The dancing patches of light on the wall stilled, as if the waves were holding their breath. Maria said nothing. The pounding began again. A trick of sea and wind, working in unison for once. The curve of the wave, held in suspense, foam whipped along the crest, as a gust of wind beat it back, before falling into its melee of navy and white. Lunch was served. A little thin soup. A mackerel, freshly caught.

"How is Bernard?" asked Maria's mother. "Still living in half your house?"

"It works well," said Maria. "It's sensible. There's no reason after a divorce why you shouldn't be friends."

"Careful of the bones," said Maria's mother. "I wouldn't want you to choke."

"And Maurice can go between us as and when he wants," said Maria, hearing the plaintive edge to her voice. Why do I have to suffer so others can be happy? I have to live beneath my ex-husband Bernard so Maurice can run upstairs to see his father when he wants: so I don't even have proper possession of my own child: so Bernard can criticise the way I bring him up: the clothes he buys, the pocket-money he has; can find fault with me if I have any kind of social life: all the while congratulating himself on his forbearance, on his self-control—living above a wife who so aggravated him when she was with him, was so frigid, so neurotic, he was obliged to have girlfriend after girlfriend just to stay sane. And how, having a child in common, and being noble, he now helps her out. She is of course a hopeless mother—absent-minded, over-emotional: Bernard can't leave Maria unprotected in the world, because of the damage she might do to Maurice. So to the detriment of his own life, his own artistic, poetic need to be free, he puts up with staying where he is, in the ex-marital home, halved by hardboard. The stairs are shared. Up the stairs go the succession of girlfriends. Turn up the music so as not to hear the moans and the groans, the creaking of the floor. What kind of example is that for a growing boy? Bernard changes the girls so often. The backs of their legs are oddly the same. Bernard seems to like girls with solid calf muscles. Maria's own legs are thin, straight up and down without much ankle. Mad legs, Bernard would call them.

"We couldn't afford to buy two houses," said Maria to her mother. "We had no choice but to do it the way we did."

Maria's mother pushes away her plate: the half-eaten mackerel lies dull upon it. The maid poaches them with the heads on. White, white sightless eyes.

"Disgusting fish," said Maria's mother. "I can't think why she buys them."

"Because they're cheap, I suppose," said Maria, and Maria's mother raised her eyebrows, in surprise that this should be seen to be an adequate motive for doing anything.

"I don't think I ever met Bernard's father," said Maria's mother, and Maria said, "He came to our wedding," and then realised it might be better not to have said it.

"The wedding," said Maria's mother. "Of course, you asked that bitch to it and didn't warn me. Do you like ginger ice cream? I'll get the maid to bring some in if you like."

It was easier to say no, but Maria made herself say yes. The ice cream came, a small single scoop in the middle of a large white plate. The "maid" was a broad local woman, with shoes trodden down at the back; local wages were low. Maria's mother spent money carefully. Maria's father spent everything there was to spend, as soon as possible, and always absently, and seemed surprised when he'd done it. He'd look at bills wonderingly; it was a family joke. Eleanor worked long hours, perforce—she was a graphic designer; she worked freelance—but her voice never hardened into reproach and complaint. Maria would listen as Eleanor spoke to confirm that it didn't, and would listen to her own voice likewise.

"It's a wild day," said Maria's mother: foam flew up the cliff and swept over the lawn and gently patterned the French windows. If the tide rose any higher it would not be so gentle. "The other side of the glass the wind will be howling. And it's a high tide. Sometimes we get the foam up here, not often. The garden's salty. Growing things is a problem."

"Twenty-three years later and you still call her a bitch," said Maria, boldly.

"She was," said Maria's mother. "And you should never have asked her to your wedding. You're my daughter, not hers."

"I didn't ask her," lied Maria. "She just came. I'm sorry. I didn't think you'd turn up. You were so against poor Bernard."

"One look at Bernard," said Maria's mother, "and you could tell what would happen next. You'd see him through college, you'd have his child, you'd take responsibility, provide all the money, and he'd wander off. Another child, like your father, not a grown person at all. I'm glad that bitch Eleanor got what she deserved. I could never understand why you were so thick with her."

She rose, as if to say the audience had ended. Her cheeks were pink: she knew she had been unduly talkative; she blamed her daughter for it. The maid came in to take the ice cream plate from under Maria's nose. Maria sat with her head lowered, as if she were a disgraced child.

Eleanor had developed breast cancer and taken four years to die: Maria's father now lived well on her life insurance money. Maria had asked him, at the time of her divorce, for the loan of enough money to buy a house at a distance from Bernard. She'd never asked her father before for money. It had been her habit to ask Eleanor. "I don't think lending you money would be a good idea," said Maria's father. "I don't want to interfere between husband and wife, even when they're allegedly exes. You two get along well enough. A divorce by mutual assent. Very civilised. If anyone can make it work, you can, Maria. I only wish your mother had been like you."

Eleanor would have understood, would have lent her the money. Maria had cried for a week when Eleanor died. Bernard said, "Crocodile tears. No one loves a stepmother." But then he was angry at the time. Bernard didn't see why Maria wanted a divorce; why she couldn't adjust to a husband's need for sexual variety, or take lovers herself to ease the emotional burden from his shoulders; Maria was rigid in her outlook, he complained: hopelessly jealous and possessive; she needed therapy rather than a divorce. And a divorce would upset Maurice. Maria had persisted. Now every time Maurice had flu, or was in trouble at school, or failed to satisfy Bernard's expectations of him, Bernard would raise his eyebrows and say, "His parents are divorced. Of course he's unhappy and disturbed. What did you think would happen?"

Maria took in Bernard's mail when he was out, looked after his cat when he was away, let in his girlfriends when they'd lost their keys. They'd look at her curiously. She wondered what Bernard said to them about her. "Isn't it time you found yourself a boyfriend?" Bernard had asked her once or twice, meeting her on the stairs. "But I suppose, since there's such a glut on the market of unattached women, you have a real problem." Maria knew better than to protest. Bernard was a journalist, a columnist: he was clever, moody, talented. He had the statistics of society at his fingertips. If she looked doubtful, he'd quote such figures as suited him to prove his point.

"I do seem to have a problem," she'd say, hoping he'd leave it there. Sometimes he did, sometimes he didn't. "Divorced women over forty," he'd say, "rarely re-marry." If she said she didn't want to re-marry, wasn't interested in men, he'd raise his eyebrows as if she was protesting too much. Maria felt uglier and uglier. At the beginning she'd given a couple of dinner parties; Bernard had asked himself down to them, and hogged the conversation, and laughed at her cooking, which was indeed bad. She didn't try again. He'd grabbed her on the stairs and kissed her once, a couple of years into the upstairs-downstairs arrangement, and said he was free on Saturday night, why didn't she come up after Maurice was asleep? Not to make it a habit, he said. Just the once to show there was no ill feeling: that she didn't hold grudges: that she wasn't like her mother, and a nag and a bore. And just the once she'd gone, to prove exactly those things, and he had been a wonderful lover, and she'd thought perhaps she could put up with all those girls after all, but he hadn't asked her up again. Maria felt worse. And the next girl, Angela, seemed a permanent fixture. Maria didn't want Bernard to marry again, she wasn't quite sure why. Especially not someone like Angela, a currant bun: tight little curls, lax mouth, stocky legs. Why would anyone want Angela when they could have Maria? Amend. Could have had Maria. These days Maria told her friends she loathed Bernard, they'd laugh at his dreadful behaviour, the things he'd done, but when he was away, when she couldn't hear the footsteps overhead, she was uneasy and nervous, though relieved of the burden of thinking about Angela and Bernard together.

Maria's mother sat down at the round mahogany table and dealt the cards again. Face downwards, blank, all but the last card in each row, face upwards. The pink faded from her cheeks.
"Be all that as it may," Maria said, "it's the present that counts, not the past. I don't mean to be defeated by a funeral. I hate funerals, but I'll go to this one."

Red on black, black on red. Death on life, life on death. Her mother said nothing.

"Bernard's father lived with us for four whole years," said Maria. "Of course I want to pay him my last respects. He was gentle and nice. While he was about Bernard behaved. It was after he left that the women got out of control. Their suspender belts in our bed. Well you know about that."

Slap, slap, slap went the cards.

"But I take a lot of the responsibility," said Maria. "I was working full-time and Maurice was still small, and I expect I neglected Bernard. I went off sex. Well, he said I did. I didn't notice. It can be like that, I suppose. It was understandable Bernard looked elsewhere. I expect I should just have put up with it. In the light of death these little dramas seem so pitiful."

Maria's mother gave a little cough.

"Well, forget all that," said Maria. "I shouldn't burden you with it. I'm grown up now. Bernard and I will go to the funeral. At least this is something we share—a particular grief: his father's dying. The end of something. There were really good times, some of the time, when I was first married to Bernard. That's why the marriage had to end: I didn't want it to get spoiled, in retrospect: unravel itself out, backwards, into nothing. The divorce was damage limitation. Do you see? In a marriage the past is forever piling into the present."

Maria's mother's game resolved itself. Four rows of up-turned, revealed cards announced finality: the imposition of order upon chaos, design over happenstance. Maria's mother smiled.

"I need a breath of fresh air," she said, and threw the French windows open, and the sounds of wild weather and pounding sea charged into the room, spray dampened their hair, the curtains billowed almost to the ceiling, Maria's mother's dress swirled around her legs, and the cards were flung about the room and in profound disorder again, as if thoroughly shuffled. Both women laughed, exhilarated.

Maria leaned against the windows to close them against the gale. Enough was enough.

"What do you mean?" asked her mother. "You won't be defeated by a funeral? Why should you be defeated?"

"It's the journey," said Maria. "The drive. You know how I hate driving. The funeral's at the Golders Green Crematorium. I hate driving into London. And I get lost." Maria had been late for Eleanor's funeral. She couldn't forgive herself for that. She'd kept missing the turning: finding herself back on the one-way system. When she did get it right, she lost more time trying to park in a space too small anyway, panicking.

"Get Bernard to drive you," said Maria's mother. "That man must be of some use for something."

When Maria got home, Maurice was back from school: he'd made his own supper. He was lying on the floor watching football on TV and doing his homework at the same time.

"Why didn't you go up to your father?" she asked.

"Because he doesn't like me watching football," said Maurice in his croaky adolescent voice. "He thinks television rots the brain. And he can't stand me rotting my brain and doing my homework at the same time. And Angela's there again, and she gets on my nerves. You know they're getting married?"

"Why her?" asked Maria, after a little time.

"Because he really only likes stupid women," said Maurice. "And Angela is really stupid. Will you come to the wedding?"

"I expect so," said Maria, bleakly. "There's no point in making things more difficult than they are already. We all have to get along together somehow. I wish he'd told me himself."

"He probably meant to tell you at Granddad's funeral," said Maurice. "You know what he's like. This is a really boring football match. I'll make you a cup of tea."

"What is he like?" asked Maria. "What is your father like?"

"How do you expect me to know what he's like?" enquired Maurice. "He's my father. But you're okay."

She had to be satisfied with that. If there was a battle, and she had tried so hard for there not to be, she was winning. Maurice was on her side. Later Maria called Bernard and asked him if he could give her a lift down to the funeral: it seemed a waste for two cars to go from the same address. Bernard said there was no room in his vehicle: it was only a sports car, he was of course taking Maurice down, and he was surprised to hear Maria wanted to go at all. Maria had in all probability triggered off the events which had led to the death in the first place. He and she were, after all, divorced. Divorce meant that his family and her family were wholly separate. And he would hardly expect to go to Maria's mother's funeral, for example. Maria said briskly that she would make her own way to the Crematorium.

Maria intended to start early: to allow at least two hours for a journey which would take Bernard one and a bit. She put on a grey suit. Black at funerals always seemed self-conscious, primitive. Widow's gear: the renunciation of sex. That's it, that's gone: the delights of the flesh deliquescing into mud. That's you served right for enjoying yourself. Black on red. Maria put on a red scarf to cheer the suit up. The hem of its skirt was unstitched. She found needle and cotton to see to it. Maurice had to be persuaded not to wear an overlarge, cannabis-worship jacket: pink curling puffs of smoke on a yellow background, and words she failed to understand but Maurice said were acceptable, Granddad wouldn't have minded. It grew later and later. Maria seemed unable to accept the dictates of the clock. Her will and the material world were at odds. Something rebelled. In the end she and Bernard left at the same time.

Bernard went down the steps in front of her; he was wearing a grey suit; he carried a portable phone. She remembered Victor long ago. Bernard seemed a stranger to her. There was a clattering behind her, and Angela pushed past. She was wearing a light shiny blue suit, and a lot of pearls, as if she were going to a wedding.

"'Scuse me, Maria. I hope you've got Maurice ready. We're going to be so late if you haven't."

"I didn't know *she* was coming," said Maurice, but he got into the car with Bernard and Angela, folding himself into the small space at the back, leaving Maria to stand on the doorstep. Perhaps it would be better if she didn't go? All that way, to what end? To stand in a dingy room, listening to melancholy music, contemplating mortality and the death of hope, the death of love, the death of her body? What sort of "respect" was it that she thought she could pay? She had failed Bernard's father in this life, she had failed to keep him alive, let alone healthy; she couldn't even stay married to his son, a failure which had distressed the old man. She could just turn back now, into her half of the matrimonial home, take the day off work, get accustomed to the idea of Bernard, married to Angela, living on top of her. Accept her role as murderer, not mourner.

But her feet walked her, almost of their own accord, towards her car. Maria wore black court shoes, worn out of shape, as she felt she was herself. Denatured: altered perforce to fit the circumstances.

* * *

The Golders Green Crematorium is sombre and leafy, concrete-pathed and well-signposted: it serves large areas of the city. Its memorial rose garden is denatured. The ashes of the dead are dug into the soil, but somehow fail to produce abundance. Little red brick chapels are used for individual services, as little individual jars of breakfast jam serve these days instead of the whole jar. Hearses come and go, quietly: coffins are carried by experts, expertly. An almost agreeable hush descends upon the little clusters of friends and relatives: the air is hard to breathe, as if the place were indoors, not outdoors, or at any rate covered by some invisible bell-jar: you might as well be in an airport, or a hospital, so devitalised the place has become, by virtue of so many human passions stultified, brought up short by the advent of death. Too late now. For who ever lived totally as they wanted to: who ever, if they have time to think about it, dies wholly satisfied? And those who remain know it.

Maria was late, but the chapel services were running even later. The deceased's friends and relatives, an official said, were gathered in the appropriate waiting room. Maria pushed open the heavy gothic door; it groaned. Blank and hostile faces looked back at her. Angela was bright in her shiny blue. Maurice came out to be with his mother. Maria and Maurice leaned against the chapel wall. Maurice smoked a cigarette. Maria hoped Bernard would not come out and catch him.

"Angela's pregnant," Maurice said. "That's the only reason he's marrying her."

Maria didn't say, "Well, I was pregnant, too. That's why he married me." Or perhaps he made me pregnant in order to be obliged to marry me and then blame me.

"Angela shouldn't be here," said Maurice. "It isn't fair. She never even met my grandfather."

"I expect she just likes to be with your father," said Maria, "wherever he goes, and so she should. Try to like her, Maurice; it will be better if you do. We have to be civilised."

A clutch of hearses approached, passed; following after them, on their black coat-tails, came a cream Rolls-Royce, which parked in a space clearly marked OFFICIAL PARKING: HEARSES ONLY, and Maria's mother stepped out. She wore a pink turban and a yellow suit, and all around were the colours of brick chapel, concrete paving, a dull sky and bare branches, on which new buds still struggled to provide just a hint of the new season. It was such a late spring: no one could understand the weather these days. "Mother? All this way!"

"I didn't want Maria to be defeated by a funeral," said Maria's mother to her grandson. "I was defeated by a wedding once. It doesn't do to be defeated by rituals."

"He brought her here," said Maria, suddenly tearful. "He had no right to do that. He was my father-in-law, not hers. How dare they?"

"Pull yourself together; you're not a child," said Maria's mother, out of some kind of dim maternal memory, "or I'll wish I'd never come." Maria was sobbing and gulping. Bernard and Angela emerged from the chapel. Bernard seemed disconcerted. Angela was pink and angry.

"I have every right to be here," Angela said, stopping to face Bernard, taking in the presence of the first wife, his ex-mother-in-law, her soon-to-be stepchild. "I love you and you love me and I want every single part of you, and that means your past as well. If you loved your father, I loved him too, he's my baby's grandfather, and I'm entitled to come to his funeral, so I don't know what you mean, Bernard, by my 'cashing in.' I don't want to hear that kind of mean, miserable thing from you ever again. I've heard far too much of it from you lately. I don't know what gets into you sometimes." Then she turned on Maria. "What are you doing here, anyway? An ex is an ex, as you'll find from now on. You depress the hell out of me, to tell you the truth. That godawful grey suit is a case in point and no one's worn a scarf for years. Self-pitying bitch."

The nasal voice stopped. It had come bursting in like some destructive gust of wind, thought Maria; everything settled, everything you clung to, was up in the air, whirling. They were all looking at her, waiting for a response. Maurice hovered half-way between Bernard and herself. Oh Eleanor, Eleanor, help me now. I married Bernard in the spring, but then the day was bright and clear. Eleanor smiled and drove my maternal mother out. Let me re-phrase that: together, Eleanor smiling, myself scowling, we held the whip that drove my mother out. Perhaps Eleanor was a false ally, after all. If she smiled it was because now she'd have my father to herself. Of course my stepmother lent me a dress. And afterwards she could afford to be generous. She'd won. Angela wants Bernard to herself, of course she does. She uses different methods, that's all—sulks, not smiles. And Bernard just spreads his hands and thrives in the warmth of our squabbling.

Even as I hesitate, I see Maurice drifting over to Bernard's side. Mother love? What's that? What's required? I want Maurice to grow up to be the best of his father, not the worst. We aren't meant to be on sides: we are meant to try to be civilised. All my life spent understanding and forgiving—but these are matters of life and death; desperate things. Red on black, black on red: understood but not forgiven. Has my mother come here today to explain that to me? She can't forgive me, she won't forgive, she must not forgive me because what I did was unforgivable; nor can she understand it. But she can still instruct me. She won't look me in the eye, she never will, but she came today to set an example, to help me.

"*My* father-in-law," said Maria to Angela, "mine. And it's you who have no business here. You can have Bernard's future, you're welcome to it, but you can't have Bernard's past. That's mine. You will not unravel my life from this moment back. Why don't you just go back to the house? Go on back, let me mourn in the peace I deserve. I came first and you came second; all you are entitled to is the dregs—"

"Bernard!" wailed Angela, but Bernard just spread his fingers helplessly, and licked his lips.

"It's her or me," cried Angela. "I'm warning you, Bernard."

"I do as I like," said Bernard. "What you do is up to you."

"This is our business, not yours," said Maria's mother to Angela, as once she should have said it to Eleanor. "You go, we stay." And she looked Angela's suit up and down as if to say this is a funeral, not a wedding; can't you tell the difference? I'm old enough to do as I like but you're not. Whoever can have brought you up?

Angela looked at Maria's mother's attire and curled her lip.

"Mutton dressed up as lamb," she actually said.

"Excuse me," said a group of black-suited, sleek-haired men, passing through, bearing a coffin on accustomed shoulders. The little cluster of mourners had to part and re-form. Maria wondered if the body inside the coffin were male or female, young or old; how they'd lived, how they'd died. Whether they were persecutor, self-interested and invalidating; or victim, understanding and forgiving, this was the outcome. Since there was no justice in

death, you'd better find it in life, however disagreeable it made
you in the eyes of others, in your own eyes too.

"Just go away," Maria said to Angela, with a snap of anger so
sharp and severe it all but cracked and slivered the sheltering bell-
jar; or at any rate a breath of cold, fresh, lively air suddenly
whipped around their legs: a memento of winter in the presence
of spring. Everyone looked startled.

"Go away," repeated Maria, "and take Bernard with you."

Bernard said, "I can't do that. I'm the chief mourner. He's my
father. I have to stay. But you don't have to, Angela. Really it's
best that you don't. Wait in the car."

And Angela walked meekly off to wait. Maurice moved over to
stand by his mother's side.

"That's better," said Maria's mother. "At last!"

"What's more, I'm not living beneath a baby," said Maria to
Bernard, "let alone you, Angela and a baby. What do you think
I am?"

"That's okay," said Bernard. "Now my father's dead I can afford
to move out. You can have the whole house."

They stood together in the chapel, and afterwards went their separate ways. Bernard to Angela and a new baby, Maria and Maurice
back home, Maria's mother back to her cards. Red on black, black
on red; red on black, life on death.

KNOCK-KNOCK

"Knock-knock," said the child into the silence. He was eight. The three adults looked up from their breakfast yoghurt, startled. Harry seldom spoke unless spoken to first. He'd seemed happy enough during the meal. The waiter had fetched him a toy from the hotel kitchens, a miniature Power Ranger out of a cereal packet, and he'd been playing with that, taking no apparent notice of a desultory conversation between Jessica, his mother, and Rosemary and Bill, his grandparents.

"Who's there?" asked his mother, obligingly.

"Me," said Harry, with such finality that the game stopped there. He was a quiet, usually self-effacing child; blond, bronzed and handsome.

Perhaps he'd been more aware of the content of their talk than they'd realised. It had of course been coded for his benefit, couched in abstract terms. The importance of fidelity, the necessity of trust, different cultural expectations either side of the Atlantic, and so on: its real subject being the matter in doubt—should Jessica go home to her faithless husband in Hollywood, or stay with her loving parents in the Cotswolds. To forgive or not to forgive, that was the question.

* * *

They'd tried to keep the story from the child, hidden newspapers and magazines. It wasn't a big scandal, just a little one; not on the Hugh Grant scale: nothing like that, not enough to make TV, just enough to make them all uncomfortable, leave home and take temporary refuge in this staid and stately country hotel, with its willowed drive, its swan-stocked lake, its Laura Ashley interior, where reporters couldn't find them to ask questions. If you answered the questions it was bad; if you didn't answer them it was worse. The solution was simply not to be there at all.

The story, the embryo scandal, goes thus. Young big-shot Hollywood producer Aaron Scheffer sets off on holiday with English wife of ten years, Jessica, and eight-year-old son, Harry, to spend the summer with her parents. At the airport he gets a phone call. His film's been brought forward, its budget tripled; rising star Maggie Ives has agreed to play the lead. Aaron shouldn't leave town. He stays; wife and child go. Well, these things happen. Two weeks in and there's a story plus pics in an international show-biz magazine: Aaron Scheffer intimately entwined behind a palm tree on a restaurant balcony. Who with? Maggie Ives. They're an item. Other newspapers pick up the story.

No air-conditioning in the grandparental home in England: how could it ever work? Why try? The place is impossible to seal. Too many chimneys: too many people in the habit of flinging up windows and opening doors, even when it's hotter out than in. You'd never stop them. And it's hot, so hot. A heat wave.

Aaron calls Jessica, much distressed. It's a set-up, don't believe a word of it. I have enemies. Jessica replies of course I don't believe it, stay cool, hang loose, I trust you, I love you.

* * *

A chat show runs a piece on spouse infidelity: featuring the phoney airport call: how to get the wife out of town without her suspecting a thing. Ha ha ha.

The heat may be good. It has an anaesthetizing effect. Or perhaps Jessica's just stunned. She cannot endure her parents' pity: the implicit "I told you so."

Harry's happy in the grandparental English garden. He is studying the life cycle of frogs. He helps tadpoles out of their pond, his little fingers beneath their limp back legs, helping them on their way. Once tadpoles breathe air, he says, everything about them stiffens. Jessica feels there's no air around to breathe, it's too hot.

Best friend and neighbour Kate, back in LA, calls to say, Jessica, you have to believe it, you need to know, everyone else knows: Aaron's been seeing Maggie for months. That's why she's got the part.

Jessica can't even cry. Her eyes are as parched as the garden. Forget tragedy, forget betrayal, how could she ever live in a land without air-conditioning?

Phone calls fly. Her father Bill frets about the cost. Aaron says not to believe a word Kate says. Kate's a woman scorned. By whom? Why, Aaron, the minute Jessica's back is turned. Come home now, Jessica, pleads Aaron, I love you.

"I'll think about it," says Jessica. She asks her mother whether it's safer to trust a husband or a best friend? "Neither," says her mother. "And Aaron probably only wants you home for a photo-opportunity, to keep the studio quiet."

The first reporter turns up on the step. Is she hurt? How does it feel? He has other photographs here; they'd like to publish with her comments. Will she stand by her man? Doors slam. No comment. More phone calls.

Aaron confesses: words twinkle across continents and seas. "Maggie and I lunched. We drank. We shouldn't have. She asked me back to her place. I went. I shouldn't have. We succumbed. We shouldn't have. We were both upset. I was missing you. I felt you'd put your parents before me. Afterwards we both regretted it. I took her to a restaurant so there'd be no embarrassment, so we could get back to being friends, colleagues, nothing more than that."

"And there just happened to be photographers around," Jessica drawls. Heat slows words.

"Her boyfriend spies on her."

"I'm not surprised," says Jessica. She's melting. But perhaps that too is just the heat. "What was Maggie so upset about?"

"I've no idea," says Aaron. "I can't remember."

"That's a good sign," says Jessica. "But if you two have to work together, and I can see you can, supposing she gets upset about something else? What then?"

"Why should she," asks Aaron, "now she has the part she wants? Please will you come home tomorrow?"

"No," says Jessica. She feels mean and angry. She'd rather he'd gone on lying. She wants him punished.

"Then I'll come and collect you," he says. "Meet me at Heathrow." She puts the phone down.

More reporters on the step. The family wait for nightfall, then slip away to the hotel. Jessica calls Aaron. He's already left for

England, says his secretary. Everyone has three days off. Maggie Ives is sick. Aaron's due at Heathrow at 11:30 Friday.

Now it's 8:30 and Friday. And Harry is saying knock-knock, who's there, me! And her parents are saying, if she hears them correctly, because they'll never say it outright, Don't go to him, stay here with us. Crisis time.

And here was home, where no one said anything outright, so at least everything was open to change. Perhaps she hated Hollywood. Perhaps she hated all America. Perhaps the only people you could trust were family, blood relatives; and husbands weren't even blood relatives. Other people had serial marriages, why shouldn't she?

If only this hotel, which claimed to have air-conditioning but had only a hideous roaring box in a corner of the dining room, was more American: if only her child didn't knock at her conscience, saying "remember me?" then she could think.

Aaron was in the air now, somewhere up above the frozen seas or the hard unyielding land, on wings of love or self-interest, how could she know which? Knock-knock, who's there? God or the Devil?

Harry put down his spoon and asked politely if he could leave the table. Rosemary said yes before Jessica could speak. He must go to his room to put on sun-block first. Harry said okay.

Bill remarked that he was an unusually good child. Jessica said yes, but she'd had him checked out with a therapist, who'd said no problem, except he might be overly mature for his age. Rosemary observed that Hollywood must be a dreadful place to rear a child: either vulgar wealth in Bel Air or shoot-outs in McDonald's, and therapists everywhere. Bill said any child was best reared in green fields in a gentle climate; Jessica should get a cottage in the village near them. Presumably Aaron would look after her financing. They'd be near, as families should be, but would of course respect each other's privacy. And so on.

Harry was now out in the garden: the other side of the long French windows. He threw a ball against the wall, hard: it bounced back off uneven bricks; he'd leap to catch it. Hurl again. The garden was remarkably pretty. English pretty. The high wall was made of slim, ancient, muted red bricks, beneath which were hollyhocks and delphiniums, pleasantly tiered. Drought restrictions were in place, but Bill said he'd looked out of his window in the early hours and seen the gardener using the hose.

"Harry's got a good throw," said Bill. "He'll be good at cricket."

"Or baseball," said Jessica. Rosemary groaned. Jessica understood, suddenly, what was obvious but she hadn't seen: that she was their only child, Harry their only grandchild. Of course her parents wanted her back in the country. She could hardly look to them for impartial advice. *Thud, thud, thud,* against the wall. Knock-knock. What about me? Father, lying but loving, v. doting grandparents? Broken home v. green fields and no air-conditioning?

"We both like Aaron," observed Rosemary, "you know that, but there's no denying he's ambitious!"

What did her mother mean? That no truly ambitious man would put up with Jessica? That she wasn't bright, beautiful or starry enough for Aaron? That it was a miracle he'd taken her on in the first place? So long as Aaron was the one persuading her to stay while she tried to leave, she could cope. But supposing it went the other way: Aaron decided he preferred Maggie Ives to Jessica? How would she survive then? She was playing games she might regret.

"I could take the car and drive to meet him," said Jessica to her parents. "He and I could at least talk. I owe him that. I'd just about make it to the airport in time."

"I'd have to drive you," said Bill. "My car has gears. You can only drive automatic."

"Bill can't possibly drive you," said Rosemary. "It's much too hot. His heart won't stand it. We don't have air-conditioned cars over here, which is just as well for the ozone layer. And I daresay you think you could afford a driver, but where would you find one at such short notice?"

Such silly practicalities! But still they stood in her way. It was Fate. Better, Jessica thought, to stick by her original decision. So public and powerful an insult from husband to wife could not be excused, and that was that. All her friends would agree. The waiter poured more coffee. "Good to see the little fellow enjoying himself," he remarked. Everyone nodded politely.

Harry came in from the garden.

"If I died," he said, "you'd forget me at once."

"We wouldn't, we wouldn't," exclaimed Jessica. "We all love you so much!"

And even Bill and Rosemary, though talk of such emotion came with difficulty to their lips, assured their grandchild of undying and unflinching love.

"No," said Harry, refusing their comfort. "I'm right about this.

I'm just not important to you. In a couple of hours you'd forget all about me. In fact if I were out of your sight for just ten minutes you wouldn't remember who I was."

And he bowed his head beneath the shower of protests and went back into the garden, to his ball. *Thud, thud, thud.*

Jessica stood up and said, "Dad, give me the keys. I'm going to meet Aaron. I'm going to bring him back here, you're going to be nice to him; then we fly back to Hollywood. I'm not leaving Aaron, I'm not divorcing him, I love him. And I have to think of Harry. Every good boy deserves a father; we've made him so dreadfully insecure. I hadn't realised."

Bill handed over the keys.

"We all have to think of the children," he said.

"We abide by your decision," said his wife. "For Harry's sake."

"Tell Harry I'll be back with his father," said Jessica. "Tell him to stop worrying."

Bill and Rosemary watched as the car lurched and shuddered on the gravel drive while Jessica got the hang of the gears. Then the car shot off into the heat haze, grating and grinding, out of the shade of the willows into the sun. The waiter hovered. Harry stopped throwing and came to stand beside them, watching.

"Where's Mom gone?"

"Mummy," corrected Rosemary. "She's gone to meet your father."

"Um," said Harry, approving but not especially so. Then he said, "Knock-knock."

"Who's there?" asked Rosemary.

"Told you so!" said Harry. "Forgotten me already! Ten minutes and see, you'd forgotten all about me. Gotcha!"

And Harry laughed uproariously, cracking up, bending over a gold and damask chair to contain his stomach and his mirth, making far more noise than they'd ever heard him make before. And the waiter was bent over laughing too, holding his middle. "I told him that one," said the waiter. "Poor little feller. He needed a laugh! We all do, this time of year."

When Harry had finished laughing he went serenely back into the garden, for more throwing, thudding, catching. The heat seemed to affect him not one whit.

GOING
TO THE
THERAPIST

SANTA CLAUS'S NEW CLOTHES

"I'm so happy we can all be together like this," said Dr. Hetty Grainger. She sat in the antique carver chair at the head of the Andrews' festive board. There was turkey for the carnivores, and nut-roast for the others, with a rich plum and chestnut sauce to go with it, to prove vegetarians can be indulgent too, not to mention sensuous, should ritual so demand. There were crackers on the table, and paper hats, and the scent of incense to remind everyone that the Hindu, the Buddhist and the Christian gods (did not the Trinity make three?) come from the same source, are of the same oneness. The Andrews were the kind who normally went to church once a year, to midnight service on Christmas Eve. But not this year.

Dr. Hetty Grainger's voice was sweet and low. She murmured rather than spoke, so that all the Andrew family, usually so noisy, fell silent to hear her speak. "I'm so happy we can all be together like this."

Although now in theory an Andrew herself, Dr. Hetty had retained, if not exactly her maiden name, at least the one she'd

259

acquired on her first marriage: Grainger. She'd done this, she said, for her patients' sake. Troubled as they were by one kind of stress or another, they hankered, or so Dr. Grainger said, for the tranquillity of continuity. To turn from Dr. Grainger into Dr. Andrew would be to rub the salt of her own new-found happiness into the wounds of her clients' neuroses. "Tranquillity" was one of Dr. Grainger's favourite words. She used it a lot. The Sea of Tranquillity on the moon, for example, was a place with which Dr. Hetty Grainger felt she had some special connection. It sent its sentient spirit out to her. Just to think of this unearthly place— so quiet, so dark, so cool, so beautifully named—lulled Dr. Hetty Grainger and soothed her when she was in any way stressed.

"She's okay, I suppose, but she's ever so sort of *astral*," said Penny, aged nineteen, on first meeting her father's therapist, soon to be her new stepmother. "I always thought the moon was just a cold lump of rock which caught the light of the sun as it went round the earth. Or is it the other way round? But apparently no: the moon is all sentient spirit and significance and stuff. Or is she just talking crap?"
And Chris, Penny's sister Petula's boyfriend, said, "No, it isn't crap. I think what Dr. Grainger has to say is really interesting. This is the New Age, after all. Everything *means* something. And at least she makes your father happy."

And, after that, opposition to Hetty Grainger within the Andrew family fell away. She made their father happy.

This year the Christmas Eve service on local offer seemed to the family a rather formal, old-fashioned and decidedly chilly event, in a church which had needed a new heating system for years and never got one. Hetty didn't want to go, anyway, so in the end nobody went. It would have felt impolite to leave their new step-mother behind.

Hetty Grainger was shortly built and mousily pretty, with soft natural hair which fell brownly around a pale plump face. But her hips were wide and filled the antique carver chair at the head of the table almost as amply as had those of her predecessor, Mrs. Audrey Andrew. Dr. Hetty didn't diet, as Audrey had. Dr. Hetty knew that if you ate a healthy, wholesome diet, as additive-free as could be managed, you would be the weight and scale that nature intended, not that fashion dictated. If fate had made you pear-shaped, so be it.

Dr. Hetty's husband, Philip Andrew, engineer, regarded his new wife fondly from the other end of the table, carving knife poised ready to start on the turkey. His chin had doubled compliantly and happily since Hetty had replaced Audrey. Now his body was heavier but his life was agitation-free. Dr. Hetty was against conventional medicine. The weighing of the body, the measuring of blood pressure, cholesterol, and so on, was just the orthodox doctor's way of adding to the stress of modern life.

Dr. Hetty Grainger should know: she'd trained as an orthodox doctor. But a patient had died under her care in the hospital where she'd had her first job; not her fault: an inquest had exonerated her; but Dr. Hetty had realised just how dangerous medical practice could be and had chucked the whole thing in. She'd wondered what to do with her life, had happened to meet Swami Avakandra, had been most impressed, had trained as an Avakandrist—a six-month residential course—and thereafter counselled in the Swami's name.

* * *

The Jungians looked kindly on the Avakandrists, who mixed the search for the archetype with a rich interpretation of symbols, made extensive use of dream and hypnotherapy, acknowledged a deep inherited collective unconscious, whilst teaching that the knowledge of ultimate reality came through sexual love rather than through cognitive processes. A state of ill health, whether mental or physical, would arise when a spiritually sensitive individual, consciously or otherwise, distanced himself from that ultimate reality. The task of the Avakandrist healer/therapist was to lead that individual back to appropriate paths of awareness. And thus Hetty had led Philip.

"I'm so pleased," Dr. Hetty Grainger went on, "that after the upsets of the last year we can all come like civilised people to the Christmas ritual!" And she raised her glass of wine to all of them, the glass being one which just happened to have been Audrey's favourite. A strand of blue ran through the clear stem. Audrey had bought it at a car boot sale which she'd gone to with Philip, just a couple of years back. The goblet had turned out to be Venetian glass—what a snip! That had been one of the couple's last outings before Philip, facing possible redundancy at work, suffering from enigmatic heart pains, had become Dr. Grainger's patient, or client, and had realised that the time had come to think about himself, not his family. Everyone's spiritual duty was to themselves.

"Yes, I'm so pleased we have managed to be civilised!" murmured Dr. Hetty Grainger. "Divorce and remarriage needn't be a source of grief and anger, if only they can be seen for what they are; a healthy re-adjustment and re-arrangement of family relationships."

* * *

And the Andrew family nodded an only slightly muted agreement. On either side of the refectory table were seated Henry, son no. 1, aged twenty-six, strong and handsome, and his pretty wife Angie with the little girls Sue and Sal; Petula, twenty-two, daughter no. 1, with her artist boyfriend Chris; and Penny, nineteen, daughter no. 2. And of course Martin, aged nine, Audrey and Philip's last child, the afterthought, the happy accident, the apple of everyone's eye. Child no. 4. Son no. 2.

Martin alone looked puzzled. Martin alone responded.

"What's 'civilised'?" asked the child. Interesting! They all waited for Dr. Hetty's reply. Dr. Hetty would know. She was the one with the insights, who knew what maturity meant, who knew how peace of mind was achieved. She it was who had brought the Andrew family all together again round the Christmas table, in harmony after the previous season's dispersal and disarray. Dr. Hetty, who that day had stood in what was once Audrey's kitchen and was now hers, and had worked so hard to prepare the turkey, in spite of her vegetarian convictions, and made the nut-roast, and the plum sauce with chestnuts, and boiled the organic pudding. Who, with Philip, the father, had strung the home with tinsel and sparkling globes, and adorned the tree with decorations taken from the cardboard boxes into which Audrey had so carefully packed them two Twelfth Nights back, before placing them in the cupboard under the stairs. Here Dr. Hetty had come across them. "So pretty!" she cried. "In some things Audrey had such good taste." Oh, Dr. Hetty was generous.

In fact Dr. Hetty Grainger was doing everything she could to repair the damage to nerves and family-togetherness perpetrated by Audrey, who had been so insanely negative, so angry, so bitter, so antagonistic to the point of insanity when her husband had fallen in love, wholly, fully, totally and for the first time, at the age of fifty-seven.

"But this marriage has been dead for years," said Philip to Audrey. "Why are you being like this? What are you objecting to? Surely it's better to be open about these things?"

"I didn't think it was dead," said Audrey, "and neither did you until you started going to see that bitch. How much does she charge you for the privilege of breaking up your marriage, your family, your life?"

"She's trying to save my life," said Philip. "You wouldn't understand. She believes in me, she listens to what I'm saying. She's patient, she's kind, sweet, gentle, never in a hurry."

"You pay her to be those things," wept Audrey. "I'm just your wife. What chance do I have?"

None, it seemed. He had walked into her surgery; Dr. Hetty Grainger had looked up from behind her desk and met his eyes and seen Osiris to her Isis. The love and compassion she felt for all her patients had blossomed at that moment into something amazingly particular. Philip Andrew was what her life was all about. Dr. Hetty Grainger, his. Both had had to wait through dreary years, but now the time of decreed fruition had come. Her marriage was over; his family all but grown. Their drudge through the material world of pre-love was at last finished. Even before the sexual contact, so intrinsic a part of Avakandrist healing, both had understood that this was destiny. The initial touch, her finger stroking his cheek, had merely confirmed a love, a connection, already in existence.

* * *

Philip Andrew, engineer, nuts and bolts man, hadn't known a thing about Isis and Osiris, but it all made sense when Dr. Hetty explained it: spouse and sister both. His own previous ignorance now horrified him: why had he waited so long to start living? Yet he was fond of Audrey; he loved his children. He did not want to hurt them. He could only hope in the end wife and family would understand.

He loved the way Dr. Hetty Grainger could explain and define not just the world but him to himself. She knew so much! But then she worked for a living; she wasn't idle; she got out into the world; she was open to fresh ideas. Audrey had always stayed home; she was a traditional wife. Her very existence could only be parasitical not just on her husband's maleness and income but on his mind. Audrey had docked her husband's spirituality as she tried to dock his sexuality, by owning it, withholding it, confining it. Not her fault, probably, but there it was. No wonder poor Philip had heart pains.

Hetty, for all her prim and gentle looks, would do anything Philip wanted, follow anywhere her patient's sexual fantasies led. This, too, was part of the Avakandrist teaching: the approach to ultimate reality through strange and winding paths, through unconditional yet unpossessive physical love. The Avakandrists didn't make much of this aspect of their doctrine in their public statements, didn't stress it too much in their publications; the world was a sexually nervous place, all too likely to unfairly misunderstand, to use scandal to condemn a life-enhancing and primarily spiritual movement. To put it bluntly, spouses, at the best of times the source of stress, would object too much if they knew too much. But now it was Christmas Day; the second since the split, the first since Philip's divorce and remarriage. Hetty was now training, at Philip's expense, as a straightforward Jungian: she'd lost her dedication to the Avakandrist doctrine—her new husband did not want her showing too many male clients the way to health and happiness, selfish of him though it might be—and the family was once again gathered together under one roof and all was peace, prosperity and understanding. Tranquillity. Thanks to Hetty's strength of purpose and the lawyer she'd recommended to Philip, Audrey had failed in her attempts to take the house and disrupt the family.

Everything was fine, in fact. Except for Martin, staring at Hetty, still waiting for an answer, his big eyes narrowed in his little face. He spoilt his looks when he scowled. A pity Martin was so much Audrey's child in both looks and temperament: Martin the afterthought, the late child; the mistake, to put it bluntly. Philip had not wanted his declining years—or so he had regarded them pre-Hetty—filled with first nappies and infant protest, then school bills and teenage trouble; Philip had thought it self-willed and selfish of Audrey to go through with a late and unplanned pregnancy. Though once Martin had arrived he was of course welcome.

"What's 'civilised'?" Martin asked again, and Hetty publicly pondered. Everyone waited. Philip noticed that the skin of the turkey was pale, dry and stretched, not brown, wrinkled and juicy as it would have been had Audrey cooked it. As she had done for the family for how many years? Twenty-six? Well, Christmas was a tricky time for everyone, as Hetty had pointed out, now so many made sequential marriages. Meanness of spirit created a "who goes where" syndrome.

When the point of the carving knife met the stretched skin, the flesh split and shuddered apart, and when the knife went into the meat the blade met a kind of pallid, stringy resistance. Audrey's turkeys dissolved to the touch of the blade, gave themselves up willingly to the feast. But then she basted. Hetty didn't bother. Philip shivered a little. Audrey was okay, though. She had finally gone to her parents in Edinburgh. Audrey had wanted Martin to spend Christmas up north; Philip felt that was out of the question. This was the house where Martin was accustomed to opening his presents; his elder brother and sisters were coming for the day; the child should not be used in the parents' disputes.

"But Mum will be all alone, Dad, if I'm not there."

"Christmas is for the children, Martin; stop worrying about the grown-ups. It's too bad of your mother to make you feel guilty."

And in the end it had been decided through solicitors—Hetty felt it was always easier on the child to deal with such matters formally—that Audrey could not provide so domestic, peopled and cheerful a festive season as could Philip and Hetty, with their two incomes, so today Martin sat at his father's table, a little niece on either side of him—how they adored him! If only the boy wouldn't try and spoil the atmosphere: like his mother, a born wet blanket.

Dr. Hetty Grainger's feeling had always been that Martin might need a little pressure to help him adjust to the new set of interpersonal relationships at home. Dr. Grainger should know. She worked with children a good deal, though having none of her own. Dr. Hetty was on something called the Victims of Child Abuse service register and spent an afternoon a week counselling at the Family Therapy centre.

"What's 'civilised'?" Martin repeated.

Martin rang his mother frequently, all the way to Scotland. That was understandable, that was okay, except his mother kept him talking and talking, no doubt on purpose. The telephone bill would probably amount, as Hetty observed one night to Martin, laughing her gentle laugh, tucking her short legs between his long skinny ones, to a few months' worth of her current retainer from the VCA.

"The trouble with Audrey," Dr. Hetty said, "is that she's one of the Pall Bearers of life. I'm using an Avakandrist term here."
"A pall bearer?"
"One of those people who blame others for difficulties they themselves have brought about. They're the hands which hold back the wheel of life, refusing ever to let go. You can tell them because they always cost you money!"

Audrey had never slipped her leg at night between Philip's. Audrey had liked to lie parallel but close, taking up whatever position her husband did: her strong, flawed, bony, cool body stretched against his. Only when Audrey was pregnant did she become warm—really warm: it was like sleeping next to a hot-water bottle. Hetty gave Philip her legs as a token but kept the rest of her body at a distance. Hetty was both intimate but remote: less familiar, less familial, more exciting, forever a challenge to be approached with reverence and respect. Sometimes he worried about sleeping in the same bed with Hetty as he had for so many years with Audrey, but Hetty said a good bed was hard to find and had performed some kind of ceremony with candles and incense which would, she said, deconsecrate the bed, free the material object from its person-past. Hetty was spiritual but not sentimental. Now, answering Martin's question, she took her time. Everyone waited.

"Civilised behaviour, Martin," said Dr. Hetty Grainger, finally, "is acting, not acting out. For example, not running up telephone bills simply to spite your father and me." She smiled as she spoke, to show she wasn't being in any way negative, merely constructive. Martin's eyes narrowed further. Audrey's eyes could look just like that, thought Philip. Martin should have been allowed to go to Edinburgh for Christmas.

"Civilised behaviour, Martin," said Dr. Hetty Grainger, "is my understanding why you do such a selfish thing, and forgiving you for it, and helping you not to do it again. You want to hurt me, Martin, because you are angry and jealous: of course you are, you feel there is not enough love in your father for you as well as for me, but there is, I promise you there is."

And she smiled again at Martin, brown eyes glowing. He did not smile back.

"Civilised behaviour," said Dr. Hetty Grainger to the whole table, her entire being alight, spoon poised over the brussels sprouts— the whole serving system (Philip, turkey and nut-roast; Henry, plum sauce; Hetty, vegetables) was held up—"is coming to terms with and controlling our negative emotions, letting go. It is the manners which come from an open heart. It is sharing and caring. It is the open acknowledgement of our passions. It is moving over to let others in. It is smiling, even when we don't want to, until the smile is real. We must try to be civilised, we must act civilised, otherwise we end up as the Serbs and the Croats, at each others' throats. Literally. Here in the Andrew family we've tried and we've succeeded, and, as I say, I'm proud of us all. That's my speech for today."

She lowered her bright eyes, her face sweetly pink with emotion, vulnerable and charming. No wonder Philip loved her.

* * *

But Martin stared on, unsatisfied. Dr. Grainger ignored him.

"Where's Granny?" asked Sal, who was four. "Why is that lady in Granny's chair?"

"Granny chose not to be here," said Philip, "and I'm sorry about that too. She was invited, of course."

"But she chose not to be civilised," said Hetty.

Now Sal's eyes narrowed. Some characteristics do seem to run in the genes: or was she just copying Martin?

"Shall we pull a cracker, Sal?" asked Philip, quickly.

"No," said Sal, pushing away her plate. "Crackers come between turkey and pudding, not now, stupid." And neither Sal nor Sue, who was three and took her lead from Sal, ate a thing thereafter. Angie apologised for her children.

"They're so fussy about their food sometimes. And of course they're exhausted. They were so excited last night they couldn't sleep. What with Santa Claus and coming to Grandpa and Granny for Christmas Dinner . . ." Her voice faltered.

"Audrey preferred to be in Edinburgh," said Philip, unnecessarily. "You know how she loved those Scottish winters."

"Mum isn't in the past tense for me," said Henry. "Not yet, at any rate."

Martin, strangely, was holding Sal's little hand against his heart. Perhaps she gave him strength.

"Let go of the past," said Dr. Hetty Grainger quietly and softly from her carver chair at the head of the table. "I would have welcomed Audrey here today, but she refused: not even for her own children would she come. That is her decision. We must accept it, rise above the sorrow it causes us. Let us raise our glasses to a future filled with love."

"I think you're a selfish bitch," said Martin to Dr. Hetty Grainger, clearly and stoutly. "You've no business sitting there. That's my mother's chair. She's meant to be serving the vegetables, not you. Those are her plates you're handing round. You didn't even heat them. You talk so much everything's gone cold."

"Little Martin," said Hetty, "I understand your aggression but there's more to this ritual than heated plates. Christmas is not about food, or presents, but about rebirth. It's the festival of starting over, and that's what we're trying to do. As for chairs and plates and so on, your mummy told us she didn't want any of the material objects in this house, that your daddy could have them all, and since your daddy and I share everything, love and life, that includes the relevant things as well. Your mother walked away from all this of her own free will because she couldn't understand love; she was not a spiritual person. And your daddy worked for this lovely house all his life, didn't he? Your mummy just sat and enjoyed the fruits of his labour until one day the bough was empty and no fruit fell. Everything is ripe for the time it's in; love must be worked for, earned. So here's to the future!"

How luminous her eyes were as she raised her glass.

"Bitch," said Martin again. "Why does nobody see she's a bitch?"

"Don't embarrass your stepmother," said Philip. But nobody was following Hetty's example and raising their glasses. It seemed she was drinking alone.

"Is that lady sleeping in Granny's bed?" asked Sal. "There was a nightie under the pillow which wasn't Granny's. I bet she is. Why doesn't Grandpa stop her?"

"Don't call him Grandpa any more," said Hetty. "Call him Philip. Grandpa is so ageing." She was barely forty herself.

"Bitch," said Martin again, and now he'd said it thrice it was Emperor's New Clothes time. The Andrews saw Hetty Grainger more clearly for what she was: a horror came amongst them. All except Philip, of course, so deep in his positive transference was he.

"Perhaps Martin had better go to his room," said Philip to Dr. Hetty, and Dr. Hetty said that was a good idea. "Aloneness quiets the unquiet spirit," said Dr. Hetty Grainger.

So Martin ran weeping to his room, into loneliness, except that Sal and Sue came running after him to keep him company, and when Martin put his head under the pillow to bury his grief, they did the same, sharing the same breath. They ended up giggling, not crying.

The grown-ups finished their meal in silence, and that evening Martin made his phone call to his mother longer than ever, this time on purpose.

"I told them," said Martin proudly. "I told them what she was. I saw her off. You can rely on me."

BAKED ALASKA

You know what it's like, Miss Jacobs, when you're having an affair? Forgetting appointments, neglecting children, running off to the hairdresser, having your eyelashes dyed; stopping and staring in mirrors instead of passing by with averted eyes—as if all of a sudden the fact that you're alive and have a body *matters*—and you're back with the sense of Mystical Connection. I'm an addict to extra-marital love: an addictive personality: one whiff of a cigarette and I'm off again: a drop of sherry in the Bombe Surprise and I'm out of my skull by dawn.

I can feel your eyebrows shooting up, Miss Jacobs, even though I can't see them. I have to lie here on this couch, which is a little too hard and rather short. What do your men clients do? Dangle their legs? Or perhaps you only get to see dwarves? I haven't been to see you for eight weeks. I'd quite forgotten how dreadful it is—talking into space like this.

What you always forget is that just because you're connected, the object of your love is not necessarily, let alone permanently, so. As if you'd made a telephone call and the other person has spoken for a little and then wandered off, and not hung up, so that not only can't you speak to them, but you can't use the phone either, for anyone else.

I know I told you I was going to Alaska, on business. That my employers had sent me on a trip to learn about Alaskan business methods. It was a lie. You mean it sounded *true*? So unlikely as to be true? Wonderful! Affairs are all lies: one gets really good at them.

I daresay even you have lovers, Miss Jacobs. There's someone for everyone: somewhere out there are men who will admire the stony bleakness of your regard, the ferocious tugging back of your hair, the toughness of your blemished skin, your unsmiling mouth. I envy you. You couldn't even begin to pretend: you are all truth and permanence as I am all frivolity and change. I know only the silly side of the coin: what it is to be loved for blonde curls and sulky looks, and that peculiar gift for idiotic discrimination I foster, which certain men find so entrancing. "Oh no, I can't possibly go there, or eat this, or see that!" With a flick of red fingernail, despising this, adoring that—men love the carry-on, for a while at least: then they get bored.

During the last eight weeks I have gone at least twice a week to the hairdresser. Nothing to prevent me blow-drying my own hair: it's just at such times you feel the need to be ministered unto. As if it takes a bevy of supporting beauties just to get one woman to meet her lover! As if she carries with her the concentrated energy of women everywhere—their desires, their fulfilment, not just her own. Takes a dozen girls to adorn one bride.

My stylist Joanna had just come back from New York with tales of high life and a mind generally at the end of its tether. The kind of stories that make you think you'd better defect: that they do things better in Moscow. I can only say that kind of thing to you, Miss Jacobs, husband Roland—well, ex-(possibly) husband Roland—being so politically serious. He married me the better to despise my frivolity. He told me only this morning that in fact he now despises me so thoroughly he is obliged to divorce me: I'll telephone home—home?—when I've finished this session with you, and if there's an answer he hasn't left and he's still my husband, and if there isn't, he's gone and he's not. Never a dull moment. I've been putting off calling home or ex-home all day. It's all right if you keep moving and keep talking—it's only with stillness and silence that the panic sets in.

Now what Joanna said—her hair is so long she can sit on it, though I can't think why she'd want to—was that in New York cannibalism is all the rage. Not whole people—*parts* of people: amputated limbs and so forth. At least I hope that's what she said. I do have this incapacity sometimes to hear what is actually being spoken. In retrospect, I can hardly have been hearing with any accuracy what Anton—that's my love, my lover: that is to say, my love, my ex-lover as from precisely seven days ago—was saying, or the end of the affair would not have been quite so unexpected; from bed to nothing in ten swift minutes. Anyway, according to Joanna, human flesh, either discarded bits of body, or—I suppose we have to face it—whole bodies, and tender young bodies at that, especially acquired for the occasion in some appalling and unthinkable fashion, are selling in New York for $2,000 a pound, and served stewed at all the best parties. And the other currently fashionable epicurean delicacy, Joanna says, is the brains of living monkeys, eaten with special long-handled silver teaspoons. Just tether your monkey and slice off the top of its skull and there you are.

* * *

I tried not to think about it. I thought about Anton instead, about wrapping my legs round his thin body and pleasuring him as he pleasured me. About a curl here and a streak there and whether a fringe is really what I need: if the hair is back from the face the character may indeed show, but was it character Anton wanted? I doubted it. And, when it came to it, what he wanted was a space in his head filled: some little wounded part made good, some little chilliness warmed. He had fun with the small words that indicated love, concern, possession, even permanence: he liked me to listen to them. He knew, I fear, that I was waiting and hoping for them—

And I? I wanted everything. I can't help it. Men run away from me in droves, as others come running towards me. I am the far end of the swimming pool: the side you have to touch before turning and swimming back. As fast as you can towards: as fast as you can away.

Doesn't it frighten you, Miss Jacobs, to think how soon we're going to die? No, nothing frightens you, because your heart is pure, your soul is good.

Monkeys' brains and long silver teaspoons. Shall I describe Anton to you? His beautiful haggard face, his lean body, his brilliant eyes, his quicksilver mind, his charm? Dear God, his worldly importance! Anton never walked if he could run. Yet I'm sure his wife saw him with more accuracy than I ever did: she would see him as I see Roland: as sheer living, walking, snoring, predictable, day-to-day folly. She would see in Anton a man re-running, decade after decade, without any alteration but with much surface embellishment, five glorious years of youth. A man for ever between twenty-eight and thirty-three, as life and event rolled by. Yes, of course, Miss Jacobs, he had a *wife*. Has a wife. Why are you surprised? Men like Anton have wives. In this brave new cannibalistic world of ours, all proper men are married, all proper women too. It's our prudence, our reality, our safe familiarity while we nibble and guzzle the private parts of comparative strangers. Oh strange new wondrous delicacies!

I try to forget amputated limbs at $2,000 a pound; I try to forget the monkeys' brains, as I try to forget, as my husband can't, the missiles gathering, forget the whole frightening insanity of the world. I try to relish only this: the conjunction of man with woman, in the face of common sense and decency.

I tell you I loved him, Miss Jacobs: it is how I sanctified disgrace: how I justified the dangerous absurdity of our behaviour: this running through the machine of a different and forbidden tape. I set up this terrible, painful affair, the little short-lived merry haphazard affair, as an actual alternative, an actual radical alternative, Miss Jacobs, and not as the optional extra that Anton saw it to be. I took it seriously. It was my escape route from death.

And yet how many times have I not myself seen my accomplice in sex as an optional extra, the affair as a trivial in-and-out relationship, when the man has believed it to be world-shaking, shattering and permanent. Ah, the biter bit!

Why Alaska, you ask suddenly? Are you keeping up with me? Why did I tell you I was going to Alaska? Because Alaska is *cold,* cold, Miss Jacobs, and one senses the ice already encroaching upon the fire, before it is even lit.

Because my mother used to make Baked Alaska, a fundamentally boring dish. Whale-fat ice cream (in her case) encased in meringue made from a packet; contents: dried egg white, stabiliser, emulsifier, permitted (who says?) artificial flavouring and colouring, put in the oven the better to shock the palate with cold and hot—nothing else is going to.

Anton was great on restaurants: accused me of being unsophisticated because I would not spend £80 on an indifferent meal for two; would rather give it to charity or feed the ducks. He would spend $2,000, I bet you, on a spoonful of the brains of living monkeys, should opportunity present.

Baked Alaska. My mother. My mother served Baked Alaska and I should be grateful. She was trying to tell us something, I think. Life is not what you think. This warm cosy meringue will turn into cold ice cream and set your metal teeth-fillings zinging!

Alaska again. Yes. Well, Anton was warm outside and cold inside. He was not swayed by feeling. By a passing curiosity, I think, because I'd got my name in the papers and he loves celebrity. Didn't I tell you that? I won the Secretary of the Year Award. Yes, little me. I can book-keep like an angel, write shorthand like a dervish, take board room minutes like a High Priestess. I could also stand on my head and run a multi-national corporation if I wanted to, only I can't be bothered. (That's what you feel like when you've won an Award—it goes to your head.) It was when I'd told Anton I could do his job better than he could—Anton is a director of an oil company, did I explain that?—he became a little cool, and then I complained of his coolness and he became colder, and then I wept and said I loved him, which of course was fatal and the end of the affair. He is the kind of man who must woo and never win. And what am I when it comes to it? Miss PA of the year.

* * *

Life, love, Miss Jacobs. Love is all we have left, and its excitements, while (as Roland keeps reminding me—you know how involved he is in the peace movement: he is so busy loving peace he has no time to love me; no wonder I run around with other men) while, as I say, the nuclear missiles gather, from Alaska to the Western Australian desert. Love. Sex. Missiles. Penises. Yes, of course there is phallic imagery here, Miss Jacobs; did you doubt it? A penetrative fear. I am the victim who invites attack. If I did not invite attack, the missiles would not gather; the men would pass by prudently; the world would be at peace. Mea culpa. Only, Miss Jacobs, this is the energy that makes the world go round, gets the children born: I can't control it. Takes more than me.

I have lied and cheated and lost over a trivial affair of the heart—because my heart was involved and Anton's was not, and that is the nub of the humiliation I now feel—and what can any of this matter? "I cannot feel," Anton said to me, "about you the way you clearly feel about me. I'm sorry but there it is. I did not mean to hurt you."

But he did. It's better to feast on the living than the dead. The taste is better. That's why I got fed upon. But this may be the last time. What I feel like now, Miss Jacobs, is the monkey. I tethered myself with my own desire. I invited Anton under my skin with his scalpel blade: slice! he went; oh, sharp, sharp—and then with a long teaspoon he supped off my living brains, trying them out for flavour, and then, finding them really not good enough after all for his epicurean fancy, he spat them out with disdain. And the monkey chatters a little, automatically, and dies. I shall go home to my husband now and calm him down. I bet you anything he's still there.

THE PARDONER

Eleanor tugged at her father's arm. She was excited. "That's her," she said. "That's her over there. That's my therapist, Daddy. That's Julie." And she waved and smiled at a demurely pretty woman of some forty years, dressed in high-necked grey, who stood over by the empty marble fireplace talking to a woman in low-necked black. The woman in grey smiled back, briefly, and resumed her conversation. Bob did not like to see his daughter so easily dismissed, but then he did not like the fact that she was seeing a therapist, and had been for two years.

The reception hall was beginning to fill up—men in tuxedos, women in long dresses. Two hundred guests were expected, for this the annual Writers' Benefit Dinner. Many stars of stage, screen, politics and literature were expected: a few would no doubt turn up. This was the first big event that Eleanor had organised for the Writers' Guild. Bob worried for her. It was important that nothing went wrong. He feared it would. Should the marble fireplace be empty? Shouldn't a fire be blazing there? And Eleanor had no doubt provided her Julie with a free ticket, otherwise why should she be there, and someone was bound to object. Didn't he, Bob, pay out enough for her? Her fees had doubled in two years; they were now two hundred dollars an hour. It was outrageous. Eleanor herself seemed much the same as usual, except that she had dieted down and could now wear his first wife Lily's clothes. But perhaps Eleanor would have done this anyway in the course of untherapied time. How could you ever know?

But Bob was in a bad mood: he knew he was being unreasonable: his black bow tie dictated a certain shirt, and the collar was uncomfortable. The tie was the old-fashioned kind, which fastened not with a Velcro strip but with a proper ribbon. Lily had made him buy it, years and years ago when she was only twenty-three, but already ambitious socially, longing to count for something in the world of parties and charity events. He knew at the time the tie would turn out to be an enduring penance. And now here was Eleanor, Lily's daughter, so like her mother it disturbed Bob to see her, wearing on her not quite lovely, slightly podgy, pale face just the same expression of discontent and disappointment that Lily wore. Only on Eleanor the look was not quite yet set: it flickered in and out and round a kind of charming eagerness, a vulnerability which Bob had always loved in her.

Her father supposed that herein lay the progress of the generations: the mother longed to go to the Ball, the daughter hosted the Ball, albeit in an official capacity.

Eleanor was wearing layers of what looked to Bob to be black underwear lace: Bob had given her two thousand dollars to spend on an outfit for this special occasion. He had done this on the instructions of Sorrel, his second and true wife. Eleanor's salary at the Guild, said Sorrel, would hardly run to anything suitable.

* * *

"Don't be shy, Daddy. You have to meet her," said Eleanor, and she dragged her father across the room past palely tall flower arrangements in elongated, fluted Grecian urns as once, as a child, she had dragged Bob to meet new friends, new toys, new pet animals, living or dead. Share my experience, Daddy.

Julie raised pale, hooded, slightly protuberant eyes to Bob's. She was younger than he had thought, perhaps in her late thirties. She was colourless. She kept her face neutral, impassive. She seldom blinked. She thinks she's looking wise, thought Bob, but actually she makes herself look merely dull.
"This is Daddy," said Eleanor.
"Don't say it," said Bob lightly. "You've heard so much about me!" Julie didn't smile, but merely nodded.

Then Eleanor was summoned and left them together, father and therapist, while the daughter welcomed, organised, panicked and chivvied guests into a reception line which kept breaking as ceremony collapsed into the pleasures of old friends, newly met; fresh friends, instantly made.

The silence between Bob and the therapist became awkward. He raised his glass to her, pleasantly. She made no effort: just stood and waited. She was drinking water.
"So you're the Pardoner," Bob said.
"Excuse me?" Her voice was soft and slow.
"The Pardoner," he said. "The one who forgives sins in exchange for money. The Pardoner of the Medieval Church: very fashionable for a time, until the abuses were such the Church backed off and cleaned up its act."
Julie looked puzzled.

"The Pardoner," said Bob, "was empowered by the Pope to accept money for the remission of sins. Since Jesus had died on the cross for us, the reasoning went, the eventual heaven of perfect content was assured. In the meantime, the more money you handed over, the sooner you'd get out of Purgatory and into Heaven. Purgatory was the kind of cleansing station you had to go to after death."

"I don't see the connection," she said. "What are you trying to say to me?"

Bob could see the imprudence of trying to press his point. He did not want the woman as an enemy. Eleanor trusted her, for some reason, with life, thought, soul. He looked around for Sorrel, his ally in this new world, but he could not see her. She was still in the powder room, no doubt. "We both have Eleanor's interests at heart," said the Pardoner.

Bob had a powerful memory of Eleanor's little face frowning over the edge of her cot, when she was too young for speech, first helplessly pointing at a doll she'd dropped on the floor, then dancing up and down with rage: furious at her father for picking the toy up, handing it over, outraged at her own dependence: out of control, in a tantrum, biting his helpful, paternal hand: tiny, sharp little teeth. Could you cure a nature born to be what it was? Should you try?

The Popes of the New Age, intermediaries between God and man, be they Freud, Jung, Janov, the Bagwhan, Eric Berne or whatever, empowered their minions to try, enabled them to make a fine living offering confession, remission of suffering, paths out of purgatory into heaven. The more the sinner paid, was the promise, the more sessions they suffered, the nearer heaven would come. The gullible, as ever, believed that heaven was possible,

happiness theirs by right, and paid up. They saw the human condition as perfectible; it was obvious to Bob that it was not.

As if little Eleanor, scowling over the edge of her cot, biting the
hand that fed her, only sporadically endearing, loveable only in
spite of herself, would ever be capable of living in, let alone creating, heaven! Poor Eleanor. When Lily left Bob, walked out on
him with her lover, Eleanor had been only five, and Bob's anxiety had been all for her, not for her little sister Kate, aged only
two, or her even littler brother Edmond. Not his baby, this last
one, he was sure of it, though he was still seeing the boy through
college.

"My heart always went out to Eleanor," Bob thought, clarifying
the notion in his head, but he did not say it aloud. Perhaps he'd
given his daughter too much of it? Sometimes his heart beat
strangely. He could feel it pounding now. He smiled at the therapist. Still she did not smile back.
"Don't we?" she persisted.
"Of course," Bob said, as lightly as he could for the hammering
of his heart. "And I do hope you'll forgive my bow tie. Pardon it,
like the Pardoner you are. It's hopelessly out of fashion; nearly
thirty years old, like Eleanor. Not a Velcro tie, mind you: I have
that to say for myself, at least I don't wear a Velcro tie; I offer
my neck for strangling."
The Pardoner looked puzzled. Such an expression seemed to sit
naturally on her face. She'd look puzzled: her interlocutor would
offer further explanation. Bob felt himself fall into the trap.
"Isn't that the function of the tie?" he asked. "To announce to
the world that the soul had been satisfactorily separated from the
body? Look at me, says the tie, look at me, you guys, I'm in command of my animal urges! No need, ladies, to worry in case I rape

or attack. These two ends are my peace offering. If I step out of line, all you have to do is seize the ends and strangle me."

The Pardoner studied him curiously, seriously. Was there no making this woman laugh? How did Eleanor stand it? Did he pay thousands of dollars a month for this? His heart was beating regularly now. He relaxed.

"I always feel uneasy at formal gatherings," Bob confessed, and Miss Julie liked that and she smiled, just a little. An Hispanic waitress with sores around her mouth offered Bob more wine from a silver tray. Something had gone wrong. Was this Eleanor's responsibility? Perhaps his daughter had no idea of how *not* to employ a servant with sores around her mouth? It was perfectly possible that she still hadn't learned that life was tough, and that you couldn't stay a warm, kind person without damaging your own interests. Perhaps that was the Pardoner's role—to preserve Eleanor's good opinion of herself.

Over at the reception line photographers became overintrusive; Eleanor drifted away, leaving the problem to others. The Pardoner excused herself and turned her back.

Bob looked round for someone to talk to, and found no one. Some of the older, grander publishers had turned up: he recognised a few faces from the old literary days; but mostly the guests were new young blood, who'd come along to pay their dues to culture, much good might it do them. And of course no one wanted to talk to Bob. The coast-to-coast chain of record shops he owned, which brought him a satisfactory enough income, scarcely edged his status with the glamour others liked to brush up against on such occasions. Lily had always longed for glamour: Bob had failed to provide it. Lily had hoped for column inches, not just income, when she married him, but had failed to tell him so.

Wasn't that Ivana Trump over there? Certainly it was. Arthur Miller? Even the Pardoner was gawping. The waitress with the pustules moved amongst them. Amazing! Bob was glad, when it came to it, that Eleanor had failed in ruthlessness. She might get married yet. At the thought, Bob could almost feel the sharp baby teeth digging into his hand. Eleanor's sister Kate had never bitten: not because she was any nicer but because she'd always been too wary, too hard, too proud ever to lose control. Kate had been born more conventionally pretty than Eleanor: blonde curls, blue eyes, hard-hearted; forever dimpling and charming, though seldom meaning it. She'd put Eleanor out of countenance and enjoyed it. He imagined that Kate made a self-righteous mother, rather than a warm one. Kate had taken her mother Lily to extremes, and done it all, Bob sometimes thought, just to annoy Eleanor: messy, uncertain Eleanor, Daddy's little girl who sometimes tried to be what Bob wanted, and sometimes the opposite, and got it all wrong anyway.

But how, in God's name, was this Julie, this rather drab and cow-like creature, so censorious, so unopen to any ideas but her own and those of whichever Pope of whatever God had given her permission to practice—how was this creature to pardon Eleanor, to understand more than a flickering of what went on in Eleanor's head? Since this Miss Julie would only have Eleanor's account of it, in any case, in Eleanor's rather limited vocabulary, Miss Julie would be on Eleanor's side, never Kate's, never Lily's, never Bob's, let alone poor Sorrel's, the wicked stepmother. Eleanor would have it easy, would never learn to be self-critical, would always stay a victim.

* * *

And if in two years, twice a week, Eleanor was still not "cured" of insomnia, or anxiety, or bulimia, or whatever symptom of neurosis had originally afflicted her, what could the Pardoner offer her client next, by way of analysis and cure?

Bob felt the Pardoner's suspicious eyes still following him. Supposing she had taken offence? He wished the conversation had not taken place. He had been hopelessly imprudent. The woman was dangerous: she had entered his life unasked, and now had unreasonable power in it, through the daughter he loved.

At last he caught sight of Sorrel, in her familiar deep blue velvet dress. He hurried over to her. She stroked his tuxedoed arm to soothe him. She knew the pattern of his agitations.

"What's the matter?"

"I so hate this kind of event," Bob said. "We're in uniform. I'm always suspicious of crowds of men in uniform. They're sinister, always in the act of justifying the unjustifiable. They smack of cabal. At least my bow tie is out of fashion. That's some comfort."

"You look very handsome," said Sorrel, and it was true. Bob had caught sight of himself, framed in a brass column as he'd entered the hall, and been almost pleased with what he saw. Still broad-shouldered, patrician-nosed, clean-chinned, a good figure of a man, in upright and energetic condition: just never good enough for Lily—"Such a fool Lily was," Sorrel said, "to let you go. But I'm glad she did, because then I got you."

Sorrel always knew when he was thinking about Lily. Knowing he loved her, she felt safe in balancing his pain with the announcement of her pleasure. The second wife understood how he still suffered from the divorce of the first, though the event was now more than twenty years behind them. He had never quite recovered from the insult, not just the loss of a wife he loved, in spite of himself, but from Lily's behaviour afterwards.

All the things that Lily had done, she'd blamed Bob for—from infidelity to desertion—and though she had to flick the whole world quite upside down to do it, she had for a time managed to persuade the children of their father's overwhelming depravity: his meanness, his lasciviousness, his callousness with others' feelings, and the rest of it. The more lavishly he had supported Lily, the more she took his generosity as evidence of his guilt. Lily had remarried: a plastic surgeon. She seemed happier now; she had the column inches she felt she'd always deserved, the woman at the party for whom the flashes pop, if only by double-proxy. Wife of surgeon-to-the-stars.

Eleanor came across to kiss Sorrel on the cheek. A Judas kiss; the thought came to Bob and made him uneasy.
"You should keep your husband in order," Eleanor said to her stepmother, and he remembered the little spiteful pre-tantrum eyes she'd had as a child. "He's really upset Julie."
"Who's Julie?" asked Sorrel, mildly. She always spoke mildly, kindly to Eleanor, avoiding danger. "And why should your father have upset her?" The familiar joke. Who's at fault? Your husband. No, your father!
"Julie's my therapist," said Eleanor. "And Daddy was being really aggressive towards her! Julie didn't want me to ask you two here tonight. I ought to be more independent, Julie says, more like Kate. And it's such a wonderful thing we're doing here tonight, and here you are trying to spoil it. I know it was stupid of me to think you and she would get along, Daddy, but you could at least have made the effort. You know how I blame myself for the separation, how difficult it is for me, how painful."

"Sweetheart," said Bob, "shouldn't you be paying attention to the function, not worrying about this kind of thing? We've been standing around too long. Shouldn't we all be going in to dinner?"

"If I'm in such a mess," said Eleanor, "it's because you find fault all the time. And now you start on poor Julie!"

Eleanor's cheeks were pink; she would flush so like this before she bit. Did children never give up?

"Eleanor," said Bob, "if you don't stop this at once, I'm not paying for any more therapy. It's not doing you any good."

"Bob," said Sorrel, warningly, "let's give ourselves time to think about this."

"That's definite, Ellie," said Bob. "You want therapy, you pay for it yourself from now on. This evening has cost me twelve thousand dollars to date, just so a bunch of chicken-shit writers can sit down to eat with a bunch of A-list performers, who'd rather, like me, be home watching TV, and all you can do is insult me for it. You could have bought that outfit for five dollars in a thrift shop and turned out looking more decent, and saved enough for three months of Miss Julie."

Eleanor's face crumpled and fell. There were tears glistening in her eyes.

"You're such a mercenary bastard," she said. "I don't know why I bother trying to please you."

And then Eleanor had gone, on her heel; over to where the Pardoner stood, gently tapping her foot, smiling vaguely. Bob wondered for a moment whether Eleanor and Julie had some kind of sexual liaison but dismissed the thought. Guests started to drift in to dinner without benefit of announcement.

Sorrel kept hold of Bob's hand, calming him down. His heart had started struggling again. By the time they reached the table, ornate with white napkins in flutes and folds, Bob's equanimity had returned. I told her, he thought to himself. I finally told her! He thought if he looked at his hand he'd see the two little red marks left by baby teeth, so he didn't look.

Sorrel sat next to Bob, leaning into him so far as decorousness would allow.

"I love your tie," Sorrel murmured, "it's the lean, sleek part of you. I don't care if you did buy it with Lily. I don't care if it's old-fashioned. It's part of you as your children are: I accept them." Thus she spoke her familiar litany and Bob smiled and felt better.

But the sense of something ominous in the air remained. Eleanor was sitting a table or so away, next to the Pardoner; she had her back to him; he could not see the expression on her face and was glad he could not.

Bob had asked as his guests old Eisenstein and his wife: and Lara the ex-opera singer and her music-producer husband Pietre, who'd just sold eight million rock reissues, quite an achievement, the music business being in the state it was. Lara seemed to be doing her best to disconcert the old dog Eisenstein, to make the ancient frog eyes of Mrs. Eisenstein blink. The pair of them had their heyday back in the fifties: Eisenstein the pianist, Sara Eisenstein the composer, into New York out of the Holocaust. They'd been to see *Schindler's List* and liked it. It had brought memories back. Any memory would do, it seemed, so long as it was of youth.

Tonight old Eisenstein was wearing one of the new bow ties; floppy, large, lush, the black gold-threaded through. The fabric cut off a weary head from a withered body, but the aplomb remained. Lara was speaking in her loud throaty voice about a current law case, a famous father, a rock star, accused of ritual

child abuse: the equally famous model wife, now suing for ali-
mony, his accuser: the child's remembrance of events, ten years
back, the stuff of fantasy and horror films; multiple rape, sexual
torture, bondage, snakes, toads, flies, all the nasty things of the
outside world internalised, introduced into the body.

"The child has sexual fantasies but understands nothing," Lara
said, in a voice which could be heard on at least four other tables.
"The child is hopelessly vague about orifices, objects of penetra-
tion, has heard cries in the night suggesting pain, knows something exciting is going on but not what, is furiously jealous
anyway, angry at being left out: works out what she can, inadvertently brings herself to orgasm. What pleasure, what horror!
How can I be so disgusting, thinks the girl child! Did these
visions really come from out of my head? I don't believe it! Along
comes the therapist in later years: quite right. 'Sweetheart,' she
says, 'you didn't invent those nasty things, you're much too nice,
much too sweet. They were real. Daddy did them.' And thus
everything is explained and the childhood guilt absolved. The
world returns to its natural order. If the universe is to be good,
the father must be bad."

Sorrel was staring at Lara, upset. Orgasm was still not part of
dinner talk, not in her book.

"No smoke without fire," said Sorrel.

Oh, Sorrel, Sorrel. You, too? Bob begins to see the future. His
heart starts to beat its promise-of-death tattoo.

Pietre says, "Lara's right. There always has to be a scapegoat, so
God can be understood as good. Once we had witches, but now
women are the ones who condemn, so it's the fathers' turn."

"Once it was us," old Eisenstein says. He has chicken soup on
his bow tie. His chin has shrunk so the fabric collects the drips,
not the flesh. "The finger of blame moves on, thank God."

The table falls silent.

* * *

After dinner, it was much as Bob expected. Julie came up to him, followed by Eleanor. Eleanor was crying.

"Now see what you've done," said the Pardoner.

"I've lost my job," Eleanor wept. "You upset me so much, Daddy, I didn't know how to handle it. I was only on trial here, you know. It was a temporary post. They said I had no eye for detail, and I tried so hard."

"Face your father," said Julie the Pardoner to Bob's daughter. "Tell him. Face the past, face yourself, finally face what happened to you. It's going to cost us all a lot of pain and money, Bob, if we're going to help Eleanor. I need a cheque for five hundred thousand dollars, and I need it here and now: it's essential that your daughter, still in her heart that poor bullied and abused little girl of long ago, witnesses this act of contrition and apology from you. The money will go to the best cause of all: what Eleanor's treatment will cost, if she is ever to recover from the trauma."

"Trauma?" asked Bob. "What trauma?"

"We worked so hard, Eleanor and I," said the Pardoner. "You've no idea how painful it is, achieving flashback memory. Your daughter ran a fever, she had pains in her joints. But she did it! And this evening, finally, it all made sense. All the memories are there, available."

"Came to her between soup and fish, I expect," said Bob. "The soup was cold, the fish was sour."

The Pardoner stared at him, at last showing signs of emotion. "You fathers are unbelievable," she said. "Still so callous! The night-time visits, the foul intruding member, the threats, the bribes, the terror! And then your wife Lily became aware of what was going on," said the Pardoner. "Lily left you in order to rescue her little girl. Of course your wife hated you: you were hateful. An abusing father."

"This way everything is explained, Daddy," said Eleanor, piteously. "Please understand. Everything is explained."

So Bob took out his cheque book and signed a cheque for five hundred thousand dollars on the spot and Sorrel came hurrying up and said, "What is going on here?"
Bob said, "I am just paying for the remission of uncommitted sins, so that I can go to heaven," at which Sorrel hit the Pardoner and Eleanor actually spat at Sorrel.

Bob took off his bow tie, elaborately untying the long silk ends, feeling the ache in his shoulders, still broad, still strong in spite of it all, and said, "This thing is strangling me."

HEAT HAZE

I am coming to see you, Miss Jacobs, because my father fears I am anorexic. I know I am not. I am simply a dancer, so the less weight I carry the better, the less strain on muscles and joints. I am not self-destructive: I mean to live a long time and in good health. But I love my father very much, and if it relieves any anxiety he may have, I am happy to go through the motions of seeing a psychoanalyst, even in relation to eating problems I do not have.

Yes, I know you are not the analyst I will eventually see: that you act as a kind of clearing house for your co-professionals. It is your function to recommend me to someone you believe will be sympathetic, someone who will like me and whom I like. Though I am not convinced that in this field "liking" is essential: some kind of intellectual rapport, yes. "Liking" just somehow sounds kind of sloppy. But do what you see fit.

Yes, I am eighteen. Yes, people do say I am mature for my age, and composed. Dancing is discipline; and to discipline the body is, albeit inadvertently, to discipline the mind. And since my mother died when I was thirteen I have been very much in charge of my own life, and made my own decisions in most things, and on the whole have done it well.

No, I have no boyfriend in the sense you mean, though I have suitors enough. Yes, I am satisfied with my appearance: ballet-dancerish; large-eyed, long-necked, long-backed, long-legged, a trifle boyish I suppose. If you stretch enough you don't get lumpy or over-muscled. A translucent look, true—but that comes from having a naturally pale skin, not I think from any nutritional deficiency. In this I resemble my mother. She died in a car accident, not from illness. I do not, you must understand, suffer from the self-doubt, the obsessional fears and the suicidal impulses which characterise the anorexic. But try telling that to my father.

Do I sleep well? It's strange you should ask me that. Actually, I don't. I used to, like a log, but since last summer I've tended to wake suddenly, and very early, and not be able to get back to sleep at all. I hate it. It makes me feel I am not properly in charge of my own self-improvement. Lack of sleep is bad for concentration, what is bad for concentration is bad for dancing.

What happened last summer? Let me put it like this. I took a decision on my father's behalf and carried it through in a way that quite shook me. I discovered a ruthlessness in myself which I fear I may inherit from my mother. What I did certainly smacked of the impetuous. Impetuously, my lovely mother ran across a road, and that was the end of her.

My family background? It was stable and ordinary enough to begin with. I lived with my mother for my first thirteen years. So far as I knew I had no father. We lived in a small house in a mean suburb; my mother worked as a secretary; all her earnings went on our subsistence and to see me through ballet school. She was not a typical stage mother, not the kind who vulgarly forces forward a talentless child; on the contrary. My talent had been obvious to everyone from my seventh year: my mother merely did her best for me. I suppose, in retrospect, that she had a tendency to the threadbare, to dramatic self-denial, to martyrdom. If we could make do with an old brussels sprout rather than a fresh and more expensive green pea, we did. My dancing tights were darned, not instantly replaced, as were those of the other children in my class at the Royal Ballet School. Yes, the Royal Ballet School. I am as good as they come, I am told. If we could save money by walking, and not taking the bus, we did. Of course I was curious about my father, but he was absent to the point of non-existence. I assumed he'd walked out on us. I knew my mother didn't want him mentioned: I knew it would be risky. I always felt she and I were in a boat together, in dangerous and mysterious seas, and that if ever I rocked the boat, both of us were lost.

But when my mother died her sister was able to get in touch with my father readily enough. He turned up on the doorstep within days of the funeral. It turned out that my mother had quite coldly and ruthlessly kept my father away: she would let him have nothing to do with us. She had accumulated large sums in a dollar account; hundreds of thousands of pounds, which he had sent for my maintenance over the years, and which she had kept but refused to touch. These sums I inherited, but, incidentally, in time lent back to my father. Yes, his income fluctuates wildly; he is a theatre producer working out of San Francisco; his great love is The Dance, as he refers to it, though I wish he wouldn't. It sounds pretentious. But my father is very particular; he loves beauty, he loves perfection: for him The Dance exists as some kind of Platonic ideal. My father is no sort of dancer himself; that is the strange thing: my mother showed not the slightest aptitude. It is as if my father's absorbing interest has been inherited in physical form by me. It is enough to make one a Lysenkoist, a Lamarckian, and believe in the inheritance of acquired characteristics.

I don't think it is that I am miraculously well-informed, Miss Jacobs, I think it is rather that the rest of my generation is so badly informed. My mother and I had no television set; we borrowed books from the library. I daresay that helped.

Yes, of course I was upset by my mother's death. It was so sudden. Five years later, and I still dream about her. Whenever I buy new dancing tights I think of her, and feel guilty because I have no intention of taking up my needle and darning. I may be composed but I promise you I am not without proper feeling. Yes, I think I have properly grieved, and properly incorporated her into my being. I am grateful to her for giving me birth, and no, I do not resent her because she hid my father from me. She lived in one world, and he so very much lived in another. She wanted to protect me; she never could understand how little protection I needed.

The sudden appearance of my father on the doorstep? No shock or trauma there. Fortunately he is a very good-looking man so it was easy to accept him as a father. Good looks help in most situations, I find. He'd called from Heathrow first, to explain himself. I'd thanked him for his interest, and for his trouble in coming all the way from the States. I asked him if he was married, if he was bringing anyone with him, and my father replied he was not married, since the law did not allow it, but he was bringing his lover. They went everywhere together. I tried to envisage her, but since I could not envisage him either, I failed, and perhaps just as well.

Two men turned up on my doorstep, hand in hand, not the man and woman I had expected. It was disconcerting for a moment, that was all. Many of the boys on my course are gay, or claim to be, or pass their adolescence as such. The acknowledgement of bisexuality, in my circles, is more and more common. I should not have been taken aback, but I was and it showed in my face. Bo said to my father, distressed, "You should have warned her first: I begged you to but you wouldn't listen. You never listen!" and I could tell they were as good as married, and relaxed.

Bo was in his mid-twenties, African-American, gentle, kind, smooth-skinned, and a dancer too; I could tell that at once, simply from the way he stood: a body at rest, but with all the waiting energy of a coiled spring, and only at rest the better to prepare for that spring. I liked him at once; well, I am like my father; I adore beauty, and Bo is so beautiful. Besides, if he loved my father and my father loved him, that was enough for me. I could hardly claim exclusive rights to a father so recently acquired, could I? It might have been much worse; he might have turned up with some blonde bimbo on his arm, or a dowdy wife; he could have had six boring children: I'd still have accepted it. As it was I was elated. If I was perforce to do without a mother, obliged to have a new life, by all means let it be with a gay couple from San Francisco. My father was one of those guys with a bald head, a good moustache, and sad, humorous, intelligent eyes. Okay, so Bo was a young and beautiful show-biz boyfriend, so what. Well, yes, a few eyebrows were raised amongst the neighbours; they may have been an ordinary enough couple in California, but they came over as exotic up and down my very suburban street.

* * *

No, I repeat, I did not find the fact that my father was gay in any way traumatic. Many a man breeds a family before discovering his true sexuality. I am a rational person. For the most part what happens does not distress me: what I am does not depress me; I can see that Fate has dealt me many good cards. It's just that sometimes what I find myself doing disconcerts me, Miss Jacobs. And I wake too early. I need someone to evaluate what is right and what is wrong. Or, in your terms, to differentiate between healthy behaviour and unhealthy, mature and immature. That's as pejorative, as judgemental, as you lot are ever likely to get. You're soft.

I decided to stay in London to continue with my training; I lived with my aunt—who fortunately had a less frugal temperament than my mother—and I was with my father and Bo during the summers. Either I went over to San Francisco or they came to Europe, and we would tour the main cities, living in the best hotels. One meets little prejudice if one sticks to the centres and can spend money. My father's credit was always good: it was only sometimes he had cash flow problems, when I was happy enough to help out. It was his money, after all.

My Aunt Serena told me I had been conceived just before my father "came out" as gay. When he told my mother she was sickened, angry and horrified; she was after all the child of her generation. She felt the best way to protect me was simply to wipe my father out of her and my life: better to pretend that I was an immaculate conception than the daughter of what she saw as a pervert. My parents had met at a production of a Sondheim musical: it seems my father was trying very hard at the time to confirm his heterosexuality but had in the end failed. However translucent, however ethereal my mother, she was still too female for him. He did his best to honour his responsibilities in relation to both of us; it was my mother who wouldn't let him. Yes, he left her for Bo.

Why should I not be kind towards this cast of characters, Miss Jacobs? Why should I feel angry? Everyone did the best they could, according to their lights. Even the truck driver who ran down my mother was not to blame for what he did. She all but flung herself under his wheels. That's why I am so glad I am a dancer; dancing like singing is an activity that can't possibly do any harm to anyone else. And if I tire my body sufficiently I have no energy left to wonder since everyone I know believes they are good, and does the absolute best they can considering the circumstances they're in, then why is the world in the mess it is? Which otherwise might exercise my mind considerably. Seven hours a day at the barre, and you have little energy left for cosmic thoughts, thank God.

Last May my father called to say he was coming not with Bo but with Franklin. He had broken with Bo, after sixteen years. I was distressed and told him so. My father said I would love Franklin as he did. Everyone must love Franklin. No, Bo had done nothing wrong: my father just felt it was just time to move on. I felt cheated. Go to college and say "my parents are divorcing" and everyone feels sorry for you: say "my father's left his boyfriend" and you'll elicit no sympathy, only at best a prurient curiosity.

A couple of weeks later I had a phone call from Bo; he wept as he talked. I could not bear to think of his lovely eyes puffy and his perfect face swollen and disfigured. I would have preferred him to be composed, not to weep. His evident distress would do nothing to help him win back my father, who could not abide tears, or sulks, or disfigurement. To act blithe and make my father jealous would be much the better way, and I pointed this out to him. But Bo was too upset to listen to what I said. Franklin, Bo claimed, was a cheat and a liar; he would sleep with anyone or anything if it paid him to; he was very charming and very slippery: my father was completely taken in by him. Bo, in fact, spoke like any wife, discarded in favour of a newer, younger model. I could not bear it; I wanted everything to go on as it always had since I'd met them: we three, through the hot summers, in perfect accord and harmony. I told Bo I would do my best to intercede with my father on his behalf, though frankly I hardly knew how to set about it. I only knew I must.

Franklin took it into his head to call me from San Francisco the week before he and my father flew over. I did not like the sound of him at all. You can tell a lot from voices, and his was somehow greasy, as if truth could never get a proper hold of it. He said he did so hope we would get on, he thought he should introduce himself in advance: I was so important in my father's life, and now would be in his. He was so looking forward to his English holiday: he'd never been to Europe before: he hoped I'd found somewhere quaint and Olde Worlde for us to stay: he'd heard our theatre was fabulous: he looked forward to fitting in a show or two. I saw no reason at all for the phone call, other than that he wanted to check up that I'd made the bookings. In the past Bo had simply trusted me; I booked as I saw fit, and I'd never let them down.

Intimidate other people? Who, me? I don't think so. In fact I think my trouble is rather at the other end of the spectrum. I am full of self-doubt. I lack assertiveness. I sometimes think I should go to classes. There are lots around.

* * *

I cancelled our hotel in Venice; I booked one deep in the English countryside. It was an Olde Worlde hotel near Stratord-on-Avon, expensive, staid, and much favoured by Americans. I got us one double room, one single, and wangled seats for a couple of "shows" through friends. Bo loved Shakespeare; so did my father: I was not so sure that Franklin would: in fact I doubted it. But shows he wanted, shows he'd get. I hoped his knees would twitch with boredom.

I met them at Heathrow; I drove them to the hotel. Franklin was attractive: I could understand why my father doted on him. He had soft, large, childlike blue eyes and a very pink and fleshy, pouty lower lip: soft and weak. He was no older than I was. He made you think of sex. Bo made you think of matters more ethereal. Franklin had a high opinion of himself: he believed he was some kind of blond, well-muscled Adonis; he looked to me like an up-market rent boy. Worst of all was the soft voice which said whatever my father wanted it to say. And my father adored him. Franklin was a coward; we had to walk right round the car park to keep in the shade; he was convinced just a glimmer of sunlight would give him cancer. And he was very pale; the pallor you'd attribute to malnutrition, Miss Jacobs, but is just a particular skin type, like my mother's, like my own. The opposite end of the spectrum from Bo: perhaps that too was part of the attraction. For my father to have left my mother for black Bo was one thing; to leave Bo for white Franklin was another. This way, it seemed, corruption and self-deception lay. I felt what I had never felt before: that it was safer to be heterosexual; that homosexuality was inherently dangerous; that a love directed towards something familiar, not something apart, could the more easily be replaced by lust, and lust in turn be overtaken by the desire for sexual excess. You had to be careful, or you ended up in the bath house. And that there was indeed such a thing as perversion: conceived by narcissism out of the homoerotic, slithering out to pollute and infect everything around, and that my father was on some kind of slippery slope that fell away into—what? Hellfire? I had no idea, but I didn't like it, and I feared for my father, and someone had to rescue him. I had a sudden notion of the existence of Evil, in absolute terms. I had always thought of evil as an adjective; now I could see it was a noun, and a proper one at that, well deserving its capital letter.

The hotel was as stately and staid as I had anticipated. There was a willowed drive, and a Capability Brown garden, plus lake with swans. Franklin fell in love with it at once. The staff were courteous to the point of servility. My father and I put up with it; Franklin revelled in it. It was assumed that Franklin and I, who were of an age, were the couple: that my older father would have the single room. When it turned out otherwise, when the porter was asked to put the men's luggage into the double room and my small suitcase into the single room, he did so, but hurried away. Pretty soon reception phoned through. Management told us with deep regret that it was against company policy for two men to share a room with a double bed. Management was embarrassed, Management was tactful, but Management was immovable.

Franklin was baffled. My father was aghast. I told them this kind of thing was not unusual outside London; I said the solution was simple. Franklin and I would share the double room: in the night my father and I would swap places. This we agreed to do. It was late, we were tired; the two men had flown a long way; simpler to give in than cry Homophobia! Barbarity! and walk out into the night.

* * *

It was hot. Indeed, there was what amounted to a heat wave. Once prolonged good weather sets in over England it tends to stay, week after week. The sky was deceptively hazy, the palest of blues: nothing like the clear bright densely blue Californian sky, of which I admit to not being overly fond. It seems too real, something actual, like a painted, arching ceiling, not the illusion, that accumulation of the next-to-nothingness of atmosphere, which "the sky" actually is.

No, I had no particular feeling about leaving my bed so my father and his lover could share it. I am not hung up about sex. I just don't do it if I can help it. I focus my sexual feelings into dance as a true priest embraces celibacy the better to realise the intensity of spiritual experience. This, to tell you the truth, is what worries my father about me: he being so much in denial of the possibility of a life not ruled by desire. And he thinks my loveless state must in some way be his fault. That by following his own passions through he has somehow prevented my own from flowering. Obscurely, too, he blames my mother for encouraging me to dance, in his eyes making matters worse. Parents seem to be like that. They blame themselves, or one another. I am prepared to take responsibility for myself. If I can't sleep, that's my doing, not theirs.

To continue. No sooner had my father laid his head on the pillow of his narrow bed in his quaint and Olde Worlde single room, complete with false eaves and flower prints on the wall, than he fell asleep, exhausted.

"He isn't going to wake before morning," I said to Franklin. "I think we'd just better let him lie there, and ignore the bed-swapping routine. Besides, the air-conditioning in our room is better."

* * *

Franklin agreed. We would share the double bed. It was only sensible. A soft night breeze blew in through the open latticed window, and played over my sleeping father's face, and refreshed it with all kinds of garden scents: I could detect lavender, and night jasmine, and violets. But Franklin slammed the window shut, and I suppose he was right: moths and mosquitoes came in a-plenty as well as the perfumes of the night. Personally, I never get bitten by mosquitoes, a quality I inherit from my father, but poor Franklin suffered dreadfully; he was allergic to bites, it seemed. We left my father's room, in haste.

Now it had seemed to me from the occasional sidelong look that Franklin had directed my way during the afternoon that his homosexuality was a decidedly moveable feast. As Bo had indicated, he would do whatever he wanted with anyone, regardless of gender, if only he could get away with it. His soft hand lay frequently in my father's, but held in itself the potential to stray. I daresay this contributed to my father's obsession with him: that he loved Franklin a whole lot more than Franklin loved him. A middle-aged man, head over heels in love with a young boy. I didn't want to see my father as pathetic, I did not want my love for him spoiled by pity. It was obvious to me that my father existed in Franklin's life to further Franklin's interests: a leg up (and over) in the theatre world to bring him a fraction nearer to the stars, to yield up the cultural background Franklin knew he needed if he was to go far as a kept man, even in the city down the coast, in Hollywood.

* * *

Franklin lay naked in the bed; I lay naked next to him. It was too hot for covers. The window was closed: the air-conditioning hopeless. We both knew what would happen. Franklin of course had no idea of the degree of my calculation, my ill will towards him, my affection for Bo; certainly not the capacity for martyrdom I had inherited from my mother. To lose my virginity thus was the cold brussels sprout; to have kept it for a loving relationship the sweet and tender green pea I, like my mother, could not allow myself. And if I think about it my sleeplessness dates from this night. I have not really slept well since.

We lay thus for some ten minutes. Neither of us was quite prepared to make the first move. In these circumstances one does some instant bonding. And I must acknowledge that what I was about to do was not all that repulsive to me. Franklin did have a really good body. I could identify with my father sufficiently to admire it, to want to have it in sexual attendance on me. I do not want you to feel sorry for me, Miss Jacobs. Sacrifice it was, but to be a sacrificial victim need not be entirely without its pleasures.

I made the first move. I said, "I suppose we ought to do what Management requires of us, in the interest of respectability and what people might think. We ought to fuck."

At which, within half a second, he was all over me. He was accustomed: I know my anatomy: my hymen had broken when I was fifteen—I remember the occasion: I was at the barre, on points, my right leg stretching. Suddenly—well, there I was, married in essence to The Dance. But I'd known that anyway: certainly that I was betrothed. But now I considered the matter settled. Symbols come along to confirm a conclusion, not to initiate one. So Franklin had no way of telling I was a virgin: I will say that to you now, Miss Jacobs, in all fairness, though of course to my father at the time I had to cry rape: see what Franklin did, and me a virgin! But that was at breakfast, the following morning.

After sex, we slept. Or rather Franklin did. I opened the window and let the mosquitoes in, and moved the sheet away from his body to give them proper access. I sat upright in the bed, knees to chest, and watched the thin, leggy things alight on the soft clammy neck, the nose, under the eyes: with an eager wave of my hand directed them to the softest, most vulnerable places. The head of the penis, the arm-pit. The creatures alighted, settled, drove their poison in, and sucked, and lost their thinness and grew dark red, and Franklin slept, the pure sleep of the jet-lagged; and pink bubbles rose on his skin, even as the hellish bloodsuckers I had summoned up departed, and the bubbles turned to red, tight, miniature volcanoes, and his manicured fingers moved to scratch the swollen tender places in his sleep, and I was glad to see it happen. Franklin was, as he claimed, very sensitive, a mass of allergies. I rejoiced. I laughed in the light of the moon. Once they had served my purpose, I shoved as many flying creatures out of the window as I could; they flew heavily, engorged. I slapped a few others to death. Food slowed them up, more fool they. Then I closed the window, and lay down next to Franklin. I shut my eyes and dreamed of the possibility of love, and permanence, and the blessed ordinariness of an everyday life which could never be mine, but which had seemed to mark my father's life with Bo, and which I wanted back again, for them.

Why could it not be mine? Well, good heavens—I had given love up, Miss Jacobs, as a bad job. I sacrificed my virginity on the altar of my father's welfare. Are you crying or laughing? Crying? Good

God! You're easily moved. I suppose in a way it is sad. I am like one of those walnuts, you know. Tough as anything: impermeably sealed; then finally you break in, and what do you find? That the nut inside is shrivelled, inedible. All potential but destined never to grow. A walnut withered in its shell, that's me.

At breakfast Franklin was a disgusting sight. All crimson lumps and bumps on a white skin, disfigured, despairing, driven mad by his itching parts, one eye half closed, mouth so swollen he could hardly talk, let alone protest his innocence while I wept into my cornflakes and confessed what had happened between Franklin and myself. What Franklin had done to me. Seduced me, abused my innocence, taken advantage of my father's trust.

My father was sickened. When Bo called through to him later that morning, on my suggestion, the car was on its way to take us away, to the evident relief of Management. We were leaving for London: Franklin was being sent home forthwith to California, paid off; my father and I would summer in Venice. Where of course Bo joined us.

Why do you think I can't sleep, Miss Jacobs? Is it so wrong to interfere in another's life? To tell lies to a good end? To pretend love while practising betrayal? Was I not balancing Evil by creating Good? Isn't that what one's supposed to do? Was I not justifying my mother's disappointment, by keeping my father with Bo, making the trauma she endured worthwhile, if only in cosmic terms? When my mother ran from the house, so impetuously, it was because I had accused her of being ruthless and tried to press her to tell me about my father; and she was hurt. I hurt, she dies, he turns up. What's a mosquito bite or so on Franklin's white skin, a false accusation of rape, in comparison to that? So many questions! You can't be expected to answer them: don't try.

But that's why I am a dancer, and will stay so all my life. No longer a virgin but that's about as far as my interest in sex will ever go. Work's a pushover compared to family life. I want no more of it.

Now that is settled, thank you and goodbye. Send the bill to my father. I will sleep well tonight.

"Run and Ask Daddy If He Has Any More Money" originally appeared in *Radio Times,* 1993, Hodder & Stoughton, 1994.

"Not Even a Blood Relation" originally appeared in *Dempsters,* in German *Marie Claire,* and in *Heat Haze,* a short story collection published in the U.K. by Orion Books Limited.

"Wasted Lives" originally appeared in *The New Yorker* and in South African *Cosmopolitan.*

"Love Amongst the Artists" originally appeared in *The Times* (London), 1991.

"Tale of Timothy Bagshott" originally appeared in *British Council Anthology,* 1992.

"Through a Dustbin, Darkly" originally appeared in *Options,* 1992.

"Web Central" originally appeared in *The Big Issue.*

"A Good Sound Marriage" originally appeared in *US Journal,* 1991.

"Pains" originally appeared in *Cosmopolitan,* 1994.

"A Question of Timing" was donated to Teenage Trust, 1993.

"Red on Black" originally appeared in *British Council New Writing 4,* 1994.

"Santa Claus's New Clothes" originally appeared in *The Observer,* 1993.

"The Pardoner" originally appeared in *Literary Review,* 1994.

"Heat Haze" originally appeared in *Heat Haze.*